W9-CXJ-596

UNHOLY LOVE

A shaft of pale moonlight fell across little Simon's coverlet as he stared at the photograph. In the dim light his mother looked so young and beautiful, and there was Christopher Hennick standing right next to her.

Simon wanted to tear the picture in half, leaving only her there smiling at him. He would tear the man up into a million million pieces and . . . and burn them. Yes, he would burn them just the way they used to burn the bad witches of the devil and the mean people who hurt the good people like his mommy.

But if he tore up the photo, his mother would cry. He did not want the new man to hurt his mommy and make her cry. He wanted him to go away. To go away in a terrible fire, like the others had gone away.

Most Pocket Books are available at special quantity discounts for bulk purchases for sales promotions, premiums or fund raising. Special books or book excerpts can also be created to fit specific needs.

For details write the office of the Vice President of Special Markets, Pocket Books, 1230 Avenue of the Americas, New York, New York 10020.

TRICYCLE

RUSSELL RHODES

PUBLISHED BY POCKET BOOKS NEW YORK

This novel is a work of fiction. Names, characters, places and incidents are either the product of the author's imagination or are used fictitiously. Any resemblance to actual events or locales or persons, living or dead, is entirely coincidental.

The quotation from *For Whom the Bell Tolls* by Ernest Hemingway is reprinted with the permission of Charles Scribner's Sons. Copyright 1940 by Ernest Hemingway, copyright renewed 1968 by Mary Hemingway.

Another *Original* publication of POCKET BOOKS

POCKET BOOKS, a division of Simon & Schuster, Inc.
1230 Avenue of the Americas, New York, N.Y. 10020

Copyright © 1983 by Russell Rhodes

All rights reserved, including the right to reproduce this book or portions thereof in any form whatsoever. For information address Pocket Books, 1230 Avenue of the Americas, New York, N.Y. 10020

ISBN: 0-671-45893-0

First Pocket Books printing August, 1983

10 9 8 7 6 5 4 3 2 1

POCKET and colophon are registered trademarks of Simon & Schuster, Inc.

Printed in the U.S.A.

*To Laird Koenig in gratitude
for his enthusiasm and support*

TRICYCLE

Chapter 1

THE COUNTRYSIDE WAS UNUSUALLY QUIET, TOO quiet. All nature seemed frozen in anticipation, waiting. The only sounds to break the silence were the creakings of ancient elms that moved painfully in the frigid air whispering across the ice-covered river and playing fields up to the ridge above. There a solemn formation of dark buildings rose bleak and foreboding against the gray, January sky. Unseen eyes behind dark windows stared down, menacing the snow-crusted meadows and tobacco fields that stretched far to the south in the deepening gloom of the Connecticut valley. Slowly nine small specks emerged in the distance. They approached, one after the other from the lengthening shadows, moving relentlessly.

The thin line of young men ran in monotonous, mechanical rhythm. They ran along rutted lanes, zigzagged through empty woods and among the trees lining the riverbank. They ran over uneven meadows and fields, their spiked shoes plodding through snow, brittle winter grass, jumping ice-filled ditches, and continued on in panting unison toward the far-off yellow lights of the gymnasium over a mile distant.

Emblazoned in maroon letters on the chests of the cross-country team's gray track suits was the proud name of the Talbot Academy.

Gradually one of the figures dropped behind the others and came to a seemingly reluctant halt. Bending down to repair a broken shoelace, the lone athlete watched as the column swung away to the north behind a stand of elms and moved determinedly on toward the Academy. He slowly straightened, his eyes searching the deserted landscape for other signs of movement. Finding none, he turned and sprinted quickly back across the frozen earth to a large, derelict tobacco barn a hundred yards off the lane. The dark red paint of its high, vertically boarded sides had peeled in wide strips over years of neglect to reveal the silvered wood beneath; its long roof sagged wearily under the burden of decaying shingles.

The youth paused briefly before the barn's large double doors. Taking a last furtive look about him, he tugged one open, slipped quickly inside and yanked it shut. His chest heaved and he leaned back against the wood to catch his breath. He waited nervously for his eyes to grow accustomed to the darkness, which was relieved only by the few rays of late afternoon light that filtered in through thin cracks between the vertical siding and the ragged holes in the roof above.

A low, gentle voice broke the silence from across the darkness. "You're late, Alan."

"I'm . . . I'm sorry," he stammered. "Coach Logan made us do two extra miles today." His knees felt weak and his throat dry. He tried to make out the figure he knew to be there.

"That's all right. It should have made you all the warmer. Come over here so we can see just how warm you are, Alan."

He swallowed hard, then moved uncertainly across the littered, rotting floor of the old barn. She stood with her back to him. The heavy sheepskin coat she wore slipped slowly down from her shoulders as he approached. She did not turn; she knew exactly how he would look. Tall, lithe, blond curls plastered to his wet forehead, a perfect face streaked with the salt of his perspiration—she could already taste it. She was thirty-four, he just sixteen.

"We haven't much time, Alan."

The boy extended his arms tentatively and encircled the older woman from behind. And then, gaining confidence, he pressed her back against his firm, young body. Its odor and warmth through the damp, gray cotton of the track suit fed her, excited her.

"You young bastard," she teased, rotating her buttocks against his groin, feeling the growing hardness there. "You rotten, bull bastard."

His hands moved awkwardly over her breasts; she pressed them hard against her, breathing in the stale, heady smell of the locker room, the unwashed socks, shorts, sweaty bodies. The rhythm of his breathing increased as his excitement rose. She encouraged the exploration of his hands over her body.

As the two figures entwined about each other, an unblinking, emotionless brown eye stared at them through a narrow gap between the peeling red boards of the barn wall.

The boy became more aggressive and she began to struggle, trying to pry herself away. "You pig bastards," she hissed as she felt the hands of others pawing her body. He held her more tightly. She forced herself around in his arms to face her teenage rapist, fighting him, cursing, her hands moving uncontrolled under the track suit over his soft, moist skin, feeling the developing muscles beneath, his broad back, the firm roundness of his small, smooth butt. She jammed it hard against her.

"Let me go, you fucker, you rotten . . ." She lapped the salt from his neck as he fumbled under her sweater. Shoving her fingers under the straps of his jock, she brought them forward to the restraining pouch. "Don't hurt me, for Christ's sake, don't hurt me. Please," she called out, wrenching down the supporter, grasping the hot, firm flesh that sprang from it. Collapsing backward, she pulled him down onto the ragged blanket spread over a mattress of old tobacco netting.

In a frenzy of excitement, the boy writhed moaning on top of her. She unloosed her skirt; he tugged it away and tore off her fragile panties, falling back onto her with clumsy, hunching movements. She looked beyond him in her mind, seeing once again the hungry, leering faces above her, feeling herself held down as dirty hands clawed at her, wrenched her tight legs apart. "Kurt, Kurt, help me, help . . ." she called out, sobbing as she guided the boy's engorged sex into her lubricated passage. His young body pounded into her without finesse as she thrashed beneath him a thousand miles away. His breath came faster, his whimpers louder and louder.

The lid of the emotionless brown eye closed to shield it from the boy's painful climax.

Too soon he exploded, their cries of joy and agony combined as he fell forward exhausted. He lay in her warm embrace panting with relief for several minutes and then slowly raised himself on his elbows to look down at her. "Gosh," he said simply.

"Gosh," she repeated, returning his smile. Anticipating the return of his nervousness and his readiness to withdraw, she stroked his bare back to reassure and comfort him while holding his young manhood imprisoned within her.

"How wonderful you were. You are my young bull," she purred softly in his ear. She caressed his body and undulated beneath him to excite the youthful libido and melt away his self-consciousness at having lain with an older woman, bringing his thoughts back once more to his own desires.

"I like you to fuck me," she said in a hungry, guttural whisper. She knew coarse, locker-room words coming from her lips thrilled him. "Do you like to fuck me, Alan?"

His hands were now moving abstractedly over her skin. "Oh, yeh." His hips began to pick up the rhythm she set for them. "Please."

Feeling his penis growing within her, she smiled. "Not now, not again, my love. Soon."

He continued to move to his own pleasure. Gently but firmly she pulled his head up from her breast and looked deep into his strong, broad face. Her eyes moved to the deep blue of his, then to his disheveled, golden hair, dimpled chin and full, sensuous lips. Straining upward, she kissed them. "Tuesday? Can you be here Tuesday?"

"Oh, yeh. Yeh, sure. Tuesday afternoon," he answered eagerly.

Rolling him away from her, she sat up. He lay in a shaft of dim light filtering through a crack in the wall. Looking down at his chest, she touched the first traces of fine, light hair and bent to kiss it. On impulse, she then kissed the end of his still erect penis, flicking her tongue over it like the tongue of a serpent. The boy jumped; she held him down.

"Remember, Alan, we mustn't tell anyone, no one, what we do here. You promise?"

"Honest, I swear . . ."

"It's our secret, my darling, just yours and mine. If anyone knew, we'd have to stop. We'd hate to have to do that, wouldn't we?"

He nodded his agreement.

The woman rose slowly and dressed, standing above him for his eyes to watch her carefully orchestrated movements. He lay on the blanket following her hands as they moved over her skin. She wondered what was going on behind that half-serious expression. "Why do you sometimes call me Kurt?" he asked.

She hesitated and shivered in the cold. Then, smiling down at him, "I don't know what you mean. I don't call you that, do I?"

"Sometimes you do . . . when you get real excited. Today you said—"

"You must be mistaken, Alan," she said abruptly, cutting him off. "I can't think why on earth I'd call you any name but your own." She looked purposefully at her watch. "I've got to go now or I'll be late. It's after four. Give me fifteen minutes head start and make sure you hide that blanket before you leave."

He nodded.

She knelt back down beside him and gave his testicles a gentle squeeze. "Tuesday, my handsome young bull." Rising, the woman pulled her coat tightly about her and crossed to the old barn door. It banged shut behind her.

The young athlete pulled up his track suit and rolled under the blanket for warmth, stretching his body contentedly. He wondered if anyone at the school even suspected he was making it with "old lady Catterby" and if any of the other boys had had her, too. She certainly hung around the gym a lot and she sure was horny. He felt very grown up and virile. I bet I do more balling than most of the seniors, he boasted to himself. He wished the other students knew; it was a real drag not being able to tell anyone. Maybe he could tell just his roommate; Frank knew how to keep a secret.

As he flexed his ego, the boy got up and hid the evidence of his most recent excursion into manhood. He rolled the old army blanket into a ball and tucked it carefully behind a high pile of rotting tobacco netting and then began running in place to fight off the cold while waiting the last few minutes before he could discreetly leave the place. He laughed to himself thinking about old man Harrothwait, the imperious, white-haired headmaster of the Talbot Academy. He envisioned the righteous old man sweeping down upon him on a cloud like God in the Michelangelo painting in the Sistine Chapel, venting his rage against the seducer of the faculty wives.

Time to go. He hoped Coach Logan was not waiting for him back at the gym. The coach had asked a lot of questions and looked at him kind of strange the last time he was late like this. He should be able to cover the three quarters of a mile in under ten minutes and he would think up some excuse to account for the lost time. A foot cramp, he had had a foot cramp. The golden boy took a last look around the abandoned tobacco barn and pushed out on the door. It did not move.

Frowning, he pushed again, harder. Then he put his whole body into it in three massive lunges. The old wooden doors creaked and strained out an inch or two, but snapped back into place. It's gotten locked somehow, he thought. Shit, she's out there playing silly games. "Okay," he called out, "let me out. Do I have to say please?" His only reply was the icy air whispering through the cracks in the barn walls. He rattled the doors in frustration.

"I can't stay here all night, you know," he shouted. "Hey, come on, open the door." He kicked at it viciously, jumping back with a shout of rage at the pain that shot up from his unprotected toes in the thin track shoe. As he rubbed his foot, he realized that whoever had locked the door was either no longer out there or would wait to let him out in his own good time. It would not be Mrs. Catterby, he reasoned. She wouldn't be playing around because it would be too risky for her. Maybe one of the guys on the team had doubled back; gosh, maybe he'd seen them. He leaned against the doors mulling the problem over in his mind.

Smoke? Was that smoke he smelled? The boy inhaled. He looked up sharply and searched the gloom. He could see nothing. Again he sniffed the air. It *was* smoke. "Oh, Jesus," he said miserably as he saw a thin flame leap up at the far end of the barn behind one of the piles of tobacco netting. He ran toward it, stumbling on a rotten floorboard, picking himself up and going on. Old Harrothwait will blame me for this, he cried to himself. He was in enough trouble with his grades without . . .

Alan grabbed up some of the netting and began beating at the burning wall. But the netting disintegrated in his hands, feeding the hungry flames. The blanket! He ran for it, returning to flail helplessly at the fire. The entire back wall of the old barn was going up.

Looking at the flames in horror, he was suddenly stricken. This was not just a case of putting out a fire so he would not be blamed; it was a matter of getting the hell out of there before he burned up, too. He raced back across the barn in panic to throw himself again and again at the double doors, calling out for help, coughing and gagging in the thick smoke that now swirled all around him. The walls. He ran along them, desperately beating on one vertical board after another, kicking at them to find a loose one.

The heat became more intense, his face felt dry as if it were splitting and peeling away, his lungs stung. He cried over and over for help. There was little smoke now; instead the air swirled with a whirlpool of blazing white ash from the flaming nets. It burned his skin, seared his eyeballs. He looked up. Overhead the beams and roof were a mass of fire spreading from one end of the long building to the other. Everything around him was red, orange, white, yellow; he staggered about in the middle of the conflagration screaming.

Outside, the flames reflected in Simon's large brown eyes as the little five-year-old sat on his tricycle watching in fascination. The pretty sparks shot skyward from the blazing tinderbox. And it was warm, so warm that he had pulled open his heavy wool coat, and, as if sitting in front of the fire at home, he sat staring into the flames, imagining faces and scenes.

Gasping for air, the golden boy pounded his fists raw against the locked doors. "My hair!" he shrieked, beating at his head. The leg of his track suit flared up. "I'm dying," he cried, "I'm dying!" Holding his face, the flaming boy whirled around in tight circles. His lungs gulped a last searing breath, then exploded within him as he toppled forward into the inferno.

Hadn't it been exciting? Simon thought, recalling the calls and shouts of the Academy's two hundred boarding students as they raced joyously, tumbling and shoving each other, down the ridge and across the frozen fields toward the huge bonfire. And then the shiny red fire engine from Wyndham Locks village, the very same color as his own tricycle, came clanging across the meadow. Of course it had come too late, and the firemen just stood about in their black slickers watching like all the others. But it had gotten too crowded, all the big boys kept getting in his way so that he could not see very well. And besides, he had gotten bored.

Leaving the group standing around the remains of the burning structure, the five-year-old pedaled awkwardly up the dirt lane toward the road running along the top of the ridge, taking great care to steer the front wheel of his tricycle onto the delicate sheets of ice that stretched across the deep ruts. The tinkling sound as the wheel shattered these thin crystal roofs delighted him. Several times Simon dismounted to cross the lane to a particularly big patch of ice. He chipped away at the beautiful, frozen design with the toe of his rubber boot and then jumped up and down on the shiny fragments with both feet until nothing remained but dull, white powder.

He was the only one in the lane at that minute and it

was dark just like at night. Simon liked night, you could sneak all around the school with no one to tell you what to do or tease or holler at you. And there were furry animals that moved at night.

Simon was so occupied in smashing an especially beautiful ice roof that he was taken completely by surprise when the hand suddenly grabbed his shoulder. He jumped back and looked up into his mother's anxious and drawn face. How long, he wondered, had she been standing up here on the ridge staring down at the burning barn.

"What were you doing down there?" she demanded.

"Watching," he replied with his typical infuriating simplicity.

"How long were you there?"

Simon bit his lip. He did not answer.

"Button up your coat."

"I can't button it." His little voice was filled with resentment. "You tied my mittens on and I can't make the buttons go through the holes."

She knelt down beside the boy and began to fasten his coat. "Was anyone in the barn?" she asked with quiet concern. "Did anyone get hurt?"

Their eyes were on the same level. Simon stared into hers for several seconds and then he smiled. "I'm hungry."

His mother looked at him in questioning silence, then patted the wool coat around his thin body. Feeling a strange bulge in his pocket, she fumbled in it and pulled out something that looked like a wooden clothespin.

"What is this?" she demanded, shaking it angrily in front of his face while searching his other pockets with her free hand.

The little boy stared at it mutely.

"It's a match gun, isn't it, Simon? A match gun!" Fear mingled in her accusation. "Who gave it to you?"

He said nothing.

His mother stood up and tore the detestable instrument apart before his scowling eyes and was about to throw away the broken pieces when she thought better of it. Looking down at them, she slipped the pieces into the pocket of her sheepskin coat. "How many times must your father and I tell you never, never to play with matches? How many times?" In frustration, she cuffed the back of the boy's head harder than she had intended and jerked her hand back apologetically, holding it stiffly at her side with a twinge of remorse and guilt. She stood silently studying the small face that stared back up at her. Instead of wrinkling into tears, it remained solemn and impassive, unnaturally mature.

"Were you playing with matches down there?"

"No."

"Promise me you weren't. Oh, Simon," she pleaded desperately, "promise me, darling. Promise on the good angel."

Again his eyes probed deeply into hers in silence.

"Why, why do you do these things?" she almost wept in anxiety and apprehension. "Why?"

"I didn't do anything," he said evenly, almost challenging her to prove otherwise.

She sighed deeply and pushed him ahead. "Go on, get home. And get ready for a hot bath; you don't want to catch your death of cold, do you?"

With one last look down across the frozen fields at the flames that still blazed brightly in the January darkness, the woman turned and walked slowly after the squeaking tricycle as the little boy who meant more to her than life itself pedaled along the road atop the ridge toward the school buildings.

Chapter 2

Two days after the tragic death of Alan Rivkin, son of Lionel and Harriet Rivkin of Grosse Pointe, Michigan, Simon sat quietly on the three steps that led up between two dormitories to the interior stone colonnade that lined three sides of the school's large colonial quadrangle. Although the sun shone brightly, Simon sat bundled up against the cold air in a heavy overcoat and his father's maroon and gray school scarf. He liked to wear his father's things, they made him feel grown and, besides, they would make him smart like his dad. His father was the smartest man in the whole school, no matter what the other kids said. He loved his dad, loved him just as much as he did his mother. She scolded him all the time, but she loved him back real hard. He knew that. The mittens, which he had managed to pull off with his teeth, hung by large safety pins from his coat sleeves. The students were all in the big dining hall at the far end of the quadrangle. He was glad because now he had the steps all to himself.

Peering intently through a piece of old net curtain

stretched across the top of the shoebox in his lap, Simon watched his latest acquisition huddled inside— a small, terrified sparrow. From time to time he lifted the corner of the fabric and pushed in crumbs from his luncheon cookie, but the unfortunate bird paid no notice. A shadow fell across the box and he looked up with a frown at the pretty little girl who stood before him. She was a few months younger than he, and just about his only friend.

"What you got in there?" Beth Sanders asked.

"A bird."

"Where'd you get it?" She sat down beside him and peeked in.

"Caught it this morning in my trap."

"Is it alive?"

Simon looked contemptuously at her and said nothing.

"Why isn't it moving if it's alive?"

"It's scared, that's all."

"Are you going to keep it?"

"Yes."

"In your zoo?"

"Yes."

"Can I hold it?"

"No." He rocked the box ever so gently and the bird fluttered its wings briefly. "See?" he said.

The two were so engrossed in the cowering sparrow that neither heard Beth's seven-year-old brother Tom Jr. and his eight-year-old friend Peter Willoughby sneaking up behind them. Too late, Simon realized his father's scarf was being yanked roughly from his neck. Crying out, he jumped up, still grasping the box as the two older boys ran gleefully into the quadrangle, waving the long maroon and gray muffler at him.

"Naa, naa, Simple Simon met a pieman . . ." Peter Willoughby chanted and Tom picked up the nursery rhyme. " . . . going to the fair. Said Simple Simon . . ." They danced around the great elms on either side of the seniors' path running the length of the quadrangle. ". . . to the pieman . . ."

"Give me that!" Simon shouted in rage. Oh, how he hated those boys.

"Let me see your wares," Peter called back, sticking out his tongue.

"Don't you touch this," Simon ordered Beth as he carefully put the shoebox down beside one of the stone columns of the portico. He looked at it protectively for a second and then ran off after the waving scarf.

"Naa, naa, Simple Simon," Tom sang, delighted at having enticed the younger boy into the hoped-for chase.

"Said the pieman to Simple Simon, show me first your penny," Peter chimed in, running easily just in front of Simon. And both boys shouted together, "Indeed, I haven't any. Naa, naa."

Peter balled up the scarf and threw it over Simon's head to Tom, who waited until Simon was just within reach before throwing it back. Frustration and rage filled Simon's large brown eyes as he rounded back toward Peter. "You'll be sorry, Peter Willoughby," he shouted.

"What are you going to do, Simple, put one of your curses on me?" he laughed, tossing the scarf at Tom, who could not quite grasp it. This time Simon snatched it from his reach and was given a bullying shove down onto the hard ground by the larger boy.

Not willing to stop the fun so soon, Peter ran over to the colonnade and, pushing Beth aside, snatched up the shoebox. "What have you got in here, Simple?" he called, taking a quick look in before shaking the box viciously over his head.

"Stop. You put that down," the little boy cried, picking himself up and running toward him. "That's my bird. Put it down, Peter Willoughby."

Throwing the shoebox high up into the air and

catching it, the older boy jeered at him. "Make me, Simple." He gave it another good shake.

Without breaking his pace, Simon leapt at the boy, throwing all his weight behind him. Surprised by the force of the charge, Peter stepped backward, losing his balance, and both boys fell crashing down the three broad steps to the cement walk, the cardboard box flying before them. Peter cried out in pain as the rough concrete cut through his trouser leg into the soft flesh of his knee. He took one look at the dark blood oozing from the torn skin and burst into tears. Jumping up, he ran bawling toward the Willoughby house as fast as he could with Tom and Beth close behind.

Simon rubbed his elbow and crawled over to the fractured shoebox lying on its side. He lifted it gently and looked inside at the dead bird, its gray feathers ruffled. The boy took it out and stroked the feathers carefully back into place, his expressionless face barely masking the hatred burning inside him. Although small, Simon knew ways of getting back at the bigger boys. As his fingers caressed the bird, a strange, faraway look came into his dark eyes and he began a small, rhythmic incantation over the dead thing lying in his hand. Simon stood up and said in a solemn voice, "The devil's curse upon you, Peter Willoughby."

Simon folded the bird very carefully into his pocket and ran, crouching, between the shrubbery and the dormitory walls, to his tricycle, looking back to see if Mrs. Willoughby was coming out of her house to holler at him. She always hollered at him. One day he would curse her, too, and then she'd be sorry.

He knew his parents would be angry about where he was going, but he wanted to put a very special curse on Peter Willoughby. Taking a final look around him, Simon pedaled furiously down River Road away from the Talbot Academy toward the village of Wyndham

Locks. Few cars ever used the road, only those coming to the school, so no one would see him if he went very fast. The road paralleled the Connecticut River for several hundred yards and then, after bridging a stream running into the school ponds, swung west across hay meadows to a narrow railroad underpass less than a mile away. That was Simon's destination, the smooth, shiny rails of the tracks. The early Saturday afternoon train going south would be passing soon. He knew, because he always watched it from the ridge.

Leaving the tricycle hidden just off the road by the underpass, he clambered up the steep bank to the top where he stood studying the twin tracks reflecting the sun as they ran over the old, strong-smelling, creosoted ties and sharp black stones in between. The rails curved to the left around a wooded bank, so Simon could not see the small, boarded-up Wyndham Locks station a half mile north, but he would hear the train stop and start there before it came into view, and he would feel the rails vibrate under the unseen approach of the powerful iron machine.

Taking the frail gray bird from his pocket, Simon smoothed its feathers once again to prepare it. He placed it on the shining rail and carefully spread out its wings in the sun just as if it were flying away with his message. The bird positioned properly on the altar, he moved back from the track about six feet and sat squatting on his thin haunches, waiting patiently while staring intently at the feathered body and its small black eyes.

At last he heard the noise of the train and braced himself. As it came closer and closer, Simon repeated his incantation and made strange, undulating movements with his hands, never taking his eyes from those of the bird. The giant, thundering, iron wheels ground down upon him, the engine horn screaming loud at the little boy squatting too close. Then, in a roaring flash, the tiny eyes of the sparrow exploded under the crushing iron; a pandemonium of wind rushed around Simon trying to throw him over with its force, but he sat unmoving, his concentration riveted to the spot as the train roared past down the track. A small smile spread slowly across his face. His curse would work; the bird was gone, the rail just as empty and shiny as it had been before. "So much for you, Peter Willoughby," he said under his breath.

Simon sat there for some time studying the rails and the way they came closer and closer until they became just like one in the distance where the train had disappeared. When he looked up at the sky he was not at all surprised to find that the sun, too, had disappeared. Dark clouds heavy with snow hung low above him and fine flakes drifted down onto his upturned face. He shivered and started the climb back down the bank to his tricycle. When he heard voices, angry voices, he jumped quickly behind a laurel bush to avoid being seen and looked down. Emerging from the underpass below him he saw a very strange sight. A woman walked beside a man who was holding onto a big dog and the man was waving a white stick out in front of him like a long magic wand. It tapped, tap, tap, as he walked. Curious, Simon thought. Could this be who the dead bird had sent to get Peter Willoughby?

"Do you really think this was necessary?" the young woman asked, pulling her coat more tightly around her. She had short, curly black hair and wore a sheepskin coat like Simon's mother. "Walking all the way from that boarded-up old station to the school? We could have taken a cab, and besides—"

"Susanne, I'm perfectly capable of walking. I've still got my legs, you know," he cut in testily. "I used to walk this every day."

"But Chris, things are different now, you're different . . ."

"Let's drop it," he snapped.

"Darling, you've got to accept—"

"I said let's drop it!"

Christopher Hennick lapsed into brooding silence, loudly tapping his stick ahead of him with deliberate, angry movements on the black tar as they moved slowly away from Simon down River Road. Their trip from Boston had been tense. Only a year ago their life together, their shared flat off-campus, had been filled with nothing but love and happiness. She was to graduate from Radcliffe with a degree in architecture, he from Harvard with full honors in English. Promising careers lay ahead. She looked forward to a job with the top design firm in Boston reclaiming the city's waterfront, and he was taking a crack at winning the newly established Benjamin Marston Fellowship for American Literature. It was a stiff competition, but once won, he would be an established scholar, the youngest to make it. And now? His relationship with Susanne lay in shambles. And his future? Did he even have one? It was all so unfair. Why him?

Susanne Laurence sighed. "I'm sorry, Chris. I don't seem to be able to say anything right anymore, do I?"

After a few minutes of further silence, he finally made an effort to rescue the awkward situation he knew he had created. Forcing a smile, he asked, "Well, what did you think of Wyndham Locks? The historic church, historic green, historic corner soda shop?"

Susanne gave a short laugh. "My honest opinion?"

"Has anything ever stopped you before?" His tone was tinged with sarcasm.

She bit her lip. She wanted their last day to be a good one, but couldn't he work at it a little bit, too? Trying to put a smile in her voice, Susanne replied, "Okay, since you asked, here's the word from your fledgling architect. Wyndham Locks looks just like every other small New England town I've ever seen.

A significant monument to some insignificant patriot in the middle of a green that hasn't seen a landscape gardener since the city fathers laid it out, a white church spire surrounded by old houses of those founding fathers at one end, and drab little mom-and-pop shops owned by foreigners lined up in protest at the other end. And if that place where we left your luggage for the taxi is what you refer to as the 'historic' soda shop, you'd better have them call in a not-so-historic fumigator unless the cockroaches double as soda jerks."

Christopher laughed in spite of himself. "Scoff if you must, but that place has tempted the jaded palates of generations of scholars, diplomats and Wall Street barons."

"So be it."

"I will have to admit, though, that perhaps the town takes a little living in before one can really appreciate its finer points. In all fairness, it must look pretty bleak right now without leaves or any flowers. The green is jammed with them in the spring. Let's hope Talbot will appeal a bit more to your ultracritical architectural sensibilities." He stopped. "We should be just about at the bend in the road. Right?"

"Right," Susanne replied, humoring him in the game he had been playing with himself ever since they left the train.

"Okay, now, over there." He pointed his stick to his right across the brown meadow. "Do you see the ponds?" He saw them so clearly in his mind. Snaring the pass, he flashed across the ice through the other skaters, slamming the puck into the goal as he stopped short in a dramatic spray of frozen crystals. The cheers rang in his ears and he felt his teammates' slaps on his back. He was the best they had that year. "There's a crowd of boys over there at the hockey rink. Right?"

"Sorry, wrong."

Christopher frowned.

"I see the ponds, a rink, but nary a boy," she said. "Deserted."

"But they should be there," he insisted. "What time is it?"

She glanced at her watch. "Two-seventeen on the button."

"Even if Talbot has an away game, there still should be a mob of students practicing over there. The sun was warm this morning; is the ice slushy, not a good surface?"

"It looks okay to me, but I'm a lowly member of the weak female race, no expert on Olympic ice conditions."

"Very funny," he commented wryly. "I tried to teach you, remember."

"Very well. I just wanted to be able to go once around the lake without falling. You had dreams of Innsbruck. We didn't talk for a week."

"Three days," he corrected absently, his mind absorbed with the mystery at hand. "Something must be going on up at the Academy today. We used to spend every free minute on the ice back when I was a kid here."

"All those many years ago." Susanne sighed in an exaggerated, nostalgic voice. "All four long years ago. You poor, decrepit, old man." Her voice lost its humor and some bitterness crept in. "And here you are, right back in the sandbox."

"Pay no attention to her, Milton." Christopher gave the dog's harness a shake. "We'll like this sandbox, you and I."

"This is all so futile," Susanne pleaded for what seemed the hundredth time. "Why not stay in Boston and work for the Marston Fellowship? You're throwing everything away. What are you going to prove by locking yourself away here?"

His voice rose quickly in anger. "How many times

do I have to tell you? I've got to prove I can make it on my own. Isn't that what you've been going on about ever since . . . ," he paused, rephrasing his words, ". . . all these months."

"On your own, yes. But that doesn't have to mean alone. We can work together like we've always done."

"Why don't you make up your mind?" he cried. "First you want me out of the womb, then back in it."

"Womb!" Susanne's patience snapped. "Is that how you think of me now? A womb? Well, you're wrong and you know it. You want out because I'm *not* a womb. And brother, you sure need one to protect that delicate ego of yours. Don't kid yourself, Chris, that's the real reason you're running back here to 'good old Talbot.' You're chicken. The great hero returns to those who revered and loved him. Make it on your own? You've got hundreds of crutches here. You know every inch of the place by heart; you don't need eyes to see here. They've probably got the cotton wool all ready to wrap up their darling as soon as you walk through the door." She glared at the man she loved. "You call that getting out and proving you can make it on your own fighting the big, cruel world? Darling, prove it by staying in Boston and competing for—"

"Shut up!" Christopher shouted, moving away from her, tapping his white stick furiously on the road. "Leave me alone."

"You're afraid, aren't you? And afraid to admit it? I'm right, aren't I?" Susanne called at his back. "You're afraid to compete, afraid of losing. For the first time in the life of the great, big, beautiful Christopher Hennick he might not come in first. That's why we haven't slept together since the accident, isn't it? You're afraid a blind man can't be as good a lover as one who can see."

"Damn you, shut up! Shut up!" He tried to blot out her angry words.

"I know what you're doing," she persisted. "This is a boy's school, a monk's cell. You're withdrawing from *all* competition." Susanne stopped abruptly, realizing she had gone much too far. "Oh, Chris, I didn't mean that," she said miserably as she ran forward to take his arm; it trembled with rage in her grasp. "I didn't mean it. I just love you so much I can't stand being pushed out of your life. I'm jealous of your precious Talbot Academy, don't you understand?"

He said nothing as he forced his way ahead. She released him, shaking her head with resignation. "Maybe it *is* for the best for us to be apart for a while to think things out," she said softly to his back. "I just don't know anymore. I'm tired of fighting you all the time."

Before he could reply, Christopher's foot caught in an unseen pothole and he lurched forward, instinctively rolling into the fall like the trained athlete he was. He lay sprawled on his back on the cold tar surface of River Road, recovering from the sudden surprise. Susanne had reached for him on impulse but pulled her hand back and stood looking down at him in helpless silence. Slowly a smile began to erase the anger on Christopher's face and he started to laugh.

"After that tirade, I don't know whether or not I dare ask you for a hand up. Do you think you could find one of those hundreds of crutches you were talking about?"

The tension broken, she, too, burst out laughing. "I know, darling, I was wondering if I dared offer it." She reached for him, but he scrambled to his feet unaided and felt for Milton's harness. Retrieving the white stick, Susanne handed it to him with a kiss and locked her arm snugly in his. "No more arguments, I promise." They walked on toward the Academy in happy silence.

After several minutes, Susanne looked back over her shoulder. "We have company," she said quietly.

"Who is it?"

"Don't know. A strange little boy on a red tricycle who seems to have appeared out of nowhere. He's been following us for the last five minutes or so. He stops when we stop, and moves ahead when we do. Could be with the CIA, I suppose."

"Probably one of the faculty kids, there are lots on campus."

She frowned. "Well, I hope the others aren't as creepy as this one. He's really giving us the once-over."

Christopher paid little attention to Susanne's chatter about the boy, concentrating instead on where he was walking. "We're on the bridge over the stream, aren't we?"

"Yes, it's frozen solid."

"Then you should be able to get a good view of the Academy from here. Well, what do you think?"

Susanne looked over at Christopher, his expectant face wet with snow, blond hair tossed by the wind, his sightless blue eyes looking ahead at a school he saw only in his memory, a happy school filled with shouting, laughing students, a school drenched with the sun she could not see. The dark brick buildings she saw atop the bleak ridge looked unfriendly, even menacing, through the snow. A gust of cold wind sent an involuntary shiver through her body as she searched vainly for some sign of life, some welcoming light behind the dark windows. The faint, melancholy chords of an organ came to her from somewhere up there. She did not know whether it was this somber lament, the mysterious little boy who sat unmoving on the tricycle, silently staring at them, or the old buildings themselves, but the place filled her with foreboding. She shuddered. Susanne felt instinctively that once Christopher passed through those doors up there, her life with him would be over.

"Yes, Chris," she said with false enthusiasm, "it

really does look nice." Susanne held his arm more
tightly as they started up the steep drive toward the
brick administration building ahead of them. On top of
its dignified white cupola, an old lead weather vane in
the shape of a running horse swung listlessly against
the gray sky in the icy wind.

The Talbot Academy consisted of a central quadrangle formed by eight large three-story, colonial-style
buildings connected by a formal colonnade running
along the interior of three of its four sides. The main
administration building that Susanne had first seen
housed classrooms, the study hall, a library and the
freshman quarters up on the top floor. It filled the
entire northern end of the quadrangle and looked
down over the Connecticut River and frozen ponds.

At the opposite end of the quadrangle stood the
smaller, more delicate dining hall, the only building
unencumbered by the stone colonnade. Its tall, two-
story windows on brighter days filled the single, large
room with the sunlight that James Harrothwait, headmaster of Talbot, so often declared essential to the
health of young, growing boys.

Three identical dormitories sat heavily end to end
on each of the east and west sides of the quadrangle.
The first two floors contained rows of small-paned
windows trimmed in peeling white paint; the windows
of the third floor angled through heavy slate roofs in
peaked dormers that were slowly frosting with snow.
The only thing to break the perfection of the quadrangle's symmetry was a chapel that extended out from
the west end of the administration building. Its interior
was a stark, white-paneled reproduction of an early
Connecticut Protestant church with high arched windows of clear glass, a choir and organ loft, gleaming
brass chandeliers hanging from the simple ceiling and a
spartan lectern from which not only the morning scrip-

tures were read by the headmaster but also announcements of the school's daily activities.

Only a dozen or so buildings were scattered outside this formal quadrangle. A 1784 white clapboard salt-box house, the home of the founding brothers of the Academy and now that of the headmaster, stood sentry to the north along the front drive from River Road up to the administration building. Along the foot of the gently sloping west side of the ridge sprawled the rambling brick gymnasium complex with its tennis courts and playing fields donated over the years by affluent and loyal alumni. Several small science buildings, the columned infirmary that assuaged the fears of even the most protective mother, a barn converted into a theatre and eight small, white-framed faculty houses ranged about the narrow road running south from the back of the dining hall along the ridge overlooking the low-lying meadows, woods and barren tobacco fields.

The only blemish on the colonial campus was the tall chimney of the school's powerhouse which could be seen through the bare trees on the wooded eastern side of the ridge that dropped steeply down to the river. During the annual spring floods, the river often crept up into the powerhouse, disrupting the school's heating system. The construction of the plant in this unfortunate location and the resultant discomfort were attributed by shivering students more to the Academy's parsimonious desire to economize on fuel than to its desire to hide an ugly necessity.

On this icy gray Saturday afternoon, the campus was indeed deserted and cheerless. No lights shone from the small-paned windows and no students called out or jostled each other along the colonnade or in the halls. Instead, the faculty and students sat glumly together in the chapel's uncomfortable pews, some to mourn in honest sadness the loss of their friend Alan Rivkin, others to mourn the loss of that afternoon's

cancelled hockey game with their fiercest rival, the
Chatham School. While they sat with bowed heads
and thoughts far from the memorial service being
conducted in sober tones by James Harrothwait,
Christopher Hennick sat nervously fidgeting in a
straight-backed chair in the headmaster's formal office.

How many times, he wondered, had he sat—or
more likely stood—in that room waiting for praise or
punishment from the old man? Memories of four years
crowded back, bringing with them a variety of emotions. Although relieved to be back at Talbot in a world
in which he felt secure, Christopher was a little frightened at facing his first teaching assignment, one made
all the more difficult by his recent loss of sight. How
would the boys react to him? He imagined how he
would have reacted to a blind English master four
years ago. Remembering his miming of a lame biology
instructor during his sophomore year, Christopher was
not cheered.

Thinking it best to leave Christopher alone to collect
himself before the interview with the headmaster,
Susanne wandered aimlessly around the paneled
room. She paused occasionally to examine some func-
tional antique object or to thumb through an interesting volume taken from the shelves lining one wall.
There were few frills in the office: chairs for sitting
on—straight up—a writing desk and several tables. No
clutter, everything in its place, neat and proper.

From time to time the administration building trembled as the massive chords of the organ reverberated
through its empty, walnut-paneled halls. The organ
made conversation nearly impossible. It also drowned
the faint, repetitious squeak, squeak, squeak of the
rusty axle of the tricycle moving cautiously down the
dim corridor toward the open office door and the dog
settled just outside it. A small, dirty hand reached

down and touched the animal's head, caressing the fur as it had smoothed the feathers of the dead sparrow.

"I'm lucky Harrothwait is allowing poor Milton at the school," Christopher said loudly over the music to Susanne to divert his thoughts from the upcoming interview. "I think the only animals he tolerates anywhere near the place are the ones caged in the biology lab upstairs. How they ever got him to agree to the snake farm project, I'll never know."

An involuntary shiver ran through her. "Ugh," Susanne gasped, putting the antique brass inkstand back on the headmaster's desk. "What's a snake farm?"

"Oh, some of the seniors came up with the bright idea of keeping poisonous snakes in the lab, rattlers and that sort, to milk the venom and sell it to the research center at the Hartford General Hospital. I guess the old man talked so much about initiative and free enterprise that when faced with a money-making venture, one that also had social benefits, he had to cave in."

"It sounds disgusting. Just make sure you stay far, far away from the biology lab. If any got out, you wouldn't be . . . I mean . . . you can't . . . She turned needlessly away from his sightless eyes in embarrassment, pretending to examine another book.

"Yes, Mother Laurence, I'll be a careful little boy," he replied sarcastically. Then his voice softened. "Don't worry, my love, snakes have always scared the hell out of me. I won't get within a hundred miles of them."

A thundering crescendo of the organ abruptly ended the music. After a few minutes of comparative silence, the chapel doors banged open, followed by a jumble of young voices broken by occasional shouts and running footsteps approaching down the hall outside. Replacing the book, Susanne walked quickly back to her chair, reaching it just as the tall, sturdy figure of James

Harrothwait, the headmaster of the Talbot Academy for the last thirty-two years, strode briskly into the room.

"Christopher," he boomed in a powerful voice, "welcome back, my boy." He took Christopher's hand and carefully looked him up and down before the young man had the chance to rise. "And this must be Miss Laurence, who you said would accompany you today. How do you do, my dear. It is a pleasure to meet you."

Susanne was struck by the craggy features of his strong face, the bushy eyebrows that rose up like wings and his full head of snow-white hair that he attributed with some pride to the eternal harassment of his youthful charges over the years. Taking his extended hand, Susanne mumbled a few awkward cordialities. Instead of her usual glib, urbane self, she felt like a stammering little girl. Her reaction did not go unnoticed by Harrothwait, who was aware of the effect he usually had on others.

"Please sit down, both of you," the headmaster said as he rounded his desk and lowered his towering six-foot-four-inch frame back into his high wingback chair, the only upholstered piece of furniture in the room. The wings made it impossible for others to see or talk to him unless they faced him directly, which was exactly the reason he had selected such a chair. James Harrothwait liked directness—he insisted upon it.

On this occasion, however, the headmaster was not being completely direct. He stalled for time, wanting to study Christopher and what changes might have occurred in him over the last four years. "Nasty business we've just gone through," he said, "but it just goes to prove my point that those who live by the sword, so shall they perish by the sword. And those who flaunt the rules laid down for their own good shall be punished by their misdeeds. Young Rivkin, a junior and a boy for whom I had high hopes—looked very much like you, Christopher—had apparently been smoking cigarettes secretly for some time in violation of the rules here. Last Thursday he left his companions on a cross-country run and sneaked," he shook his head sadly, "oh, how I dislike people who sneak. Rivkin *sneaked* into one of the old tobacco barns in the south field to smoke. It is quite obvious that due to his own carelessness he set the place on fire and the poor, misguided boy perished in the flames. Such a tragedy. Such a waste. I only hope this will serve as a lesson to all others here who are tempted to break the rules." The headmaster also hoped it would serve to stop further fatal accidents. Two deaths in as many years had been difficult to explain to the anxious parents of his charges.

"Christopher," he continued, "make a point to instill the importance of honesty and honor in your pupils. They must learn to live by the laws of society. Their parents send them to us not only to develop their minds and bodies, but to develop in them the high moral standards that will guide their actions and those around them for the rest of their lives."

"I'll certainly do my best, sir," Christopher replied sheepishly, remembering his constant infractions of the rules while a student at Talbot.

"But now for Christopher Hennick. Terrible, my boy, this trouble about your eyes. The doctors say there is no hope, none at all?"

"Not now. Perhaps some time in the future."

"If it is merely a financial problem, rest assured we at Talbot will help, but you must let us know. Your parents are good people, Christopher, but they are of modest means. I feel sure they would want us to help if we could. To lose one's sight is a difficult handicap for a man to bear. But it is not insurmountable."

Susanne was dumbfounded at the old man's frank

discussion of this sensitive subject. She had scarcely dared mention the word *blind* to Christopher since the accident seven months ago.

"I am informed you have been offered a chance for a fellowship at Harvard to continue your studies in contemporary American literature," the old man said. "You are not trying for it. Why? Your blindness?"

Christopher nodded.

"A pity. In your present state the competition would have been difficult, but knowing you, you would have come through with flying colors. It would have been quite a feather in your cap. Perhaps one day you—"

"No," Christopher declared bluntly. And then lowered his head.

The headmaster's eyebrows rose. He observed the anger in Christopher's tone and the stubborn set of his jaw and decided the subject was best left to another day. But that day would come; James Harrothwait was not one to let his students run from challenges. "That is your dog out there in the hall?" he asked.

The young man's jaw relaxed. "Yes, sir, Milton. Thank you for letting me keep him here."

"Well, there was no help for it. Milton. That is a strange name for a dog, is it not? Called after the poet, John Milton, I suppose?" The headmaster smiled.

"Yes. His situation was rather analogous to mine."

The old man looked hard at Christopher and his smile faded. "You are referring to Milton's blindness?"

"And his poem 'Paradise Lost.' "

James Harrothwait had not spent forty odd years as a teacher without having gained some insight into the moods and motivations of others. He was genuinely saddened by what he saw before him. He knew this boy perhaps better than he knew most of the students at the Academy. Christopher had fitted the Olympian image of grace, education, honor and manliness that he liked to think he was building in the boys here.

Physically, Christopher looked like a young god to the old man, with his curly golden hair, square, honest face and broad shoulders. How well he had led the school to victory in football and hockey, and on the occasions he had seen the boy on the trampoline, how his well-formed body had soared high through the air as if on wings. But, as in everything, there had been the counterbalancing negatives. The boy had been too self-oriented, too competitive, too proud of his athletic and intellectual accomplishments. Not because they showed his personal development and growth, but because they showed him superior to others. The vain fall hard, he thought, sighing.

"As with Milton's angel, Lucifer, do you look upon yourself as having fallen from grace, Christopher?"

"Well, after all, I . . ."

"Or, like the first man, do you feel others responsible for your loss of Eden?"

Christopher Hennick sat silent, unable to verbalize his emotions, his feeling of injustice.

"I sincerely hope you are not feeling sorry for yourself, Christopher. Are you?"

The young man bit his lip and lowered his head as if trying to escape the piercing eyes of the headmaster that he knew from past experience must be boring into him at that very moment.

"Self-pity is a very negative and unhealthy attitude for one of your age. I call your attention to the fact that the blind Milton not only wrote 'Paradise Lost,' but also later wrote 'Paradise Regained.' I hope you will be inspired by this man's strength and brilliance as a writer, not wallow in a patently inaccurate and demeaning analogy to his earlier poem." He paused to let his words sink in.

"Now, to your duties. The other masters in the language department have pitched in to take over your classes until your arrival. It was most inconvenient that you were unable to be here for the start of the winter term, but I can understand that it must take time to get used to working with a seeing eye dog. A German shepherd, is he not?"

"Yes, sir. I was very lucky to get one on such short notice. There is quite a waiting list." Christopher's voice sounded thin and uncertain.

"So I understand. I trust you will not encourage the students to make a pet of him. You know my feelings about pets at school."

"You have nothing to worry about. In Boston they stressed that Milton's effectiveness would be destroyed if his loyalties were confused and others allowed to distract him."

The headmaster nodded his head approvingly and looked down at the open folder lying in front of him on the highly polished surface of his desk. "You will take over a total of five English classes. Two will be for the first-year students. You will drill into them the standard classics of English and American literature, none of the modern, sensational trash people mistakenly call classic today. Those, I fear, the boys will read on their own time no matter what we say. I want them well grounded in the right literature so they will have a basis on which to evaluate the quality of all written works." He turned toward Susanne, his eyes twinkling with a sudden surge of mirth. "Even pornography should be written well."

He returned his attention to the file before him. "Christopher, you have the list to which I refer. Among them are: Dickens, Thackeray, Fielding, Poe, Hawthorne, Thoreau, Longfellow, Harte . . ." As the names flowed from his tongue, he smiled at the pleasure the authors had given him. "These classes will meet three times weekly and you will have twenty students in each.

"You will also conduct two classes three times weekly for third-year boys on the history and appreciation of literature. There will be twelve in each class and you will have more latitude in selecting the poetry, novels and biographies from not only this country and England, but the rest of the world as well." He paused, a fine smile spreading across his lips. "And you might include Milton's 'Paradise Regained.' " The crusty old man looked up to catch Christopher's reaction. There was none.

"Finally, I have decided to take advantage of your creative bent, which seems to have flourished so well at Harvard. You will conduct a creative writing course for those senior students who, through their past efforts, have shown themselves capable of profiting from the training and stimulation you can give them. This is a pet idea of mine. I believe this school should encourage and develop budding young authors; not enough good writing is being turned out these days. From time to time I would like to receive samples of the boys' work. Reading it will make a most welcome and interesting change from the more mundane tasks with which a headmaster must deal." Harrothwait closed the file and pushed it from him. "I envy you, my boy. Nothing is more rewarding than watching the growth of ideas and the ability to express them in the minds under your care."

"Shall I start classes Monday?"

"I think not, Christopher. It will take you several days to accustom yourself to the school and the routine of the faculty. You will find it a far different life from that which you led here as a student. Talk with the masters who have been conducting your classes to determine the relative abilities of each student and the material they have covered to date. Plan to take over your first freshman class on Thursday."

Christopher concentrated on all the headmaster was saying, the earlier humiliating lecture temporarily forgotten in the discussion of his duties. During his student days he had grown accustomed to the headmaster's gruff exterior. He suspected that under his rigid facade the man had a true affection for each and every one of his students and faculty. "Favoritism is the founder of petty jealousy," the headmaster often said, "and distracts the faculty from its real job, that of teaching, just as it distracts a young mind from its real job, that of growing." Like Solomon, one expected impartial, stern and just treatment from James Harrothwait.

"You have not yet met your superior, Arthur Catterby, head of the language department. He joined us at Talbot the year after you graduated." The headmaster turned to Susanne. "He and his wife—a most charming woman—have invited you both for dinner this evening." Susanne sensed his reference to Mrs. Catterby was made without real enthusiasm. Turning back to Christopher, he continued. "You and Arthur will be able to make your arrangements for the next days at that time. I am sure you two will get along famously. Arthur is a fine teacher, and he and Mrs. Catterby will make every effort to ease you into the social life of the faculty here at Talbot."

"I look forward to meeting them," Christopher replied.

"Now, one last piece of business. I know you propose to rely solely upon tapes, records and other modern equipment the blind use in situations of this sort. Unfortunately I am a little old-fashioned and understand next to nothing about all this fancy paraphernalia. And so I propose to add one more arrow to your bow, a primitive one that I *do* understand. Christopher, I have taken the liberty of assigning a scholarship boy to help you for two hours every afternoon, a pair of eyes, shall we say. Well, what do you think of that?"

Christopher did not know what to say. He resented the light dismissal of his carefully arranged plans.

"Lucas Howe is a very bright and good boy. He comes from fine people and has many of the excellent qualities of leadership you exhibited at Talbot. Unfortunately, English is Lucas's Achilles' heel, and so it is my desire that while he helps you in reading and preparing your lessons, you, in turn, will help him. He is, by the way, almost as good a quarterback as you used to be."

The placing of his athletic prowess in the past tense made Christopher flinch. After all, he had won the Ivy League title for Harvard only last fall. A twinge of jealousy flickered against the unknown boy.

"You made quite a mark for us on the football field. Now I expect you to make as good a mark for us in the scholastic area," the headmaster said while getting up and approaching his new English master. He laid a large, firm hand on Christopher's shoulder. "It is good to have you back with us. As in the past, I am sure you will make us all proud of you."

Before Christopher could answer, the old man boomed out, "Lucas, please join us now."

An alert, slender but athletic-looking boy of sixteen walked into the room and stood somewhat nervously on the edge of the group. He had obviously been waiting outside in the hall all this time and Susanne wondered how much of their conversation he had heard. He smiled at her, brushing a mop of straight, dark hair from his eyes.

"Miss Laurence, may I present Lucas Howe," Harrothwait said as the boy took her hand, "and this, Lucas, is Christopher Hennick, with whom you will be working."

The speed of events confused Christopher. He stood, extending his hand into the blackness, hoping it was toward the boy he had not expected and who had not yet spoken to indicate his position in the room. Seeing his distress, Lucas spoke quickly and reached over to grasp the uncertain hand while moving to stand in front of him. "Very nice to meet you, Mr. Hennick. I know all about those records you set here and we all followed you at Harvard. You really creamed Yale last year. Fantastic." His voice was filled with obvious admiration which served to soothe Christopher's ruffled ego and embarrassment.

As the two shook hands, James Harrothwait beamed his approval and Susanne sighed with relief at how well the sixteen-year-old had handled the situation. The headmaster suddenly consulted his watch.

"Oh, dear, I regret I must leave; I have a most pressing appointment with the parents of young Rivkin who are now with Mrs. Harrothwait. Lucas, will you please take Miss Laurence and Mr. Hennick to his room and help him settle in." He took Susanne's hand. "It has been a pleasure meeting you and I am sure we shall see each other again soon." Susanne thought she detected a conspiratorial wink from the old man. "Christopher, you are in good hands. We will talk further tomorrow after Sunday chapel." James Harrothwait strode quickly from the room and disappeared down the long, shadowy hall of the administration building, leaving them standing awkwardly in his office.

Lucas broke the silence. "While I was waiting, the taxi from the village came with your luggage, sir. I've already hauled it up to your room."

"Thanks very much. I assume that as junior man, I'm up on the third floor next to the freshman barracks?"

"Yes, sir." The boy smiled, remembering the hell through which he and his friends had put their freshman floor master. "But they're not up top now. Mr. Harrothwait assigned them all study hall after the memorial service to keep them out of trouble; they'll be locked up in there until dinner time. Shall we go on up?"

As they walked from the office, Susanne noticed that the strange little boy who had followed them earlier that afternoon was standing in the hall beside the German shepherd. Quickly withdrawing his hand from the soft fur of the dog's head, he looked up at her with a mischievous grin and then looked over at Christopher. The smile slowly faded, his mouth fell open in a look of surprise, surprise and what seemed to be fear. He backed away, his small fists clenching and unclenching at his sides. The large brown eyes narrowed and she watched his face turn into a mask of pure hatred so malevolent that it frightened her. He moved back into the recess of the door across the hall, only the whites of his eyes showing in the darkness as he watched Christopher take Milton's harness and follow Lucas Howe down the long hallway.

Unnerved, Susanne turned away and dashed after the two young men, grabbing Lucas's arm. "Who is that little boy, the one who was in the hall with you?" she whispered, pointing back down the shadowy corridor, knowing that even though she could no longer see him the boy was there, his eyes following them. His tricycle stood silent, waiting.

"Oh, that's Simon Catterby. The other kids call him Simple Simon. He's a weird little kid, that one."

"What do you mean, 'weird'? Weird in what way?" she persisted.

"Gosh, I don't know, really. Just weird. Doesn't get along very well with the other kids and he's always roaming around, even at night. You never know where he'll turn up; he seems to be everywhere, always watching. He's a real pain."

"Why was he out there with you?"

"Don't know. Maybe the dog. Simon doesn't say much, he just looks. They say it's because he's a genius or something like that, has fantastic powers of concentration. Well, here we are," Lucas said, indicating the wide wooden staircase at the eastern end of the administration building. "Your room is at the top."

"Don't remind me," Christopher replied, starting up the stairs. "I must have made this trip ten thousand times. My freshman advisor had that room. Come on, Susanne. If you ever wanted to see the black hole of Calcutta, now's your chance."

"I think I'm in it now," she countered. "Don't they ever turn on the lights in this place? Those little wall brackets hardly light themselves."

"You get used to it, don't you, sir?" Lucas replied. "It's all the dark paneling. But when the sun shines, there's plenty of light, isn't there?"

Christopher's back stiffened. "I'm afraid I'm the wrong one to ask about the relative merits of light and dark, Lucas," he said coolly.

"Gee, I'm sorry, I didn't mean . . ." The boy's voice trailed off unhappily. Lucas said nothing more as they climbed the broad staircase, each step creaking under their weight in the silent building.

The corridor running the entire length of the second floor was just as gloomy as the one below. The glass-paneled doors opening into rows of classrooms on either side admitted only faint traces of gray afternoon light. Reaching the third floor, Lucas crossed the corridor and threw open the door that faced the top of the stairs. "Here it is."

Susanne walked into the middle of the small room and looked about her. "Don't say a word," Christopher said from behind her. "Let's see if it's changed in the last four years. Around twelve feet square?"

"Closer to fifteen, I think."

"Single bed against the wall on the left, desk straight ahead in front of a dormer window—the only window?"

"Right," she replied.

"Curtains in a drab maroon pattern to match the bedspread and cushions? The walls a dingy cream?"

"You're batting one hundred."

"Little fireplace to the right with a chair on either side. There's a closet there someplace. Oh, yes, and a bureau against the wall behind me."

"Hey, you're terrific," Lucas said in honest admiration. "What a memory."

"Don't flatter him too much," Susanne interrupted. "He forgot the coffee table in front of the fireplace and the bookcases under the window."

"I did not," Christopher countered, laughing. "They must have been added since I was last here."

"Well, I don't care what either of you say about it," she lied, "I think it's a cozy, nice room. It's not at all like the black hole of Calcutta. Oh, there's a hot plate. We'll have to get some cooking things and—"

Christopher interrupted her false gaiety. "Sorry, only a pot and some cups. Cooking's strictly forbidden if I recall correctly. Coffee, cocoa, tea and sympathy. That's all we're allowed to brew up in these rooms."

"Gee, I wish we could have hot plates," Lucas sighed enviously. "The student council was pushing for it last spring, but then Hugh Snyder smuggled one in against the rules and set fire to his room. That was the end of it for everybody."

"Was it a serious fire?" Susanne asked.

"Yeh, I'm afraid so. Hugh must have left it on when he went to sleep that night. He was killed."

"Oh, my God, how terrible." She turned to Christopher, taking his arm. "You will be careful, won't—"

His initial burst of good humor vanished. "For Christ's sake, get off my back, will you," he snapped, wrenching free of her grasp. "All you've done since we got off that damn train is to . . ." He stopped abruptly, remembering Lucas Howe's presence in the room. "Lucas, you don't have to hang around any more. I'll be able to unpack and get things settled without your help."

"I don't mind staying, sir. And what about taking you over to the Catterbys' for dinner?"

"Just tell me where they live and I'll walk over there all by myself with my own two legs," Christopher replied testily.

"Oh, yeh, sure," the boy stammered awkwardly, glancing at the dog and Christopher's white stick. "They live in Sherman Hall, north side. That's the third dorm down the quad on the right."

"I know Sherman Hall and its location very well, Lucas. Thank you. Miss Laurence and I will manage for ourselves."

"Okay, sir, I'll shove off now." Lucas backed toward the door. "See you tomorrow at four? That's when Mr. Harrothwait told me to meet with you. I don't have football practice in the afternoon anymore and so . . ."

"See you at four, Lucas," Christopher interrupted in a long-suffering voice.

"Four tomorrow afternoon," the boy confirmed miserably, unsure what he had said to upset the new master.

"It was nice meeting you," Susanne said with all the warmth she could put in her voice. "I hope I'll see you again soon."

"Goodbye, Lucas," Christopher cut in. "And will you please close the door after you." He stood rigidly in the center of the room until he heard the latch click shut; then his taut muscles relaxed and his body seemed to sag. Feeling his way over to the bed, he collapsed onto it and stared blankly up at the ceiling. "Thank God that's over," he sighed.

Susanne was tempted to blast him for his rotten treatment of the boy but held her tongue for the sake of preserving peace during their last few hours together. "Do you want me to unpack your things and put them away?"

"You might as well. Put them the way I used to keep them at our old apartment," he said, talking to the ceiling.

Her stomach tightened at his mention of the two small rooms they had shared for the last two years while he was at Harvard and she at Radcliffe. Both their families had known about the arrangement but had said nothing, sure that their children would sanctify the relationship with marriage after graduation. And they had planned to do just that, but then the accident. All their plans had gone up in smoke. That reminded her; Susanne went quickly over to the bookcase and examined the electric hot plate. It was almost new and had no frayed wires. She moved it as far from the window curtains as possible.

"What are you doing now?" he demanded, annoyed at her constant fussing.

"Just arranging a few things to make the room look more attractive."

"Thanks," he retorted sarcastically. "It will be very reassuring to know how attractive my room looks—to other people." Christopher rolled over on his side, turning his back to her.

With a sigh, she began to unpack the rest of his things, filling the bureau and closet without saying another word. From time to time she looked over at him as he lay facing the wall. Christopher's breathing was smooth and regular. Susanne knew he was exhausted. If he were to get through this evening with his new boss without losing his cool, she had best let him sleep.

Moving to the window, she stood quietly looking down through the bare branches of the great elms across the quadrangle as night slowly fell over it. The snow had stopped, leaving gray patches on the slate roofs and ground below where several small figures ran back and forth scooping it up in an impromptu snowball fight. Their shouts drifted up dimly to her ears.

She thought of the little boy, the strange little boy. "Weird." "Genius." Those were the words Lucas Howe had used to describe Simon Catterby. Susanne remembered the look of intense hatred that had contorted his face when he saw Christopher closely for the first time. Why would he have such violent emotions about a complete stranger? In her mind she saw Simon's narrowed eyes burning in the shadows of the long, empty hallway below. He was probably only five or six years old. And yet she was afraid of him.

Susanne wondered what he had been doing to Milton. She wondered where he was now.

Chapter 3

THE HEAVY AFTERNOON CLOUDS HAD GIVEN AWAY TO a cold, clear, night sky filled with bright, twinkling stars. Dormitory windows blazed with warmth and the long colonnade surrounding the quadrangle was bathed in soft light. Through its high windows, the great brass chandeliers glistened in the dining hall, casting long rectangles of yellow across the frozen earth. Susanne watched the last of the snowballers hurrying toward their evening meal. In contrast to the afternoon gloom that had made Talbot seem so dismal and foreboding to her, this evening it looked cheerful, warm and full of happy activity as she stood beside Christopher on the steps of the Catterbys' front door in Sherman Hall.

He had awakened from his nap refreshed and relaxed. After shaving and showering in the communal bathroom that he shared with twenty of the freshmen, he had even allowed her to select his evening's wardrobe without protest. As Christopher had decided to be very Ivy League on his first public appearance, she chose a blue button-down shirt and rep tie to match his brown tweed sport jacket and gray flannel trousers.

Now that he had had time to get over the severity of the Harrothwait interview, much of his confidence had returned. He was back at the old school again, he had roots, he had a warm and secure room waiting for him. Whatever nervousness Susanne now observed in his behavior was directed only at making a good impression on the head of the English department and his wife. He faced Susanne on the stoop. "Do I pass inspection?"

"With flying colors." She smiled and brushed back a stray blond curl from his forehead.

"Okay, then in we go to beard the proverbial lion in his proverbial den. Where's the bell?"

"Just to your right. There, you've got it."

Pressing the button, the two waited with their best smiles to greet the Catterbys. The door was jerked open by a pleasant-looking man in his late thirties wearing a shapeless and well-worn corduroy suit that bulged at both elbows and knees. Arthur Catterby introduced himself briefly with a hearty but unmemorable welcome and ushered his two guests in from the cold. "What about your dog?" he inquired. "Does he stay outside or come in? You know we're not very used to animals on campus."

"I'd appreciate it if he could be inside with us," Christopher replied. "Milton's almost like a brother to me at this point, and I'd hate to think of him sitting alone out in the snow."

"Milton, as in the poet?" Christopher nodded. "Well," Arthur said, laughing, "I wouldn't want it said that I refused the great John Milton entrance to this humble house, now would I? Come in, come in and meet the family. We've been looking forward to your arrival for quite some time." Christopher warmed to the sound of his voice and the hospitality in it.

Taking the young master's arm, Catterby led them through the small entrance hall to a living room on the left decorated for casual comfort with overstuffed furniture whose floral patterned slipcovers sagged unevenly to a worn carpet. Although several tables and side chairs looked to Susanne like fine antiques, they showed obvious neglect. The room overflowed with a jumbled litter of books, papers and toys.

As they entered, Arthur's wife unwrapped herself from a curled-up position on the couch and casually tossed a copy of *Vogue* onto the already crowded coffee table. With bored nonchalance and drink in hand, she moved forward to them. Once again Susanne witnessed a strange reaction to Christopher. As she got a closer look at the young man, Karen Catterby's step faltered and her face drained of color; she swayed forward, spilling her drink. Quickly forcing a smile, she extended her hand to Susanne and Christopher, then moved unsteadily aside, brushing the Scotch from her velvet trousers while trying to regain her composure. Seemingly oblivious to his wife's discomfort, Arthur Catterby ushered his guests past her into the living room.

Leaning down, Christopher removed Milton's harness and settled back into the deep, overstuffed chair to which Arthur had steered him. He felt the dog's chin come to rest protectively on one of his polished loafers. The room smelled of good things bubbling and baking somewhere in the kitchen; it smelled the way a home should.

As his host chatted banalities while mixing drinks, Christopher was unaware of the little boy who sat on a red tricycle in the hall studying him silently from across the room. Simon studied the way the man's yellow hair curled, the dimples that appeared in each cheek whenever he smiled, the nose and perfectly proportioned lips—the man looked just like the picture in his mommy's dressing table drawer that made her cry. And his eyes were blue, too. Simon hated the pretty man. He hadn't come to hurt Peter Willoughby at all; he had come to hurt his mommy—the way the others had.

Karen Catterby came up behind Simon and put her hand on his shoulder, squeezing it reassuringly. She pushed him into the room. "Darling, get off your tricycle and say hello to our guests. This is Miss Laurence," she said, proudly standing the boy in front of Susanne.

"Hello, Simon." She looked up at Karen. "Simon and I met each other informally this afternoon while we were walking over from the station," Susanne said in a friendly gesture to make some sort of peace with the boy.

His mother whirled him around. "You weren't at the tracks again, were you?" she demanded sharply. "How many times must—" Karen Catterby broke off the start of a scolding in deference to the others. The boy glared daggers at Susanne, but it was nothing compared to the look on his face when forced to stand before Christopher. "And this is Mr. Hennick, darling, who has come to help Daddy. Isn't that nice? Now shake his hand."

Christopher leaned forward; he could sense the boy's face close to his. He held out his hand and waited. For a second or two Simon stared into the unseeing eyes only inches from his own. They were funny eyes, they did not look right at you. He looked up at his mother's anxious face and back at the man before him. He could feel the tenseness in her hands as her fingers began to dig into his shoulders. She was afraid, he knew it. With a fierce grimace, he hit Christopher's hand aside as hard as he could with his small fist.

Startled, Christopher jerked back as Karen grabbed the boy, restraining his arm before he could strike again. The blow had not hurt at all, but what the hell was going on? he wondered. "I'm sorry, I . . ." he blurted out in his confusion. If only he could see.

"Here, here, Simon," Arthur interrupted, "that's no way to behave, son. Not to a guest. Now apologize and shake Mr. Hennick's hand."

The little boy stood firm, looking from his father to Christopher. His lips pressed stubbornly together and he shook his head slowly back and forth, making no move to offer his hand.

Although his face was a mask of stern parental disapproval, Susanne noticed that Arthur Catterby seemed almost amused by his son's bold reaction to the new master. His wife, however, was in a state of flustered agitation out of all proportion to the triviality of the childish incident. She knelt beside Simon, trying to soothe him as her eyes moved anxiously between her husband's face and Christopher's. "Simon . . . darling, please." Finally she broke the deadlock, pulling the boy away. "I'm terribly sorry, Christopher. Sometimes Simon plays a bit too hard and gets tired and out of sorts."

"Yes," her husband agreed, "and this afternoon he had a bad shock. One of his little friends, the Willoughby boy, fell sliding on the ice and broke his arm. A very nasty accident, wasn't it, Karen?"

Christopher wondered if it were his imagination or had Arthur Catterby subtly emphasized the word "accident"?

Simon looked up at his mother, a smile slowly spreading across his face. "Stop that this instant," she snapped, shaking him, "and go to your room." Wriggling silently against her grip, he reached out vainly for his tricycle as Karen Catterby hauled him from the living room. Simon's protesting footsteps and her scolding voice ended with the abrupt slam of a door somewhere overhead.

"Well, now that you've received your official welcome to the Catterby home from my son, Christopher, can I refresh that drink?" Arthur asked jovially. "We've got to catch up with Karen."

Confused as to exactly what had happened, Christopher smiled and held out his glass. "Thank you. I hope I haven't done anything to upset your boy."

"Oh, I'm sure you haven't. Simon's a very sensitive and high-strung little five-year-old with a great deal of imagination, that's all. And I'm afraid I encourage that imagination, much to my wife's displeasure." Christopher felt Arthur's large, soft hand press reassuringly on his shoulder. "One never knows how he's going to react to people. He seems to have an uncanny ability to reach deep into their minds and read their thoughts even before they have them. You're not planning on thinking evil thoughts while you're at Talbot, are you, Christopher?" Arthur Catterby teased, briefly tightening his grip before taking the young man's glass and moving to the bookcase, part of which had been converted to hold liquor bottles and glasses.

How Christopher wished he could see the little boy, the curious little boy who Susanne said had followed them earlier that afternoon and whom his own father described so strangely. But still, children were children. They were all the same to a young man like Christopher—unpredictable. And they cried a lot. "I'm afraid I'm not much of an expert on little children."

"No one really is," Arthur countered.

By the time Susanne and Christopher received their refills from Arthur, Karen Catterby had returned from upstairs with additional apologies for her son's behavior. Without waiting for her husband's help, she poured herself another highball. From the sound of the liquor gurgling from the bottle, Christopher knew it to be a strong one. Karen curled back up on the sofa and joined the others in a casual conversation about school life. Her voice seemed strained and forced to him.

As she talked, Susanne studied Karen from across the room. She looked to be in her early thirties and was physically quite attractive. A trace of German

accent made her seem all the more sensual and pro-
vocative. She was a woman fighting to hold off the
years, Susanne thought. The curves of Karen's body
were all too apparent under the tight, blue, turtleneck
sweater and velvet slacks. Gold chains of various
lengths hung from her neck, falling around and attracting attention to the swelling contours of her breasts.
She wore only a shadow of mascara and her high
cheekbones further accentuated large brown eyes that
were deep, expressive duplicates of her son's. Carefully groomed eyebrows arched teasingly when she
smiled. In contrast to the passion Susanne sensed in
this woman, Karen Catterby's long, straw-colored
hair, ivory complexion and pale, glistening lipstick
gave her a cool, high-fashion look that seemed more in
place within the pages of *Vogue* than on the campus of
the Talbot Academy.

Susanne could not help feeling that Karen was an
unhappy woman whose life had not been easy. And
she was bored, terribly bored. In contrast, Arthur
Catterby looked as if he had been contented and
spoiled all his life.

He was not particularly good-looking, a bit under
six feet tall and too plump for Susanne's taste. His
thinning black hair was combed carelessly across his
scalp, failing to hide approaching baldness. The marks
of his thick, horn-rimmed glasses were deeply in-
dented on either side of his broad nose. She wondered
how this singularly unexceptional-looking man had
managed to snare and hold onto anyone with Karen's
looks and apparent sophistication. It was a question
that puzzled not only Susanne but every faculty husband and wife on the campus.

Karen, too, was making observations as they talked.
She had hardly taken her eyes off Christopher, only
averting her gaze when she became aware of Arthur's
eyes on her. This young man nearly fifteen years her

junior both frightened and excited her. He was perfect in every detail; he transported her back to those precious years in Heidelberg.

Looking at Arthur, she knew he would be no problem, he never was, tied up in his gloomy library with his nose buried deep in his books. Poor, boring Arthur. But Simon. He would know, wouldn't he? He always seemed to sense the attraction. He certainly had tonight. If what she feared were true, she would have to be very careful this time for both his and Christopher's sakes.

All through cocktails and later as he pretended to enjoy dinner, Christopher was aware of the undercurrent of friction between the older couple. Karen seemed the aggressor, finding not-so-subtle ways of venting her frustrations on Arthur. He appeared not to notice her sarcasm and innuendos while chatting amiably with his guests. Replying to Christopher's question concerning her German accent, Karen explained that she and Arthur had met six summers ago at the University of Heidelberg where he had been engaged in research.

Christopher caught the caustic tone in her voice when she said, "One day the world will finally be allowed to read the fruits of all those years of research, Arthur's magnificent and definitive tome on the Faust legend. How many years," she asked, "have we been waiting for it now, darling?"

For the first time, Arthur Catterby's face flushed in embarrassment. He spoke defensively. "I'm afraid Karen believes that study and scholarly research are an overnight affair."

"Overnight?" she laughed, draining her wineglass. "How many nights are there in a decade? Two decades?"

"Do you enjoy living in America, Mrs. Catterby?" Susanne asked quickly, hoping to change the subject.

"I had looked forward to it," she replied, "but foreigners are not always accepted in the more puritan enclaves of New England." Karen smiled acidly at Arthur. "Arthur's mother, poor dear, still looks upon me as a peasant from Hitler's youth movement."

"You do exaggerate, darling," Arthur laughed lamely. He turned to Susanne. "Life has been difficult for Karen," he explained. "She's a very intelligent woman who does not find the intellectual and artistic stimulation she enjoyed at Heidelberg in the environment of a boys' school such as Talbot. One day soon my appointment to the University will be confirmed and there, I hope, she will find the interests and excitement she lacks here."

"Well, you seem to have had a bit of excitement recently," Christopher said. He felt sorry for poor Arthur, who seemed such a nice, pleasant man and who was under attack by a wife who obviously had had too much to drink. "I understand that you had quite a fire here last Thursday. Mr. Harrothwait said a student died." Christopher could not imagine the effect of his statement on Karen—it was like a slap across her face.

"Yes, indeed," Arthur sighed. "It was such a tragic and needless waste of a fine, virile, young boy, wasn't it, darling?" Karen looked down at the plate before her, saying nothing.

The head of the English department looked intently from one person to another as he spoke. Christopher detected a strange, almost sadistic tone in his voice. "The link between fire and death is a fascinating one. It has played an important role in almost all religions known to us today. The Christians used it to purge sin. On the altar, flames have carried human spirits as sacrifices to pagan gods. On the pyre, they carry the spirit to heaven. Ever since Prometheus stole fire from the gods and gave it to man, fire has both ennobled and terrified man. Its fascination is inbred in us. Just look

how small children stare hypnotized into the flames."
Karen raised her eyes to meet his. "How they are
drawn irresistibly to fire, the delight they receive from
striking a single match. Why Simon is only five and
yet—"

"Arthur!"

Karen's cry sounded like a plea to Christopher.
Arthur paused in midsentence and looked at his wife.
"Are you all right, darling? You look quite ill."

"You know how this kind of talk upsets me," she
said, standing unsteadily and picking up several plates.
"Don't you and Christopher have some business
things to go over tonight? Why don't you two do that
now while Susanne and I take care of the dishes. You
don't mind, do you?" she asked, turning to her guest.

"Not at all," Susanne replied, rising. "It's the least I
can do to thank you for such a delicious dinner."

Arthur rose slowly and led Christopher into his
littered study opening off the far end of the dining
room while the women stacked and carried dishes to
the kitchen. Karen wrapped an apron around her waist
and tossed one to Susanne. "There's a little more wine
left in the bottle. Why don't we split it?"

As Karen passed her one plate after another, it
slowly became apparent to Susanne that in addition to
drying china, she was in the kitchen for another reason, to satisfy her hostess's curiosity about Christopher Hennick. They discussed Christopher's activities at Harvard and their hopes and dreams for the
future. As she answered Karen Catterby's questions,
Susanne sensed an antagonism gradually growing between them almost as if the other woman were jealous
of whatever past intimacies she might have shared
with Chris.

To Susanne's relief, the men called them back into
the living room, where, for most of the remaining part
of the evening, she took the role of observer as the
others talked. She marveled at the contrast and con-

flict between husband and wife that lay submerged beneath almost every word that the Catterbys spoke to each other. Why, she wondered, had Karen Catterby chosen to remain in a situation she obviously detested. Christopher also pondered these questions as he and Susanne made their farewells. In comparison to that of his parents, their life together seemed ugly to him.

As they walked slowly toward the taxi waiting to take her to Springfield where she could catch a late bus back to Boston, Susanne described Karen's and Arthur's physical appearances and related everything she had seen at the Catterbys' that evening, emphasizing Simon's violent and emotional reaction to him. "Darling, he may be only a little boy, but he frightens me," she said, her voice filled with concern. "Little boys can do all sorts of nasty things to hurt people they don't like. You should have seen his sick little smile when Arthur told us about the boy who broke his arm today. Please, do be careful of him."

"I think I can take care of myself there." Christopher laughed, brushing aside her warning. "But from what you say, I should be more careful of his mother. You make her sound like one real sexy babe for her age."

"It's not a laughing matter," Susanne protested.

He smiled, squeezing her arm. "Don't worry, I have absolutely no intention of getting mixed up with my boss's wife. Remember the old expression, 'Never dip your pen in company ink'?"

"Then you'd better lock and bolt your door at night."

"Sorry, my love, I'll just have to take my chances. No keys allowed."

"What?" Susanne looked at him in alarm.

"Too dangerous. Someone might lock himself in during an emergency—get sick, a fire, something like that and help couldn't reach him. It's an old Harrothwait edict."

"Oh, Chris, do be careful, I—"

"Hey, little worrywart," he cut in, "where's your face? I want to give someone a goodbye kiss." The humor left his voice. "No matter what I said before, I'm going to miss you." Christopher paused and softly added the word he had not spoken for so long a time, ". . . darling. I was thinking about you all through dinner. Who am I going to holler at and blame for all my troubles?"

Susanne took both his hands. "We don't really have to do this, you know. We could still . . ." Christopher put a finger to her lips.

He shook his head stubbornly. "We'd just end up back at each other's throats all over again. And who knows," he said desperately, trying to smile, "you may forget all about the nasty blind man."

"And you," she countered softly, "may say, 'Hey, I think I still love that silly girl.' May I phone you?"

He turned away evasively. "I'll call you . . . when I get more settled."

They were standing by the cab now, its driver studiously avoiding their conversation by studying his fingernails.

"I guess this is it," she said.

"Yep." The happy times they had had together flooded through his mind and his throat went dry with the loss he felt.

"Goodbye, darling. I love you."

"Goodbye." He paused. "I may not have acted like it, but . . . well . . ."

Reaching up, Susanne pulled down his head to give him a quick, hard kiss and then slid into the back seat of the cab, her eyes filled with tears. "All right, driver."

As the taxi pulled away from the west side of the ridge, Susanne looked back through those tears at the lone figure standing with his dog in the snow. She watched as he, too, wiped his eyes with the back of his hand and then, with Milton at his side, turned and slowly felt his way up to the Talbot quadrangle. She looked away and spoke aloud to the black tar road up ahead caught in the headlights of the cab. "God damn you, Chris Hennick. God damn you."

Long after his mother had put aside the goodnight book and tucked him in with an affectionate kiss, Simon lay in his bed patiently waiting for all the sounds of the house to stop for the night. A shaft of pale moonlight fell across the coverlet. He stared at the photograph he had sneaked out from his mother's dressing table drawer. In the dim light his mother looked so young and beautiful, but there was Christopher Hennick standing right next to her. Simon wanted to tear the picture in half, leaving only her there smiling at him. He would tear the man up into a million million pieces and . . . and burn them. Yes, he would burn them just the way they used to burn the bad witches of the devil and the mean people who hurt the good people like his mommy; he had seen pictures of them in his daddy's books. But he could not tear up the photo or his mother would cry. He had seen her sitting in her room looking at it and crying. It made him feel sad and frightened to hear her cry. Mothers were not supposed to cry—only little kids like Beth Sanders and Melissa Ann Benton were supposed to cry. He did not want the new man to hurt his mommy and make her cry. He wanted him to go away. The others had.

Creeping out from under the covers, his thin little body shivering with cold under blue and red Superman pajamas, Simon went to his desk. Using a black crayon (black was a bad color), he painstakingly drew a figure on a piece of paper from his pad. Although to an adult it might look like a strange, out-of-proportion stick figure, to Simon it looked just exactly like the man in the photograph, just like Christopher.

Holding his drawing up in the moonlight, he jabbed a sharp pencil through the paper over and over until the man was all filled with holes. Then, carefully emptying the metal waste basket beside his desk, he turned it upside down, being sure not to make any noise. He carefully smoothed out the ragged drawing on top of it. That done, Simon tiptoed quietly across the room and opened the drawer of a table on which sat several cages of animals: his hamsters, a white rat and a tank of turtles. Far at the back of the drawer he found the old tin Band-Aid box in which he hid his most precious possessions, including the two matches. He took out one and crossed back to his "altar."

Simon sat solemnly before the overturned basket, the coldness of the room overshadowed in his mind by the importance of the ceremony. While moving his hands back and forth over the drawing, he mumbled the incantation he had made up specially to get the bad man. Then, looking about him furtively, Simon struck the match once, twice, three times on the floor. He frowned and struck it a fourth, fifth and sixth time. Finally it flared into life, the brightness of its first flame briefly lighting the room before it lowered and began moving slowly, greedily back along the wooden stick toward his fingers. Simon held his little torch before his face, staring into it, and then lowered it ritualistically to the paper on the altar. As it caught, the edges of the drawing turned black and curled inward, the figure contorted, writhed and twisted in agony in the pyramid of fire.

Simon smiled.

Across the quadrangle, sleep also evaded Christopher Hennick. His mind went over and over the harsh, probing words of the headmaster, mixing them with images of his life at Harvard and the Academy. Sometimes he hated the man, sometimes he loved him. Christopher thought of the Marston Fellowship and

then of the days ahead of him at the Talbot Academy.
They would certainly be different. He rolled over,
wondering what the boys' reactions to him would be.
He tried to fit Susanne's description of Lucas Howe to
a living, breathing body and to visualize the Catterbys.
He liked Arthur. He seemed an amiable, gentle person, and Christopher felt comfortable and at home
with him. He imagined Karen Catterby, a slightly
faded sex goddess lying naked and spread-eagle across
the centerfold of *Hustler* magazine and smiled dreamily as he mentally opened and closed the magazine
until her open legs fell off.

The jumbled thoughts finally gave way to sleep, and
Christopher moved through a pageant of dreams. He
floated free in the air, soaring high from the trampoline. He knew how graceful he looked against the clear
blue sky, he felt the smooth flow of the muscles in his
body as they stretched and contracted in slow, gliding
somersaults and turns made high above the taut canvas. Christopher hardly felt the trampoline as he came
down to meet it and then soared high again in a gradual
loop, his body arching back to swoop over and around,
to fall back to . . . the headlights of the car reflected on
the rain-wet street shattering his windshield, he spun
around and around as the screams, the shrieks came at
him from all sides, lights were everywhere, coming
closer, and the horns blaring, the . . . Christopher's
body jumped back instinctively on the bed, jerking him
into panting consciousness.

Where was he? He lay there gasping for breath. He
felt the cold perspiration on his body and yet his face
was hot, his eyes smarted, he couldn't breathe. Christopher coughed, and then came fully awake with sudden realization—my God, there's smoke in here. He
sat bolt upright, his stomach knotted in panic. Holding
out a probing hand into the blackness, he moved it in a
wide arc along the side of his bed away from the wall,
pulling it back quickly as he felt intense heat coming

up from the floor nearby. His mind flashed a picture of what was there: the bed, little side table near it, the waste basket—he remembered carefully emptying his ashtray in . . . You idiot, he screamed at himself, you've set the fucking waste basket on fire.

Coughing in the smoke, he slid to the floor and carefully edged toward the heat on his knees, his hands like sensors reaching ahead toward the basket. He yelped from the sharp pain that burned his fingers as he touched the hot metal. Reaching back, Christopher snatched the blanket from his bed, balled it up and in one quick movement jammed it down into the flaming waste basket. He sat on the floor for several minutes, pressing the blanket down hard against any ember that might still glow beneath it and waited for the beating of his heart to slow. All was silent, black, he could have been in a vacuum. Then his ears picked up a strange noise. It was sort of a rhythmic squeaking sound, squeak, squeak, squeak, squeak, getting fainter and fainter as if something were moving away down the long, empty corridor outside. Then silence.

Chapter 4

THE PANDEMONIUM IN THE HALL OUTSIDE HIS DOOR told Christopher that morning had arrived and the freshmen were well into the start of another typically boisterous day. Even though they were granted an extra hour in bed on Sundays, their internal clocks could not adjust to this once-a-week luxury, and so the majority ended with an extra hour in which to snap towels at each other, wrestle, shout, leap and bully the smaller ones before breakfast.

Lying in bed, the young master listened to the activity while working up the courage to get up and go out to introduce himself. As they shared the same bathroom, there was no way of avoiding them. Sooner or later he would have to bite the bullet and meet the boys. Fortunately the problem of inertia was solved for him. A sudden cessation of shouts in the hall followed by lowered voices just outside his door indicated that Milton, who had spent the night there, had been discovered and was now the center of attention. A tentative knock sounded on his door.

"Just a minute," he called, getting out of bed and

feeling his way to the closet as quickly as possible. Bumping into a chair, Christopher cursed under his breath as he pulled on his bathrobe. "Come in," he called.

When the boys entered, they saw the handsome and famous new English master perched nonchalantly on the edge of his desk, looking in their direction. "Excuse me, sir," the self-appointed leader of the expedition said, "we were wondering if you'd like us to walk your dog for you before breakfast."

"He's a German shepherd, isn't he?" another voice broke in.

"Shut up, Colin," the first boy snapped authoritatively, and then his tone became more humble. "We'd be real happy to give him a good run, sir."

"That's very kind of you . . ." Christopher paused. "I didn't catch your name."

"Oh, sorry, sir. Raymond, Raymond Hoyte."

"Well, as I said, Raymond, that's very kind of you and the others, but I think I'd better do it. The headmaster feels very strongly about you boys not making a pet out of Milton."

"He's a seeing eye dog, isn't he, sir?"

Christopher tensed at the question but kept an even smile on his face. "Yes, he is."

"See," Raymond said aggressively to some unseen person near him, "I told you he was."

"Sir, Mr. Fowler down at the other end of the hall said we were to take turns making your bed and tidying up your room for you. He's made up a schedule for us. Do you want us to do it now, before breakfast, or after?"

A sudden surge of anger flashed through Christopher. How dare some complete stranger take it upon himself to arrange a personalized maid service for the poor, helpless, blind man down the hall. He tried to control his temper, but the boys sensed it in his voice. "I think, Raymond, we'll leave the question of my room alone for the time being until *I* decide what *I* want done with it."

"Gee, I'm sorry, sir, we just thought . . ."

"Let me do the thinking, will you, Raymond?"

There was a deathly silence in the room and then Christopher heard the shuffle of feet as probably six or seven boys filed out. Behind the closed door he heard the murmur of their voices in quiet outrage discussing what had just happened.

Pretty dumb, he chided himself. You sure know how to get off on the wrong foot, don't you, Chris old boy? His anger now subordinated to the need to correct the unfortunate situation he had just created, Christopher grabbed up his shaving kit and towel and walked to the door, pulling it open to silence all conversation in the hall. He knew that dozens of eyes would be fixed upon him. "Mr. Hoyte?" he asked, turning his head from side to side as if looking around for him.

"Sir?"

"Raymond, thanks very much for your concern. If you are the first man on Mr. Fowler's duty roster, I would appreciate your making my bed now and tidying up the room. I had a little trouble last night, so will you make sure you check the waste basket and, if necessary, find me a new blanket."

"Yes, sir, right away, sir," the boy replied, his eagerness fired to a great extent by his curiosity over the new master's "little trouble."

"And after breakfast, I'd like all of you who've been assigned to me as advisor to come in for a get-acquainted session. Will you please pass the word?"

Christopher moved on into the communal bathroom and noted with satisfaction that the hall once again filled with the babble of voices and running feet. No longer having anything sensational to gossip about and no strange new master to ogle, the boys had gone back to their normal, exuberant Sunday morning routine.

By the time he returned to his room, Raymond Hoyte had brushed off the singed wool from his blanket, made the bed and emptied the waste basket. "Boy, sir, you had a *fire* in here last night, didn't you?" he asked with obvious enthusiasm.

"Yes, Raymond, and the less said about it, the better. I vowed last night that I will never again smoke in my room, so you won't have to concern yourself about it happening a second time. A good lesson to remember when, and if, you should ever take up the evil weed."

"Yes, sir. Is that all?"

Raymond Hoyte was obviously dying to rush off to the others with the news, but it could not be helped. To try to hush it up would only assure its greater news value and so send it all the faster through the school's highly efficient grapevine. "If the room looks neat to you, Raymond, that's all. And thanks. I appreciate your and the other boys' help."

"That's okay, sir. Fat Jack will take care of it tomorrow." The door closed behind the fleeing Raymond.

Christopher could not help smiling at the name Fat Jack. He knew exactly what the unfortunate boy would look like—pimply face, round as a tub with knees that sagged inward to touch and feet that pointed outward like a seal's when he walked. There was a Fat Jack in every class.

He dressed, slipped the harness on Milton and took the dog down for his morning walk. As they passed along the east colonnade, Christopher snapped open his watch and carefully felt the time. He had almost an hour before joining the Catterbys for breakfast, an invitation urged upon him by Arthur last evening. Turning, Christopher headed down the ridge to the oval cinder track that ran around the football field for some strenuous exercise. There was little snow on the track and its surface felt smooth under his feet. He

would be able to feel it as soon as he strayed off onto
the rough grass on either side. Not needing his stick,
he tucked it under his arm and began walking faster
and faster, ending by jogging with Milton running
happily at his side.

Karen Catterby sat at her dressing table brushing
the long strands of straw-blond hair while looking
absently out the window, lost in thought. Below on the
west side of the ridge her eyes slowly focused on the
distant figure with a dog beside it running around
the track. Her brushing arm slowed as she studied the
figure. Although she could not see the face, she knew
it by heart. She would send Simon out to play before
Christopher arrived for breakfast.

Christopher spent the next four days meeting the
freshmen living on his floor and busily preparing to
take over his classes. He joined Arthur Catterby for
breakfast every morning to discuss the basic objec-
tives of each course and the interpretation of the
various literary works he would be covering with the
boys. Simon was never present at these meetings,
always seeming to have just dashed off to play before
Christopher arrived. And to his surprise, after their
first breakfast together, Karen Catterby made only
minimal appearances, remaining strangely aloof. In
fact, he became acutely aware that she was actually
making an effort to avoid being with him. He thought it
particularly amusing in light of Susanne's dire predic-
tion of his imminent seduction by his boss's wife.
Probably for the best, he reasoned. From the guarded
remarks he had heard about her since his arrival at
Talbot, Karen Catterby seemed a most controversial
character, one to keep far away from.

At the time he certainly had no way of knowing the
fears that lay behind Karen's strange behavior or of
her terrified reaction when the student grapevine had
first delivered the news of the fire in Christopher's

room. In a frenzy, she had ransacked her beloved Simon's room, praying she would find nothing. Instead she uncovered the charred fragments of his drawing and a match in his sacred Band-Aid box. When confronted with this evidence, his responses were typically and infuriatingly vague and elusive. He promised not to play with matches in his room again. That night Karen's twisted dreams had been full of her dead brother, the flames around him, the screams of innocent victims in the old tenement buildings along the Heidelberg wharf, the wail of sirens. He had reached out to embrace Simon. "Leave him alone," she had cried a oud over and over, "leave him alone," waking cold and trembling in Arthur's arms as he tried unsuccessfully to comfort her.

And so, torn between her desperate attraction to Christopher and her strong, protective instinct to shield her son from some real or imagined fate, from that day on Karen had refused to approach Christopher or talk with him openly. But her eyes and thoughts were constantly on him. She watched him jogging early every morning from her window and from the kitchen as he talked with Arthur in the study. She looked for him as he passed on the way to the dining hall and noticed when his hair needed combing, his tie straightening. Thoughts of him consumed her day.

As yet Christopher was far from expert at reading Braille. Most of the novels and poems he planned to cover in his courses he knew nearly by heart or had on tapes and records to play before class to refresh his memory. He relied on Lucas Howe to read aloud and tape those works that were new to him or unavailable in libraries for the blind.

He had to admit that the headmaster's "primitive" gift of a pair of eyes had been a wise one. And Lucas was not a bad sort at all—in fact, they got along very well together. Lucas was mature for his age, his voice calm and low, and so without benefit of sight, Christopher came to regard the sixteen-year-old more as a contemporary than a student six years his junior. Intuitively, he felt Lucas liked him and had a real desire to help, to make it all work. On his own initiative, the boy had designed grade books and charts to make it easier for Christopher to maintain a permanent record of his students' progress—or lack of it—throughout the year. He had sufficient trust in Lucas's discretion and honesty to allow him to record Christopher's daily impressions without fear of his repeating them to the other students.

Between work sessions, Christopher took long walks through the dormitories and classroom buildings and around the campus to familiarize himself with how many steps it normally took to walk the length of each colonnade, how many steps in a flight of stairs, which doors had high thresholds, which did not, which opened in, which out. Occasionally Lucas accompanied him to point out physical features of the land, show him through and describe the classrooms he was to use and refresh his memory on the overall layout of the ridge and the paths that crossed it. Christopher wanted to be able to move quickly and confidently about the Talbot Academy. He hated the idea that others might be watching the new, blind master, watching and waiting for him to fall.

The last place into which he ventured had been his favorite, the gymnasium complex. It should have held sweet memories for him, but now it reminded him bitterly of his limitations. As he stood alone in the locker room visualizing the long rows of tinny-sounding, metal lockers separated by long, thin, wooden benches, he was intercepted by Neil Logan, director of the athletic department and head coach of the Academy's moderately successful football team.

"My God, Chris, it's good to see you," Logan boomed out, pounding the young English master on the back and vigorously pumping his hand up and down. "Heard you were back, but Marcia and I thought we'd better give you a little time to readjust to the place before having you over to the house. I guess we can offer you a drink legally now that you're a member of the faculty. No more sneaking the stuff from a bottle behind the bleachers, eh, boy?" He laughed, his large stomach, the result of sagging muscles and too much beer, bouncing jovially. "Never guessed I knew what you guys were up to, did you? Well, I thought, what the hell, what damage is a little booze every now and then going to do 'em, it's all part of becoming men." He slapped Christopher on the back again. "And if I'd reported you, I'd have lost my whole fucking team, and you know how the alumni like a winning team, eh?"

"Hey, speaking of alumni, have you seen the new swimming pool?" Christopher stood silent and perplexed. "Oh, yeh, hey I'm sorry, I forgot." He paused. "Well, don't just stand there, come on, I'll describe it to you." Logan took Christopher's arm and propelled him forward. "It's right up your alley, fantastic. We're setting up a real swimming team this year. I can't remember—you used to swim, didn't you?"

"Sorry, Mr. Logan," Christopher said desperately, pulling his arm from the coach's grasp. "I've got to go now. I was just on my way to . . ."

"Look, Chris, call me Neil now. It's Neil and Marcia, right? We don't stand on formalities at our place, boy."

"Right, *Neil*, it was nice talking to you. We'll get together real soon." Christopher fled down the gym corridor as fast as he could, so eager to get out and away that he failed to heed Milton's warning movement and crashed into the door at the end of the hall. As he pushed down on the horizontal bar to swing it out, he heard Neil Logan call after him. "Hey, that's some dog you got there, Chris. Marcia's real crazy about dogs. You bring him with you, eh?" The door slammed behind him, cutting off the word.

"Boy," Christopher repeated angrily under his breath. " 'Bring him.' What the hell does that stupid son of a bitch think I wander around holding onto a dog for. *He* brings *me!*" That ended his visits to the gymnasium.

The headmaster was not known for making unannounced visits to the rooms of his faculty members, but Wednesday night before Christopher was to take over his first class, the old man made the effort to huff and puff up two long flights of stairs to see Christopher Hennick.

"I see you're keeping a neat and tidy room, Christopher," James Harrothwait remarked for openers. "Students don't respect a man who lives and dresses sloppily, no matter what the current crop of be-one-of-the-boys teachers say on the subject. A tidy room and a tidy body make a tidy mind. I'm glad you've remembered that." He lowered himself into the chair to the right of the fireplace. "It's why I insist on coats and ties being worn in the dining hall and chapel—a sign of respect to oneself and to others. So many of this generation today need to learn respect. But enough of that. How are you faring?"

"Oh, very well, sir. I take over my first class tomorrow."

"I know, I know. How is Lucas Howe working out?"

"Perfectly, I'm glad to have him. Thank you for—"

"Good, I think that boy has all the makings of a first-class leader. I want this school to be proud of him one day." He looked down at his hands. "And you are prepared for tomorrow?"

"Yes, I think so."

The headmaster looked back up at Christopher after a long silence. "And your blindness, do you find it a handicap to you? But that is a stupid question," he said, chiding himself. "Of course you find it a handicap. Let me rephrase myself. Is it hindering you in establishing a good relationship with the boys?"

"I don't think so."

"Good."

"I seem to be getting along very well with my freshmen up here."

"The other faculty members say you never talk about your accident, about your blindness. They say you're not very sociable, hold yourself apart."

Christopher was aware that his face had reddened. "We don't seem to have much to talk about together as yet. I think they're a little embarrassed when I'm around. I'm doing my best to appear just the same as I was, the same as everybody else."

Again Harrothwait sat silently, thinking over Christopher's words. "Perhaps," he said slowly, "it is unwise to try to be 'just the same' as you were. You are very different from the person you were. Christopher, you are blind now. Your entire personality has to be affected in some way by that. How can you lead an honest, content life unless you admit it openly, come to grips with it and adjust to it?

"Everyone here is clearly aware you are blind. You only hurt yourself by trying to hide it. How can you expect them not to be embarrassed in your presence when they sense your own embarrassment? How can you expect them to speak openly and frankly to you when they are unsure of your sensitivity to what they may or may not say? Think about that, will you?"

Why the fuck doesn't he make up his mind? Christopher thought angrily. First it's don't dwell on it and feel sorry for yourself. Then when you try to act normal, he tells you you're not normal and not to forget it. Why doesn't he just take his fireside chats and shove them. I don't need his nose in my business.

"Yes, sir, I will," Christopher replied aloud.

"Now, tomorrow, my boy, be prepared for the worst. Be prepared for the cruelty that the young know so well how to inflict, not so much by word but by attitude. Start strong and do not falter. And above all, don't let them see they can hurt you or, by God, they will use that weapon. Demand their respect by your attitude, by your bearing, by your determination to *teach*. Remember, you are conducting the class, not they. You are the one who calls the tune, not they. I want you to develop a rapport with your students, but a rapport through their respect for your ability and desire to help them, not a rapport through a mistaken attempt to win their friendship. Once you have gained their respect, their admiration and friendship will follow.

"Look at Mr. Witherspoon, 'the Hook,' as his students call him behind his back. He is perhaps the most iron-fisted member of our faculty. I hear he boxes ears and, on occasion, has ricocheted blackboard erasers off the heads of the malcontents. Yet I tell you there is not one of his boys who would not stand up and fight for his honor. Remember that, Christopher. Gain their respect and you gain their minds."

"I'll do my best, sir." Christopher was impressed with what the headmaster had just said even though it violated many of the rules he had been taught in his education course at Harvard. He had studied mathematics under "the Hook." The headmaster was right; he knew of no other teacher at the Academy he respected more or who had taught him more than that old man.

"Well, Christopher, I just dropped by to wish you luck tomorrow. Let me know how things go on your first day, will you?"

Christopher had no doubts that James Harrothwait would know almost to the minute how things were going on his first day. "I will, sir. And thank you for taking the time to come by to see me."

The old man nodded and stood up, the scraping sound of his chair indicating to Christopher that it was time for him, too, to rise.

"Good night, my boy."

The door closed firmly, leaving Christopher once more alone behind the facade of confidence he had tried so hard to build during the last four days.

Chapter 5

DAWN WAS STILL SEVERAL HOURS AWAY. IT WAS Thursday, the twenty-fourth of January—Christopher Hennick's personal D-Day. He lay in his bed listening to the unaccustomed silence and thinking of the day ahead. His stomach was tied in a knot.

Activity, Christopher thought, that's it, I need some physical activity. Slipping quietly out of bed, he pulled on his track suit and a pair of sneakers. Awakened by his master's movements, Milton stood ready to greet him in the hall with tail wagging. Like coconspirators, the two stole silently down the old, creaking staircase.

The early morning air was icy, biting into the young master through his thin track suit as he hurried down toward the oval. He had become quite used to making this trip and now knew almost within inches where to anticipate steps and how long it would take to descend the ridge to the athletic fields. As soon as he felt the cinder surface of the track under his feet, Christopher broke into a liberated run, letting go of Milton's harness and relying only on his feet to guide him. How wonderful it felt to run free, to let his muscles exert themselves, stretch, strain, to feel his heart increase its rhythm, the rise and fall of his chest as his lungs called for more and more oxygen, the tingle of warming blood coursing through his veins. Christopher forgot everything else, his mind centered completely on the hedonistic pleasure of his body's movements.

By the time he returned to his room relaxed and exhilarated, the freshmen were beginning to wake and stumble about the hall, preparing to meet the minor challenges of their day. He showered and shaved while carrying on a one-sided conversation with Raymond Hoyte. The boy stood staring blankly into one of the mirrors over the row of washbasins absently brushing the teeth on the same side of his mouth over and over. He managed to mumble after Christopher as the young master was going out the door. "I'll see you later, sir. You're my first class."

Christopher turned in the door. "That's right, Raymond, and I hope you're up on your *David Copperfield.*"

"*David Copperfield,* sir? Oh, no, we finished that last week. Please, do we have to go over it again? Mr. Engel said—"

"A little review never hurt anyone," Christopher interrupted confidently, but his stomach was once again beginning to tense under the first student complaint, even if it were a minor one thrown out by a sleepy young boy.

"Chris, there you are," Arthur Catterby called out as the young master tapped his way toward the classroom. "I missed you at breakfast this morning."

"Oh, Arthur, I'm sorry. I lost all track of time." Christopher shook his head at his own rudeness. "I was reviewing today's tapes one last time before class."

"I thought you might at least have dropped by the house for a few words. Nothing wrong, is there?"

"No, just eager to get started," Christopher replied with exaggerated cheerfulness.

"You're sure? Karen or I haven't said or done anything to—"

"Gosh, no," Christopher interrupted quickly. "You've been just great, and I've hardly spoken to Mrs. Catterby."

Arthur smiled, then frowned. "And Simon?" he asked. "His attachment to his mother is so terribly strong that," Arthur paused, ". . . well, sometimes Simon does jealous little things he doesn't really mean. He hasn't . . .?" The question was left unasked.

"Honestly, Arthur, everything's fine."

"Good." Arthur brightened. "Then we'll keep it that way, Chris; everything just the way it is now, eh?" Arthur took his arm lightly. "Well, shall we ride forth and do battle with the little dragons?" He guided Christopher into the classroom, where the two men faced twenty fledgling English scholars. Christopher sat on the corner of the desk in an attempt to look a confident, relaxed, old hand meeting his hundredth group of new students as Arthur launched into his speech.

"Boys, although you are freshmen at Talbot, I'm sure you really need no introduction to Mr. Hennick. You've all heard by this time that Christopher was one of the school's best athletes, not to mention being an All American at Harvard. But that is only one facet of Mr. Hennick's life. Aside from his skill in sports, he is also a very talented, if not brilliant, student of American and English literature. We are all very lucky that he should elect to return to Talbot as a master rather than remain at Harvard to compete for a most prestigious fellowship, the winning of which would be the envy of many an English scholar." Did Christopher detect just a trace of envy in Arthur's voice? No, impossible. "I am sure you will come to count yourselves extremely fortunate for this extraordinary and unselfish decision on his part."

Arthur's rather stilted, unimaginative remarks were

delivered with such gravity that at first he could not
help but impress the boys sitting before him. They
were still too new to the life of private schools to have
acquired the veneer of cocky boredom sported by the
older students. The unexpected mention of the Marston Fellowship had caught Christopher below the
belt; somehow it made him feel almost like a coward,
feel that Arthur Catterby thought he had unwisely
abandoned the field of combat and should return to it.
Arthur continued to speak slowly and a bit pompously,
looking from one young face to the next, his eyes
trying to hold theirs. He told how he expected them to
conduct themselves with their new master and the
respect and cooperation due him. As he talked on,
Christopher's attention began to wane and he found
himself reluctantly admitting that although he liked
Arthur, the head of the English department was really
rather tedious and uninspiring. As with their morning
breakfast meetings of the last four days, Christopher
had to struggle to keep his mind on what Arthur was
saying. His thoughts and voice lacked animation and
the spark to whet young appetites. How on earth, he
wondered, could this man inspire the boys? He was
thankful he had not had a teacher like Arthur Catterby
when he was at Talbot or his love of literature might
never have had the chance to flower.

But wasn't he being unfair? He could put Arthur
down as a comfortable, genial bore, but there had to
be more to him than that. After all, he was a department head in one of the country's best schools and he
had managed to marry and hold on to what Susanne
had described as a Bavarian bombshell. And there was
something else—he did not know quite what—something lying beneath Arthur's warm, pleasant manner,
something that intrigued Christopher. He had detected
it in the occasional strange phrase Arthur let drop, the
subtle emphasis of a word, the messages he seemed at

times to be sending Christopher, messages that Christopher could not quite grasp.

After ten minutes, Arthur finally abdicated the spotlight and made an elaborate show of shaking the younger man's hand as a welcoming gesture before leaving the room. There was a barely audible sigh of relief from the boys as the door closed behind him. Christopher now faced a quiet and curious class alone.

The boys sat in two rows of solid, wooden chairs, each with a single, wide armrest for writing. They formed a semicircle before his desk. Two walls of the classroom contained small-paned windows, the wall behind him held a long blackboard with some of the traces of yesterday's work still on it. He had the physical layout of the room firmly memorized. Now he wanted to place the students within it so he would know which way to look when he called upon each of them in turn.

"Well, boys, after that talk from Mr. Catterby, I don't think there's very much left for me to say except how happy I am, personally, to be able to work with you and to have the opportunity to introduce you to some of the world's great literature, novels and poems. I hope they'll bring you as much pleasure over the years as they have given me in just the short time I've known them.

"Now outside the romance of literature, I have a pretty orderly mind, so the first thing I want you to do today is to arrange yourselves alphabetically from my left to right. Okay, everyone up." Christopher heard mumbled voices, some complaining about being moved away from friends or favorite places, and the scraping of twenty heavy wooden chairs. "John Cullaghan, as C, you're first on the list. Over here to my left," he said, pointing in the direction of the desired seat. "Raymond Hoyte, you next to John, Ray. Sandford Jones? Do I call you Sandford or have you a favorite nickname?"

"Sandy, sir, that's what everyone calls me."

"All right, Sandy, will you take the chair next to Ray." And so it continued until the class had been completely arranged to Christopher's specifications. As he looked ahead into the blackness, Christopher now saw twenty names clearly printed out in two rows before him. They're all there, it's going to work, he told himself with relief. His confidence was high.

"You boys finished reading *David Copperfield* last week. What did you think of it? Did it interest you? What do you think about the times in which it was written? Anyone?"

There was no answer.

"John," he pointed directly at John Cullaghan, "tell me what it must have been like to have lived in England during the time of David Copperfield. For example, what kind of food would you be eating?"

"Roasts, sir, they ate lots of roast meats . . ."

"And goose," another voice added from the R or S section of the room. After a few sessions, Christopher knew he would be able to recognize the speaker with the help of his mental chart.

"That's right," John Cullaghan continued, "goose at Christmas. But I don't think the people—the poor people, that is—had very much to eat at all. Everybody seemed awful hungry most of the time."

"Why do you think Dickens wrote so much about the poor people in England, Ray?"

The rest of the hour was spent in earnest discussion of the novel in terms of the times in which it was written. The boys appeared genuinely interested in talking about the political and social ramifications of the book now that they were being asked for opinions and ideas rather than the typical recitation of memorized names, places and quotations they had come to expect. When he dismissed the class at the end of the hour-and-a-half session, Christopher felt well pleased with himself. Not only had the classwork gone smoothly, but his lack of sight had not hindered him in any way. In fact, he felt sure that after the first few minutes he had handled himself so carefully that the boys either forgot or were unaware that he *was* blind. Well, the freshmen are out of the way, he thought; now for the juniors.

Taking the white stick he had left standing in the corner by the door when he had come in, Christopher walked confidently down the corridor and up the stairs to the room on the second floor by the biology lab where he would conduct his second class that day before lunch. As before, Arthur Catterby stood outside waiting for him.

"Everything go well?"

"Yes, I think so," Christopher replied with the modesty born of knowing that all *had* gone well. "The boys really seemed interested in our discussions. We're going to get further into the political times of Dickens tomorrow. I've assigned them some work to do on English history."

"At least Mark Shepard of our history department should be happy," Arthur said without apparent humor, leaving Christopher in some doubt over Arthur Catterby's happiness with his all-embracing approach to literature. Before he could consider the matter further, Arthur indicated by his touch that the time had come to enter the classroom. "You know your aide, Lucas Howe, is in this class?" he asked, reaching for the door.

"Yes, he's been a big help."

"Well, I hope he comes through for you," Arthur said noncommittally. "Let's go on in."

The head of the English department once again began his ponderous welcoming speech and his request for cooperation, but this time Christopher sensed the bored restlessness of the boys. When Ar-

thur explained that he and the other interim teachers
had reviewed each student's progress with Mr. Hennick, a general groan rose from the class accompanied
by a hoot or two and some derisive laughter. Arthur
dealt with this by ignoring it and raising his voice over
the noise until it subsided. This minor insurrection
reminded Christopher that he now faced an entirely
different kind of animal from the more respectful and
meek freshmen. Last night's words of the headmaster
came back to him. "Be prepared for the cruelty that
the young know so well how to inflict."

Unable to gain the boys' full attention, Arthur pos-
tured a bit more, then cut his speech short and retreated to leave Christopher alone with his class. The
young master knew that this, not the previous hour,
was the real test of his ability to teach. Self-con-
sciously, he repeated the few opening remarks he had
made to the freshmen, becoming more and more aware
they seemed woefully inadequate, trivial and almost
condescending when directed at this older group. He
could almost feel the derisive smiles on the faces of the
twelve students sitting before him.

"Hey, sir, I hope you're not going to introduce us to
the *complete* works of William Shakespeare," a good-
natured voice called out of the darkness. It was followed by some laughter. Christopher could not help
thinking that this anonymous familiarity would not
have been tried on him if he had been able to see the
speaker.

"Don't you like *Macbeth?*" Christopher asked.
"I'm told you should have finished it for today's
session."

"Yeh, it's okay, but enough is enough. We've had
Romeo And Juliet—which, by the way, is no great
shakes from the sex standpoint—*Hamlet*, and now
Macbeth. When do we get to the really exciting stuff?"

"*Macbeth* is exciting, just as exciting as . . ." His

instincts told him to cut the discussion short and not get into an argument until he had established his authority; the boys were taking the class away from him. ". . . as any of the war novels, and a lot better written."

"Frank's not talking about shoot-em-ups, sir," another voice broke in, "he's talking about sex. That's the only thing that excites old Frank." More laughter followed. Christopher thought he heard Lucas's voice ineffectually trying to cut off the ensuing banter. Things were out of hand. In his growing panic he resorted to the power inherent in his position.

"By Frank, I assume you are referring to Frank Cannel. And who are you?" he asked in a coldly superior voice.

"Tony Arnacella."

"Antony Arnacella? Well, Mr. Arnacella, I'm glad you spoke up. Your initials are A.A., head of the line in the alphabet. Will you please change your seat to the one over there on the far left."

"Why me, sir, why do I have to move? I didn't do anything."

"It's not just you, Tony, I'm putting the whole class in alphabetical order so I can keep track of you, that's all."

A general uproar erupted as the students complained to each other and to their new master both at the same time. "Jeez, sir, we don't have to do that in any of the other classes." "That's a lot of kid stuff." "Whose paper will I copy if I can't sit next to 'Brains' Fleischer?" "Hey, come on you guys, what's the problem?" That voice Christopher recognized as Lucas's. "Why the hell should we move; it's stupid." "Mr. Engel let us sit where we wanted."

Mr. Engel can see, you crummy little bastards, Christopher wanted to yell at them. Instead he shouted, "Quiet!"

The hubbub ceased instantly.

"Now I, not you, am running this class and you are going to sit where I tell you to sit. Is that clear?"

This time he was answered only by mumbles and under-the-breath whispers among the boys.

"All right. Tony Arnacella, first chair on the left, Frank Cannel next to him. Then Alan Fleischer, Dwight Garret, Lucas Howe, Bruce Kirschbaum . . ." The angry movement of feet, unnecessary banging of chairs and purposely dropped books filled the room as he continued to call out the names he had memorized. "Howard Langley, over here on my right. Now for the back row. Paul Moore, you'll start off on the left, then David Roon, Steve Van Buren, Peter Weiss and Henry Young." Christopher waited until the movement had stopped. "Okay, are you all set?"

"Yes, teacher dear, we're all in our places with sunshiny faces," came the sarcastic reply from a voice Christopher thought he recognized.

"Good, then we'll let *you* start off, Frank."

"Why me?" the boy complained in offended innocence.

"Because you seem to have a very big mouth." Christopher's retort brought a supportive and enthusiastic roar of laughter from the boys.

"How'd you know it was me?" Frank Cannel answered back, feigning outrage. "Jeez, sir, you couldn't see me; you can't see any of us."

The other boys waited in eager anticipation for Christopher's next sharp put-down, but the promise of his earlier quip was not fulfilled. Instead their new master seemed to wither and, turning to his right away from the challenger, called upon Howard Langley, his question barely audible over the snickers and whispers circulating throughout the room.

"Excuse me, sir?"

"I asked, Howard, if you remembered much about the classical mythology you studied last year?"

"Oh, yeh, I know most of it. Why?"

"Do you see any similarities between Macbeth and King Darius the third of Persia?"

"King Darius?" the boy asked in astonishment and paused, trying to make a connection. His silence made the continued whispering of the class all the more blatantly apparent.

Christopher raised his voice. "What about the Oracle at Delphi, Howard? Does that suggest anything to you?"

"Oh, you mean the Oracle is like the witches in Macbeth; they both prophesied the future."

"They both prophesied the future, but in riddles, didn't they?" Christopher asked, his frustration increasing at the noise continuing in the room and the occasional scrape of a chair. Turning to his left again, he directed the next question to Tony Arnacella. "Tony, what were the riddles of the Oracle and the witches that misled both Darius and Macbeth?"

"I'm over here, sir," Tony said from Christopher's right. "I was just getting a book I left under my old chair."

As he whirled around to face the out-of-place voice amid giggles and snickers, the class awaited Christopher's reaction to this latest blatant disobedience. His whole body tensed. "Get back to your seat, Arnacella," he barked angrily. There was more laughter that could only have been caused by a rude gesture made at the blind English master.

"Alan Fleischer, Mr. Hennick," a voice said to Christopher's front left. "The Oracle told Darius that if he crossed the river into battle, a great kingdom would fall. Darius crossed, but the kingdom that fell was his own and he was later killed. Macbeth's witches said he need fear only man 'not born of woman.' As he considered all men had to be born of women, he went ahead thinking no one could hurt him. He hadn't counted on Macduff, who was prematurely taken by Caesarean operation from his mother and who killed him."

Under normal circumstances Christopher would have been impressed with the knowledgeable answer to his question, but now he felt it almost an intrusion made by a boy who apparently pitied his current predicament.

"Thank you, Alan," he replied acidly as punishment for the student's unwanted sympathy, "but in the future please wait until called upon before giving us the benefit of your wisdom."

"Up yours," he heard Fleischer mutter, and the sentiment was echoed by others in the room.

Christopher felt himself drowning. "Paul," he called in desperation, "do you think *Macbeth* would have been as interesting a play if the concept of predestination, as introduced by the witches, were not present?" He asked the question, not because he felt it right in the present circumstances, but because it had been next on the mental list he'd prepared last night and he could not think of anything else to say or do to save himself.

"Come on, Paul," a sarcastic voice laughed. While obviously trying to collect his thoughts, Paul Moore was now the center of some good-natured kidding. "Gee, sir, I'm not . . ."

"You'd better define 'predestination,' Mr. Hennick," another voice joked, "our Paul isn't the brightest." More laughter.

"Who said that?" Christopher snapped.

Laughter surrounded him now. "Guess," an anonymous voice challenged.

"Cut it out," Lucas's voice hissed.

"Jerk off, brown nose," jeered a voice sounding like that of Frank Cannel. Several chairs scraped against the floor and a shuffle of feet . . .

"Sit down, sit down, all of you," Chris shouted. "I want some order in this class."

Clapping and sarcastic cheers welcomed his pronouncement. He had lost all control. His dead eyes pictured the derisive expressions on the faces of the twelve boys before him. He had to keep going.

"In what way do Lady Macbeth and the witches parallel each other in the plot?" he fired out desperately, and then, realizing the question had been directed at no one, added, "David Roon," calling out the first name that came to mind.

"They were all women, sir." The facetious reply was greeted with the expected response from the class—laughter.

" 'Ataboy, Roon, you really know your sex," Frank Cannel called out. "There's some hope for you yet."

"Quiet!" Christopher ordered, striking his fist on the desk.

"Hey, sir," another voice laughed, "they were pretty lousy cooks, too. They . . ."

"Quiet, I said," the frantic young teacher shouted over the laughter.

" . . . overseasoned their cauldrons with too many eyes of newt!"

A stunned silence fell over the room. Only a few embarrassed giggles and some muttered outrage against the bad taste of the last speaker could be heard. The sympathy of the class now swung to Christopher, but too late. As if a fist had ploughed into his belly, the young English master gasped and stood with his mouth gaping open trying to formulate some response. Nothing came. He turned and, forgetting his white stick, felt his way clumsily toward the door using the blackboard as his guide. He left twelve boys sitting straight up looking sheepishly from one to another and at the dark streaks his fingers had made on the chalk-gray slate of the board.

Lucas left his chair and walked quickly after Christopher, finding him standing down the dim corridor, his forehead pressed against the coolness of the wall, his body tight as a spring ready to snap. "Chris," he said, "I'm really—"

"Sir, to you, Lucas," Christopher lashed out, and then turned, holding out his hand to find the younger boy's shoulder. "I'm sorry, Lucas. Forget what I just said; I heard you doing your best." He paused. "I really blew it in there, didn't I?"

"It wasn't so good," the boy agreed reluctantly. "But it'll work out; they're really a great bunch of guys. And they're real sorry, I know it."

"What went wrong?" he asked miserably. "No, don't answer that, I know damn well what went wrong."

Lucas hesitated. "We're not that much younger than you are, Chris, and it feels sort of funny to be treated like . . . like . . ."

"Like kids by a kid," Christopher finished. "That's what you mean isn't it?"

By not answering, he affirmed Christopher's statement. "But your questions were really interesting, honest," Lucas said with exaggerated enthusiasm. "I never thought about those things before."

Christopher squeezed Lucas Howe's shoulder. "Thanks for trying. I'd better go back in there and pick up at least a few of the pieces. You go on in ahead of me; you don't want to get branded as the friend of the bad guy."

"Hey, that doesn't—"

"Go on, I'll follow you in a minute or two." Christopher heard Lucas walk off in the direction of the classroom as he stood alone trying to compose himself. His thoughts were slowly distracted by an odd and yet strangely familiar sound. From what seemed far down the long hall, he heard a squeak, squeak, a rhythmic squeak of metal against metal coming toward him. It got louder and louder until it seemed right beside him. Then it stopped.

"Hello," he said. "Who is it?"

No sound came, just the faintest whisper of breathing.

"Hello. Who are you? What do you want?"

Still no reply.

Reaching out, Christopher felt the air before him and moved toward where he thought the sound was coming from. As he stepped forward, the squeaking started again and then stopped, almost as if the noise itself were trying to stay away from his touch.

"Come on, stop playing games. Who is it?"

Silence.

Fuck it, he said to himself, I've got enough problems to worry about without playing hide-and-seek with some idiot. He turned and walked back along the wall to his class.

Pausing with his hand on the doorknob, Christopher took a deep breath, turned it and walked several steps into the now silent room. "Okay, guys, I don't think there's much point of going any further today; we've both got a lot of thinking to do. It's a shame about *Macbeth*. You might have become friends, but let's put the king back in his coffin. Your next assignment should be more to the taste of the humorists in the class, the *Comedy Of Errors* by Mr. Cannel's favorite author, William Shakespeare—all of it."

He turned on his heels, grabbed the white stick and left the room without bothering to wait for the reaction of the boys to either his obvious crack about their behavior or the length of the new assignment. At this point he really did not care. All he could think about was that he had failed miserably; everything he had been afraid of had happened. The boys could not accept him because they could not form a rapport with a blind man. He had to talk to someone. Arthur Catterby's face flashed in front of him. That was it; he would talk it out with good, old, comfortable Arthur.

As he felt his way along the length of the hall toward

the stairs leading down to the west colonnade, Christopher heard footsteps behind him; some passed, others hung back. They would be the boys from his class on their way back to their rooms or just going outside to enjoy the unexpected gift of the hour's freedom he had just given them. He pictured their pitying faces staring at him as they passed. In actuality, most of the boys refused to pass or slunk sheepishly by averting their eyes in embarrassment. They were not particularly proud of themselves. Harrothwait would have been pleased to know that some of his moral teachings had managed to seep into their "thick" skulls.

Christopher stood for a long time on the Catterbys' doorstep trying to think how best to tell Arthur of his failure before ringing the bell. When he did, there was no answer. He pushed again and waited. Shrugging his shoulders unhappily, he turned about to leave when the door opened behind him.

"Chris," Karen Catterby exclaimed in surprise. She glanced quickly to the right and left.

"I guess Arthur's not in?" he asked awkwardly.

"No, he has a class." She looked sympathetically at his distraught face.

"Oh. Oh, well, I just wanted to . . ." He paused. "Things didn't go so well with my junior class."

"I know," she replied gently.

"You know? Already?" His voice was filled with anguish.

"One of the boys in the dorm stopped by. A case of the guilts, I think. He said they gave you a rough time."

"Yeah," he said simply.

Karen was undecided about what to do as she looked at the miserable young man. His utter dejection was more than she could bear. "Look," she suggested, "why don't I get my coat and we'll take a walk. Right now you look like a man who could use a friend."

He had mixed emotions about the wisdom of confiding in Karen Catterby, but her voice sounded warm and encouraging. Christopher thought for a minute. What harm could it do? "Yes," he said, "yes, I'd like that. I thought Arthur would be—"

"Arthur would be a nice person to talk to, but I think maybe right now you need someone who's not so nice and who'll talk back. Be warned, you may not like what I say." Karen waited for a negative reply to her threat. When none came, she walked back into the house for her coat.

Karen Catterby's heart raced with excitement, her throat felt tight and dry. Was she mad to be doing this? She knew the risk. But he was here and he needed her. They would be together even if it were for just a short time. And, as Arthur had said so often, maybe she was letting her imagination run away about Simon. Where would he be now? Oh, yes, he was playing down the ridge by the gymnasium with the Sanders girl. The safest thing to do was stick to the colonnade running around the quadrangle. Most of the boys would be in class for the next thirty minutes, and if any of the faculty bitches saw them together there, their gossiping tongues would have nothing very exciting to repeat, not that that bothered Karen much any longer. In the past three years she had often found herself the target of jealous whispers from the wives and sly winks from their husbands. The more the whispers, the greater enjoyment she found in encouraging the winks. Was it her fault? No, she reasoned, not if the other women could not satisfy their men. Let them spend more time pulling themselves together and less pulling their competition apart.

Struggling into her sheepskin coat, Karen joined Christopher on the steps. "Let's walk down the colonnade," she said lightly, preceding him the few paces to the columned walk, where she waited. "It's such a wonderful day, isn't it? Blue sky, hardly a cloud, sun . . ."

"I wouldn't know," he said despondently as he joined her.

"But surely you can feel it, can't you?"

"Feel it?" he asked in surprise.

"Certainly. I had many friends who lost their sight in the bombings when I was a child, and they could tell you what kind of a day it was from its feel. You know, if it was muggy the sky was almost sure to be hazy or overcast, and if the air felt crisp and dry, the sky was most probably clear and blue. They could tell spring by the fresh smell of the earth and fall by the musky scent of fallen leaves. They loved to turn their faces up into the warmth of the sun." Karen looked over at his blank face. "You don't really know what I'm talking about, do you?"

"I'm not sure, I haven't thought much about it," he replied almost too casually. He wanted to leave this rather embarrassing and silly topic of conversation.

"But you've got to think about it."

He said nothing.

"What have you been doing ever since that accident, hibernating? Blind people function perfectly well through their other senses once they learn to use them, once they stop clinging to the illusion of sight. My young friends did it and you're a lot luckier than they, you—"

"Me? Lucky?" he interrupted, almost contemptuous of her apparent naivete.

"Compared to them, you are. You lived a much longer time before losing your sight. You've seen so much more for your mind to remember and visualize when you hear, smell or feel things. The kids at the orphanage were young, some blinded almost from birth. And what little they did see was ugly—death and rubble. I wonder if today they can really understand or visualize the beauty of a flower garden or how a wide, manicured lawn looks after the rain." She fell silent and shook away all her memories. Then, clearly wanting to change the subject, she said, "Tell me what happened. It can't be as bad as you and the boys both seem to think."

Christopher explained in great detail everything he and his students had said and done from the time Arthur left them. As Karen listened, she could not help studying the young man who walked beside her tapping his stick from side to side. Her eyes moved over his face, the way his hair curled at the nape of his neck, brushing his collar with golden softness, the subtle arch of his eyebrows. When he talked, deep dimples cut into his cheeks, his lips were moist and full. Several times she reached out tentatively to take his free hand but pulled back, almost fearful of the contact, a contact that could set something in motion she knew she would not be able to control. She forced herself to be content with the occasional brush of their shoulders as they walked.

"But why on earth did you want to put the boys in alphabetical order?" she asked, turning her mind away from his physical presence.

"So I'd know where each one was."

"They were in the same room with you, wasn't that enough?"

"No, not if they're going to change their seats every day. I wouldn't know in which direction to look. I want to be able to look directly at them, face to face, when asking questions."

"Is that so important? As soon as they answer you, you know from their voices where they are."

"It's not the same."

"But they know you can't see them."

"I don't have to keep reminding them of it, do I?" he snapped back at her, and then added quietly as a justification, "It's more natural to look at the person you're talking to."

"Chris, you are either very silly or very stupid, I don't know which. You are blind. Why do you feel the great need to pretend you're not? You're not fooling anyone around here. If you want the boys to accept you, then you better learn to accept yourself as you are."

"You sure come right out with it, don't you?" He laughed nervously, not wanting her to see his hurt. "You and Harrothwait."

"Good for him; he's right."

"You talk as if it's not important, being able to see," he challenged.

"Quite honestly, your blindness isn't all that important to anyone but yourself. I don't care, I really don't," she said coolly, taunting him the way she used to taunt her brother to break through to him. "And I'm sure most of the other people on this campus, young and old, couldn't care less. What's it to them. You're the only one who's making all the fuss about it around here."

Anger replaced his hurt. She had no right to say those things. He wanted an understanding ear, not a vicious attack. "It's my problem," he said curtly. "I'll work it out for myself."

"Ha," Karen sneered derisively, "you know as well as I that that's a cop-out, that . . ." She paused in midsentence as a thought struck her. "You know, I've suddenly realized something. You're probably just like Arthur—weak! You can't face the truth either. He dreams of the University appointment that will never come and his great Faust paper that will never be published because he'll go on writing and rewriting it until the day he dies, afraid to admit to himself he hasn't anything new to say about Faust. And you, you go on pretending that that athlete's body of yours is still perfect because you're afraid to admit to yourself it's got a flaw."

He went rigid.

"You're afraid," she continued, boring in. "I've never heard you even use the word 'blind.' Today is the first time I've ever heard you even deign to discuss the subject, and that's only because I'm forcing you to. You are afraid to admit it." She emphasized every word.

"That's not true. Get the hell—"

"Then prove it." Karen suddenly stepped in front of him and grabbed both his arms, pinning them to his sides. "There. Now I'm standing right in front of you, Christopher Hennick, staring directly into your eyes. Can you see me? No. Say it, say it out loud, say 'I'm blind, I can't see you.' "

He struggled, but she held him. The muscles of his face contorted.

"Say it, coward," she ordered, feeling his body cringe at the disgust in her voice. She tightened her grip and shook him. "Say it, say it so I can hear, so everyone in this lousy place can hear it."

Rage, pain and frustration all mingled together on his face as he broke. "Damn you," he shouted at her. "I can't see, I can't see. Does that make you happy? I'm blind. Now are you satisfied?" He tried to shake off her hands, wrench himself free from her.

"Yes," Karen said softly, "I'm satisfied."

He stood trembling, vulnerable, tears—his first since the accident—filling his eyes and running down his cheeks as his body slowly relaxed after its explosive release of tension. And slowly Christopher became aware of Arthur's wife, of her compelling strength, of the heavy scent from her hair that surrounded him. He became aware of the stirrings of attraction and desire that flowed between them through the touch of her hands on his arms.

The faint squeak was like a knife of ice piercing Karen's brain. Jumping back, she released Christopher and whirled from him to look desperately around her, her eyes searching the colonnade, the quadrangle. There, across from them on the west side, sat Simon, his body rocking back and forth as he stared at them. Even from that distance, his eyes caught hers and seemed to probe deep into them.

"What is it?" Christopher asked.

"Darling," Karen called to the little boy, "come over here."

"Who is it? Arthur?"

"Simon."

Christopher heard the noise of the tricycle as Simon slowly pedaled it around the brick walk of the colonnade toward them. "I've heard that squeaking before," he said. "What is it?"

"It's his tricycle." She lowered her voice and asked urgently, "Where did you hear it?"

"This morning outside my second class. I asked who it was but got no answer. I'm afraid your son doesn't like me very much."

Karen seemed relieved. "No matter what Arthur does, no matter how much oil he seems to use, that damn back axle still squeaks." Her voice tapered off to a whisper as the little boy approached. "We'd get him another, but Simon's a fanatic about that machine, won't let it out of his sight."

Karen's tone changed from conspiratorial to one of open cheeriness. "Say hello to Mr. Hennick, darling."

The boy sat ten feet from them looking up at both with accusing eyes. He saw the man brush the wetness from his cheeks.

"Simon, let's not go through this thing all over again. Say hello," Karen ordered.

"Hello," the small voice said grudgingly. Christopher sensed the animosity and defiance in it.

"Hello, Simon," he answered brightly. "Was that you I spoke to this morning in the hall?"

The little boy said nothing, just sat looking up at the blind master.

"Simon, was it you?" his mother persisted. "Answer Mr. Hennick."

The boy remained silent.

"Chris, I've got to go now, it's time for Simon's lunch," Karen said in exasperation. "I'm afraid I wasn't much help solving your class problem. Perhaps Arthur *is* the better one to talk to . . ." She paused and then added, ". . . if you still want to hide." Turning to Simon, she said, "Mr. Hennick came to talk to Daddy this morning, darling. We must remember to tell him, mustn't we?"

Christopher reached toward her. "Can we—" he began hesitantly.

"Talk to Arthur," she cut in, her voice cool and detached. "Come along, darling, I'll fix you something special." Karen started off behind Simon as he turned his tricycle around and pedaled off in the direction of home.

He called after her as he heard her move away. "But I . . ."

"Goodbye, Christopher," she said firmly over her shoulder.

Facing the direction in which she had gone, Christopher stood in a state of confusion brought on not only by their heated conversation but also by the brief intimacy and then coldness in their relation. He wished he could see her as she really looked; the image he carried of her from Susanne's description no longer seemed to fit. She was a far more complex woman, a compelling woman. If he could only see her, touch her face.

Shouts coming up the colonnade behind him signalled the end of the last morning class and the thundering, bellowing stampede to the dining hall for lunch. Christopher let himself be nudged and hustled by the throng, turning without thinking to chide an aggressive boy who accidentally elbowed him aside. "Hey, open your eyes and watch where you're going. Do you want to borrow my stick?"

Chapter 6

THAT NIGHT, SIMON ONCE AGAIN SLIPPED OUT OF BED and pulled on his bathrobe while puzzling over what steps to take. The picture of his mother holding onto that Mr. Hennick's arms and struggling with him went round and round in his head. What had he been trying to do to her? She had acted funny all afternoon and pretended nothing had happened, but Simon knew better.

He wandered slowly around the dark room, his feet oblivious to the cold floor as his small fingers carefully traced the outlines of the cages in his zoo, prodding a sleeping hamster through thin bars. The startled rodent ran back and forth in his cage. Simon really could not see the tropical fish or the turtles in their watery homes, but the light from the waning moon fell across the old, cracked aquarium with the weighted glass top where the twisted, striped bodies of the garter snakes lived. He squatted down to get a closer look. Once his father had showed him pictures in a book and told him about how some men down south danced with snakes around their necks. His mother had been mad at his father for doing that; she hated snakes. Simon liked them. His dad had a lot of stories about snakes. Snakes were bad angels; God had got mad at them and taken their legs away.

The door to his room suddenly opened. Startled, Simon squinted up at the dark figure silhouetted against the bright light of the hall outside.

"Why aren't you in bed?" his father asked softly. "It's way past your bedtime." Closing the door, he entered and knelt down by his son, putting his arm around the little boy.

"Mommy was with Mr. Hennick."

"I know, Simon. She was trying to cheer him up. He had a very upsetting experience today."

"I hate him."

Arthur smiled at the vehemence of the typically childish assertion. "It's not nice to hate people."

"Yes, but I hate him anyhow." Simon angrily nudged the old aquarium before them. The head of one of the serpents lifted up slowly from the dry leaves. He watched as it swayed stiffly and then sank back down. It was an awful lot smaller than the big ones in the biology lab.

"Come on, Simon, be daddy's little soldier and get into bed." Arthur lifted him gently up and crossed the room to his bed, tucking the covers tightly around him.

"He was crying."

"Who?"

"That Mr. Hennick."

"Oh?"

"Mommy was holding him. He was going to hurt her."

Arthur ran his hand lightly over the boy's hair. "Now don't fret. Mommy's safe and we'll keep her safe, you and I. Go to sleep and have wonderful, wonderful dreams." He leaned over and kissed his son's forehead.

*   *   *

Christopher hurried to his second and final Saturday class. He had spent too much time after his first class with Raymond Hoyte and a few of the other freshmen who wanted to keep talking about Dickensian England, and now the halls of the administration building were nearly empty of students. Friday had gone quite well for Christopher. He had been introduced to his second freshman and junior groups and, using a new, more relaxed approach with them, had had few problems in setting up a good relationship with both sets of boys. Now he was rather looking forward to the challenge lying ahead of him—trying to win over Tony Arnacella, Frank Cannel and their classmates.

After his traumatic confrontation with Karen Catterby, he had done a great deal of thinking and soul searching. What had he been trying to prove? Anything? Or had he merely been taking his problem out on the world the way he must have done with Susanne? She had put up with it because she loved him. These boys had no reason to do so. Anyway, he felt more relaxed now; he saw (if he could indulge himself with the use of the once-banned word) things in a more positive, challenging light. He had even called Susanne that morning. Their conversation had been stilted at first, but he had finally found his tongue and admitted he missed her. She had cried. They had made tentative plans to spend a weekend together at Talbot early next month.

He was just a door away from his classroom on the second floor when his stick hit something sitting directly in his path. Coming to an abrupt and puzzled halt, Christopher tapped the metal-sounding obstruction curiously. It moved back with a squeak. "Simon?" he asked, "is that you?"

He got nothing but silence as his reply. The young master sensed hatred around him in the silent hall.

"Simon, for Christ's sake, say something. At least tell me why you don't like me."

He stood waiting for the answer when he heard footsteps running toward him. "Hi, Chris," Lucas Howe called. "Sorry I'm late, but Coach Logan wanted to see me at the gym."

"That's okay. Say, maybe you can help me get Simon to talk."

"Simon Catterby?" the panting boy asked in surprise. "Well, sure. When and what do you want him to say?"

"Now," Christopher replied, pointing his white stick. "Ask him why—"

"But Simon's not here," Lucas interrupted.

It was Christopher's turn to be surprised. "He's right over there, he . . ." His voice trailed off in confusion.

"He probably scuttled off when he heard me coming," Lucas said casually.

"That kid's starting to give me the creeps. I don't know what he's got against me," Christopher said, shaking his head.

"Don't worry, I told you the day you got here that he's a little weirdo. Coming in?"

"Yep."

Putting thoughts of Simon behind him, Christopher followed Lucas Howe into the room and without a sign of hesitation went straight to his desk, laying his white stick across the top of it in full view of the class. He turned toward the boys who sat silent before him in their alphabetically assigned seats waiting curiously for what would come after the last, disastrous session.

"Good morning, gentlemen," Christopher said. "First, I want you to know that I'm burying everything that happened here Thursday along with poor old Macbeth. As far as I'm concerned, it's a dead issue and I hope you will treat it as such."

The small chorus of murmurs he heard sounded happy and positive.

"Now, as to the seating arrangement, the only reason I asked you to do it alphabetically was to help me know who was talking, at least until I became familiar with your voices. As I can't see, I have to identify you by your voices, not your faces, although in a few cases I think I have a pretty good idea of what you look like. I'd say that Frank is the Don Juan of the class and Tony more like one of the Marx Brothers."

Appreciative laughter swept the room. "Dead on, sir," someone said.

"If you men don't want to go the alphabet route, sit where you like. I only ask that you identify yourselves the way Alan Fleischer did Thursday before speaking. And by the way, Alan, I'm sorry I took your head off Thursday. You gave an excellent answer, I just wasn't in the mood to accept it."

"We don't mind sitting this way," Dwight Garret said, his statement seeming to find general agreement.

"Who spoke?" Christopher asked.

"Oh, sorry, sir. Dwight Garret."

"Okay, Dwight, before we start the play for the day, why don't you tell me something about yourself. Where do you come from, your activities here at Talbot, what you think about literature in general, who your favorite authors are and, if you don't have any, who you hate the most."

The class laughed.

"I'm going to ask all you fellows to tell me the same things so that we can get to know each other better."

"Peter Weiss, sir. Are you going to tell us something about yourself, too?"

"Sure, turnabout is only fair play. Do you want to start off with me?"

"Yeh. Is it true you were almost expelled from the Academy for putting Mr. Harrothwait's car on the roof of the track house?" Laughter followed and Chris joined in.

"Boy, if you know about that, you must know all there is to know about me. The answer is yes. Some of the guys on the hockey team and I took it apart, hauled it up there and reassembled it. The headmaster was pretty upset at the time, but I think way down deep somewhere he had to admire us for pulling it off. At least he didn't toss us out, but it's certainly not the type of initiative he usually likes to encourage."

That answer opened the floodgates and soon Christopher was deluged with questions about his athletic career both at Talbot and Harvard, his number of completed passes, yardage gained running, number of goals and so on. The question had to come and he was ready when he finally heard, "Steve Van Buren, sir. How did you lose your sight?" A hush fell over the room.

"I guess the easiest way to answer that is by saying, stupidity. A few days before graduation at Harvard, we 'jocks' and our dates rented a house on the Cape for a farewell blast—a typical wine, women and song affair. We all thought we were pretty big men on campus and tried to keep ahead of each other in everything, and that, unfortunately, included booze. Driving back to Harvard the last night, our car skidded in the rain on the 'B School' bridge and went out of control." As he spoke, Christopher relived the traumatic, physical terror of the accident. "We turned around two or three times and went over into the Charles River. I cracked open my skull in the impact. One of the other guys pulled me out as the car went under and managed to swim to shore with me. That's it."

"Jesus," someone gasped, "you're lucky you didn't get killed."

Christopher smiled to himself. That was the second time in several days he had been called lucky. "I guess you could say that."

After a bit more probing into the circumstances of the accident, the boys moved back onto Christopher's athletic career and the reasons for his wanting to become a teacher. So that was it. They no longer seemed interested in his blindness; they were more interested in the positive, more constructive aspects of his life. He answered a few more questions and then threw it back into their laps. "All right, now it's your turn. Tony, tell me about yourself."

Tony Arnacella stood up. He didn't really know why, but he did. He started haltingly to tell the young master about his background, life and ambitions. The honest atmosphere that Christopher had established when speaking of himself held, and Tony spoke truthfully without being silly or playing for gags. To his happy surprise, he saw his fellow students were interested in what he had to say. Although all the boys had palled around together for almost three years, each in turn was surprised at how little they really knew about the others and basically how much more interesting they were. This form of "show and tell" would have an important benefit for the boys in that it would tie them all closer together, breaking down some of the small, internal and snobbish cliques that had grown up in the class.

At the end of the hour, all the boys had had the chance to talk and Christopher skillfully brought them back to their classwork. "Now how about hearing from Mr. Shakespeare? What say we start digging into the *Comedy Of Errors*. What was your overall impression of it, David?"

"Frankly, sir, I thought it was pretty silly."

"Isn't that what a comedy's supposed to be, David?"

"I guess comedy changes over the years. I didn't get much of a laugh out of it."

"That's an interesting comment about comedy changing over the years. In this particular case we have an example of a piece of comedy that has survived over two thousand years."

"Oh, come on, sir . . . excuse me, I'm Paul Moore

. . . Shakespeare wrote that play only about four hundred years ago."

"That's quite right, Paul, but William Shakespeare was not the originator of this play. The original was written in ancient Greece by Aristophanes. Shakespeare stole it."

"Stole it!" The class went into an uproar.

"Or perhaps it would be more charitable to say he adapted it from Aristophanes' *The Twin Menacmie*. And that's not all. You may have seen its more modern musical comedy adaptation, *The Boys From Syracuse,* on television. The show was written by Rogers and Hart and its film version starred, among others, the Marx Brothers."

With this revelation, the *Comedy Of Errors* took on a new light in the eyes of the junior class and the jangling hall bell calling the end to the period caught both the boys and their English master by surprise. It was gratifying to Christopher that his class did not immediately bolt for the door and dining hall, but straggled out of the room carrying on their separate arguments and discussions about the three plays in one. He remained seated at his desk, savoring the joy of triumph as the sounds of voices and footsteps faded in the hall.

He thought about Karen Catterby and all she had said, and he thought of Neil Logan. The coach had tried to be friendly. So he was awkward and said the wrong things—Coach Logan always said the wrong things. Karen said it was he who was making everyone nervous. He had been pretty rude running off like that after Logan had invited him over for a drink, and he sure could use a little company and a shot of Scotch. Why not take him up on his invitation? It would be good to talk again with somebody who was really knowledgeable on sports, and as he remembered, Logan's wife was sort of nutty. It might really be fun. He would see Logan tomorrow.

Christopher wondered if it would be safe to use the trampoline if you couldn't see. He remembered that beginners often used training harnesses as a guide—he certainly already had the feel for the canvas. Lucas might help him, or Logan. He longed to do something more athletically creative than just jog around that damn track. Swimming? The new pool would have lane markers if they planned to use it for competition. Those would make good guides for a blind person. He'd try.

His thoughts returned to Karen Catterby. He felt her hands on his arms again, felt the warmth, strength and intimacy that had flowed through to him. He did not know what to make of her. She intrigued him. He tried to compare her to Susanne but could not. She was older, more worldly. He'd get Lucas to give him a detailed description of her. Christopher's mind was so absorbed that in the silence of the drafty old building he did not hear the classroom door slowly swing shut.

After lunch on Saturday afternoons, the Academy held no classes. Instead the boys were expected to compete on the athletic fields for the honor of dear old Talbot. Being the winter term, that meant the swimming pool, basketball court and wrestling mats would be filled with enthusiastic players, cheerleaders and spectators. James Harrothwait believed that strong, healthy minds and bodies were developed simultaneously.

Christopher toyed with the idea of attending one of the events, but decided a long walk was a better idea. Perhaps the Catterbys would be interested in joining him. As he hated sports, Arthur certainly would not be at the gymnasium. If not, there was always Milton. He was considering the alternatives when his attention was caught by an alien sound. At first he could not fit it into the context of a New England classroom. When he did make the connection, Christopher froze in terror.

The sharp, rustling rattle came from somewhere on the floor to his left. That would be near the door that connected his classroom to the biology lab. It's always kept closed, he thought in panic, but now it's open. What in hell is it doing open? The whirring noise came again, or was it two now? It was closer. Oh, God, he screamed to himself, they've got out.

A picture of the glass tanks of the snake farm in the lab next door flashed through his mind. He could remember his revulsion upon first seeing it years ago, his fear of the banded serpents that entwined about each other. Now in his mind he visualized the tanks broken, the snakes slithering over the tops or through the broken glass sides, slithering across counters, falling to the floor and, in their sliding, gliding motions, moving toward him across the wooden floor.

He had to run, to get out of that room while there was still time. Placing both hands firmly on the top of his desk, he slowly rose, making ready to launch himself in a headlong plunge for the hall door. A series of sharp, short rattles to his right triggered by his movement froze him once again. They were all around him. He almost sobbed as he sank slowly back into the chair. In his mind's eye he saw one of the five-foot snakes pulling its length into a slithery coil before the hall door, its head rise up swaying to look at him, the dry, horny rings at the end of its tail vibrating in an angry warning. Christopher sat stiff as a statue; his hands felt like ice. Think, damn it, he told himself as he tried to force his unreasoning panic down, don't do anything rash or stupid. First, you can't move, not an inch. He was sure rattlers would not strike unless frightened or angry. You've just got to sit here until someone comes along to help.

Lucas Howe and David Roon bolted down the last of their fruit Jell-O and milk and received permission from the master in charge of their table to leave the dining hall early. "Hurry up, Lucas. I've got to get down to the gym and set things up for the wrestling match this afternoon," David urged as they trotted down the ridge. "Are you swimming today?"

"No," Lucas answered, "the team has a match with Hillory at two-thirty and Logan isn't very happy about nonteam members fooling around in the pool before a match. I'll give you a hand with the mats."

"Great, then we can get a good seat for the basketball game. You don't have to work with Mr. Hennick this afternoon?"

"We usually don't get together on Saturdays, and he didn't say anything about this afternoon." He paused. "Maybe I should ask him."

"Don't take the chance, he might say yes. Come on."

Lucas smiled and followed him down the path. "It was a good class today, wasn't it?"

"Yeh, not bad. He seems like a nice guy, too. Boy, can you imagine crashing off a bridge into a river? I wonder what happened to the car."

"You know, Roon," Lucas laughed, "that's typical of you—a real materialistic bastard. I hope you remember me when you're rich and famous." He opened the side door of the gym and pushed David in ahead of him.

The silence of the classroom was almost more terrifying to Christopher than the occasional whirring sounds; at least they told him where the serpents were. Minutes seemed like hours as his cramped muscles held him immobile. Where was help? Why hadn't someone come along to find him? He knew all too well. The entire school was in the dining hall having lunch and, to his horror, he realized that after that most of the faculty and students would head for the gymnasium for the afternoon's sporting events. Why would anyone come back to the administration building on a Saturday afternoon? And if they did, why would they come to this room? The clock in the cupola overhead struck two. He had been frozen there for almost two hours. Another whirring rattle came from the horny rings below him by his left foot. Please, God, help me. Won't someone come and help me?

"How did Christopher's junior class go today?" Karen asked as she watched Arthur Catterby pour himself another cup of coffee.

"I talked to a few of the boys at lunch. They said they had an interesting discussion about *Comedy Of Errors*. One asked me if I knew that William Shakespeare stole the play from a Greek. Honestly!" he blustered, shaking his head. "I had better have a good long talk with Chris about his teaching methods. The headmaster won't be at all pleased with the idea of him denigrating his favorite playwright."

Karen laughed. "Did he steal it?"

"I haven't the slightest idea."

"Well, it's probably the most interesting thing those poor kids have learned in their English classes in the last two years."

"I don't find it very amusing," he retorted acidly. "And it's about time you realized that teaching is not a joke. Young Hennick should stick to the standard course, not go skylarking off into history and little-known, wholly irrelevant facts. I might as well talk to him about it now; there's no point in putting it off. He'll probably be in his room. I didn't see him at lunch. And that's another thing," he complained. "This will be the second time this week he's skipped his dining hall responsibilities."

"Oh, Arthur, don't pick on him today. He's having enough trouble adjusting to life here without another lecture."

"You seem to know a great deal about Chris's

problems," Arthur commented, watching her reaction while sipping his coffee.

"I told you, Simon and I met him Thursday. He came to see you and we talked a bit."

"Well, all right," Arthur sighed. "If you feel I should hold off for a while, I will. But no more of this 'stealing' business, I'm warning you." He got up and walked toward his study. "I've got some German translations to do. Will you check them over?"

"Is it really all that important?" Karen asked wearily. "Will they make any difference in your finishing that damn paper of yours?"

"Of course they will. If you want me to—"

"All right, all right," she interrupted. "I'll do it when I get home. I promised to take Simon to the matinee movie in Wyndham Locks this afternoon."

"He's never wanted to go to the movies before. Why the sudden interest?"

"I don't know. I got the impression you put the idea into his head. But what's the difference . . . anything to get off this island."

Arthur looked hard at her, then turned, closing the door to his study after him.

James Harrothwait hurried from the Talbot Homestead across the drive in front of the administration building, glancing at his watch. He had to make appearances at all three athletic events of the day and it was nearly time for the swimming meet. He was very proud of the new pool; it was a testimonial to his ability to squeeze money from the school's alumni and also a testimonial to their regard for him as headmaster of their "beloved" old school. Often he had thought wryly that absence certainly made hearts—and purse strings—grow fonder.

He looked up at the overcast sky that threatened either snow or more rain. With some annoyance he noted lights on in one of the second-floor classrooms.

He'd have to remember to speak about conserving electricity at the next faculty meeting. Some of these masters thought money grew on trees; they didn't understand how hard it was to keep the school going in these times of rising costs. The headmaster rounded the corner of the building and hurried down the path to the gymnasium.

Every cramped muscle in his body screamed in agony, but Christopher still sat motionless. Once, perhaps thirty minutes ago, he had felt one of those disgusting things slither over his foot—his foot! It had taken every ounce of control he possessed not to shriek and jump for the door. He was obsessed with the picture of his body, bloated and blue, lying on the floor covered by a mass of writhing serpents. He saw one flat head after another rise up and, with mouth wide, strike at his dead body, sinking in its long fangs over and over again. A rattle behind him brought Christopher back from the almost trancelike state in and out of which he had been drifting for the last hour. The rapid whirring died out, but another sound came to him. It was farther away, out in the hall. Christopher concentrated on it, trying to interpret it. Footsteps, yes, there were footsteps coming down the corridor in his direction. Should he call out? He waited, praying as the steps approached the door. They stopped, and he heard the muffled voice of the school janitor speak to him through the glass panes of the closed door. "Sorry, Mr. Hennick, I didn't know you was in there working. Mr. Harrothwait said he saw lights burning up here."

Without moving the rest of his body, Christopher turned his face slowly toward the door and screwed it up into the worst frown he could imagine while shaking his head negatively from side to side. The janitor looked through the door at him, realizing something must be wrong—but what? That poor blind boy looks in pain, he thought, reaching for the doorknob.

As soon as Christopher heard the latch click open, he whispered as loudly as he dared to warn Croucher of the danger into which he was walking. "Stop, stop. Don't come in." He nodded at the floor.

Emil Croucher paused, the door open only about three inches and looked with puzzlement at the young man.

"Snakes, the rattlesnakes are out. Get help." Christopher's voice broke into a sob. "For God's sake, get help." A vicious, whirring rattle sounded beside him.

The startled janitor looked down at the floor, his old eyes picking up first one snake near the door, then a second by the desk. Then the others. He pulled the door shut gently and turned on his heels.

Faster, Christopher prayed, run faster. He knew he could not keep still much longer; various muscles were already twitching spasmodically. Sooner or later a leg would thrash out or he would lose complete control and topple from the chair into the midst of the frightened and angry snakes.

Emil Croucher ran in a sort of lumbering fashion, his bowed legs moving as fast as his sixty-odd years would allow down the ridge to the gymnasium. Good Lord above, he kept mumbling to himself, them snakes loose and all around that poor blind boy. Good Lord above, oh, my God. As it had been the headmaster who had sent Emil to turn off the lights after their chance encounter outside the gymnasium, it was back to Harrothwait the old man went to tell his terrible news.

He half-ran, half-hobbled down the gymnasium corridor to the doors of the basketball court. A hullabaloo of noise met him as he pulled them open and searched the spectators for the shock of white hair belonging to the headmaster. He could not find it. Letting the doors bang behind him, Croucher continued down the hallway to the pool after a quick glance into the sparsely filled wrestling room. James Harrothwait was not up in the balcony over the pool but down in one of the chairs by the contestant benches giving encouragement to the boys. The old janitor walked as fast as he could around the edge of the pool, mumbling to himself and attracting the attention of those he passed with his just audible pleas to the Almighty. "There goes Mad Emil," one of the students laughed, nudging another.

Reaching the headmaster, the distraught man grabbed his arm in a demand for attention. "Lord help us, Mr. Harrothwait," he rasped, "that Mr. Hennick is up in that classroom you told me about, the one with the lights on."

"Calm yourself, Emil. If he's there, then there is nothing to worry about. You told him to turn them off when he leaves?"

"That ain't it. Them snakes is out. They's all over the place."

Harrothwait shot him a stunned look. "Out? What are you trying to tell me, man?"

"That boy's sittin up there blind as a bat and there's snakes all around him on the floor. They's gonna get him."

The headmaster was on his feet before Emil Croucher finished his last pronouncement. "That blasted project," he muttered as he strode several paces to the swimming coach who stood waiting for another event to begin. "Your whistle, Mark," he ordered, holding out his hand. The startled history master took off the silver starting whistle hanging around his neck and handed it to the determined older man, who immediately put it to his lips and sent a shrill, piercing blast echoing off the high glass and tile walls of the pool room to silence the spectators. All eyes turned to the dominating figure standing before them.

"James Taylor, Jesse Baily, Noah Fleischmann," he called out, "come here at once."

A stir ran through those in the bleachers and the swimmers as two senior boys, trying to remember what horrible offense they had committed and for which they presumably were about to be chastised, scrambled over the seats toward the headmaster. "Sir?" young Taylor asked, the first to arrive.

"Where is Jesse Baily?" James Harrothwait demanded in a contained voice, seeing the Fleischmann boy approaching.

"I don't know, sir, probably watching the basketball game. That's his—"

"Find him at once, James, and get up to the biology lab as fast as your legs can carry you. Your snakes, gentlemen, have gotten out."

Jim Taylor's eyes bugged.

"Don't just stand there, boy, move! And tell no one about this. Noah and I will go straight to the room now."

Taylor dashed along the side of the pool and out the door, followed by the headmaster, janitor and second boy as the curious spectators watched the unexpected drama with fascination. "Back to the contest, gentlemen," the headmaster called out in his booming voice. Turning to a faculty member standing by the door, Harrothwait ordered softly, "No one is to leave until I give permission."

"Can I be of help?"

"No one is to leave," the old man repeated over his shoulder. "Now, young man," he said to Noah Fleischmann, who jogged by his side, "Mr. Hennick is in his classroom with those snakes. As you know, he cannot see. We must get him out. Tell me how to do it."

By the time the headmaster arrived at the classroom, the other two boys were close on his heels. As Noah had directed, Harrothwait approached the glass-paned door slowly so as not to alarm the rattlers and looked in to make an appraisal of the situation. He, too, shared an unreasoning fear of the reptiles and his heart went cold as he saw Christopher's desperate face and the snakes, several coiled near him. "Are you all right, have they bitten you?" he asked just loud enough to penetrate the glass between them.

Christopher shook his head slowly.

"Steady, my boy, we'll get you out." He saw the heads of two of the serpents elevate and turn gradually in his direction, their small, black eyes penetrating the source of disturbance. Swallowing, the headmaster took a step back. "Taylor, Baily and Fleischmann are out here. They know how to handle those things. Don't move."

Seeing Christopher's head nod very slowly to acknowledge his words, Harrothwait moved back to address the boys, who had been holding a whispered conference. "I place Mr. Hennick's safety in your hands now, boys. Please be careful for all your sakes."

Noah and Jim slipped into long leather gloves taken from a locker placed outside the biology lab door for just such emergencies. Taking up long poles with wire loops at their ends, they nodded at each other and moved toward the door.

"You'd better stand back, sir," Jesse advised the headmaster. "We're going to open the door now and divert their attention from Mr. Hennick."

"Jesse," Jim whispered, "you can see the tanks in the lab from here; the tops are open. All nine rattlers are out."

"I see at least two of them near his desk, and one right here by the door," Noah said. "When I push it open, I'm going to disturb it."

"You've got to," Jim advised, "but do it slowly. He can't strike at Mr. Hennick from here. Let's just hope he doesn't get too mad."

Turning the doorknob, Noah pushed the door in

about eight inches. When it touched the rattler, the snake's body began to coil, its head and tail lifted in an angry warning. As Noah continued to push the door open farther and farther, the reptile struck out at it in a lightninglike blow, its head thudding into the glass. The headmaster backed away, feeling sick to his stomach. The snake recoiled and struck again, leaving drops of pale venom splattered on the glass. Then it retreated slowly away from the door, losing itself momentarily from view among the maze of chair legs.

"Mr. Hennick," Noah called softly, "stay real cool. There are only two snakes near you now and we're going after them first."

Again the young English master slowly nodded his head in acknowledgment. He heard sharp, rustling rattles coming from several areas about him along with the creaking of old floorboards as the two boys edged inch by inch into the classroom.

The snakes by his desk began to coil as the boys approached, the horny rings at the ends of their tails whirring furiously at the intruders. "Don't worry, Mr. Harrothwait," Jesse assured the headmaster, who stood transfixed in the hall outside. "They can only strike about two and a half or three feet, two-thirds of their length. Jim and Noah won't get that close." The old man hoped the knowledgeable young Jesse was right. "We'll goad them into striking and slip the nooses over their heads before they can recoil. They're helpless then. You know, the rattlesnake, or Crotalina," the boy continued, "represents the highest type of serpent development and specialization."

"Your words leave me strangely unreassured, Baily," Harrothwait said wryly. He was about to say more when a snake struck out at Noah and the ensuing battle between boy, snake and pole captured his horrified attention. The fact that the undulating, four-foot-long body was finally lifted by its neck at the end of the pole by the triumphant boy did little to cheer the headmaster.

"Only one left before we can get you out, sir," Jim whispered across the room to Christopher. "It's under your desk about ten inches from your right foot."

Christopher's foot moved involuntarily in shocked response to the words and was answered immediately by an angry rattle that seemed to be right under him. He was going to be sick to his stomach; he fought to keep the vomit down.

"Don't move, for Christ's sake," Noah hissed.

Christopher wanted to smash him for those unnecessary words of caution. The skill with which the boys were apparently handling the situation served to remind him that it was all their fault in the first place. Them and their damn snakes—he'd strangle each and every one of these kids when he got out of this.

His sudden surge of rage against his would-be rescuers distracted him momentarily from the battle that was about to take place around his legs. It was not until he felt the sudden movement of the reptile brushing his leg that he realized it had struck at whichever boy was moving toward it, and for the next few seconds he sat in terror as he felt both the pole and rattler's body, which part he could not know, slap against his feet and legs.

"Got it, sir," Jim said quietly as he held the snake away from himself with a gloved hand. Noah stood facing the two rows of chairs under which he counted at least three other furious reptiles. "Come in and get him, Jesse," Jim called quietly.

Leaving the headmaster, Jesse Baily cautiously entered the room. "Okay, sir, you can move now," he said, "but do it real slow. I'm going to touch you on your right arm. When I do, stand up and let me guide you to the door. Don't panic."

"Don't panic," Christopher hissed through clenched teeth. "What the hell do you think I've been doing for the last—" He felt the touch on his arm and started to get up, but his legs would not move. He tried again but fell back into the chair.

"Noah, help me," Jesse whispered. "Is it safe, Jim?"

"Yeah, but hurry; one's moving and looks real mean."

Christopher felt a hand under each arm pulling him up and, with their help, he managed to shuffle clumsily and slowly ahead to his right. When he heard Jesse Baily say, "You're okay now, sir, you're in the hall," he let himself sink to the floor.

"How do you feel, Christopher?" Harrothwait asked.

"Awful," was all he could manage. His body began to tremble uncontrollably.

"As soon as you get some of your strength back, you are coming right over to the Homestead for a stiff brandy and a lie-down. Mrs. Harrothwait will insist." He patted the young man's shoulder reassuringly while looking back into the classroom where the boys had just captured a third rattlesnake. Now that Christopher was out of danger, he allowed himself time to admire the maturity and skill with which his pupils had handled the emergency. They are good boys, those three, he admitted to himself. But as to the future of that reptile farm of theirs? Someone's carelessness had almost cost a life. He would not tolerate that danger at the Academy. A full inquiry into it would be started tonight after those boys had made sure every last one of those beasts was locked safely away.

As Christopher slowly regained his color and strength, the headmaster asked gently, "Did you go into that biology lab this afternoon?"

"Go into that lab?" Christopher replied in surprise. "Never. I didn't even know the door into it was open. No one in my last class said anything about it. I thought it was always kept closed."

"It is supposed to be kept closed at all times," Harrothwait confirmed. "Not necessarily because of any danger involved, but because of the smell those animals make." He lapsed into silence, considering various possible reasons for the violation of his edict. It occurred to him that it could be no careless accident but a purposeful act carried out by someone with a grudge against one of the three owners of the farm. He earnestly hoped that were not the case. He would hate to think one of the boys at Talbot would be so base in character as to settle a dispute in this fashion.

"If you weren't in the lab," he continued to probe with concern, "did you hear anyone else moving about after the period was over? I want to be absolutely sure that no one tampered with those cages before I have my discussion with young Taylor, Baily and Fleischmann."

"I didn't hear anything."

"I see. Thank you."

They remained in the hall until the boys completed the capture of all the reptiles and had locked them back in their tanks. They were then directed to return to the gymnasium to tell Andrew Benton, the science master, that the headmaster had given permission for those at the swimming meet to leave whenever they wished. They were also warned to say nothing of this misadventure. "Nothing, absolutely nothing, is that perfectly clear?" James Harrothwait insisted.

"Yes, sir," the three voices replied in almost perfect unison.

"Good. And boys, even though we are going to get to the bottom of this unfortunate occurrence and the apparent carelessness that caused it, I do wish to thank you for the bravery and skill with which you rectified it." A quick smile flashed across their faces but faded when he continued. "I will see you in my study at the Homestead this evening at eight. Be punctual."

Chapter 7

As much as the headmaster tried to keep the incident of the escaped rattlesnakes quiet, it was too much to expect with the superefficiency of the Talbot Academy grapevine. Several days of subtle inquiries on Harrothwait's part failed to uncover the identity of the person who must have removed the tank covers and so, even though he was inclined to be sympathetic toward Taylor, Baily and Fleischmann when they insisted they had not been careless, he was forced to insist upon the removal of the reptile farm before the parents of his other charges descended upon him in outrage.

Christopher harbored none of the headmaster's sympathies for the three boys. It took him days to unwind from the ordeal. The constant questions of the freshmen on his floor and the students in his classes did not help him forget the trauma of those three hours, and for quite some time after that, serpents slithered in and out of his dreams at night.

With this single exception, the next three weeks were relatively happy ones for the young English master. Each day he gained more and more confidence in himself as a person and as a teacher and became increasingly popular with the boys. By mid-February, the headmaster had received several requests for transfers to Christopher's classes and he anticipated a sizeable demand for his new creative writing course that would start in the spring term.

Perhaps the greatest reason for Christopher's relative contentment lay in his coming to grips with his blindness. He no longer bothered to conceal it, he even joked about it (although some pain still remained beneath the humor) and was making a concerted effort to pick up and pattern an active sports life within the confines of his visual limitations. In the afternoon he worked out with the gymnasts on the trampoline, rings and parallel bars, and at the request of Neil Logan, put on exhibitions for the boys. He also swam fifty laps in the school pool each morning before classes and, when time allowed, joined the weight lifters.

His new interest in indoor athletics was fortunate because his jogging and long walks over the ridge had come to a halt due to the abrupt change in the weather that February. Freezing rain or snow fell almost every day in the Connecticut valley, piling up drifts across paths and against buildings, turning the trees into delicate ice sculptures that bent low and creaked under their burden of glistening crystal. The plows from Wyndham Locks barely managed to keep River Road open to the Academy by pushing the ice and snow up into steep walls almost six feet high on either side of the narrow opening.

While Christopher's weekend with Susanne had to be postponed twice because of the vagaries of transportation, the students reveled in the snow. Weekends were filled with increased activity as the growing membership of the ski club trained on nearby hills.

Early one morning in the middle of February, the headmaster stood looking through the windows of his office. A frown was etched deeply across his forehead.

Harrothwait loved the primitive beauty of New England winters, but his practical nature did not like the threat of spring floods that increased with every new inch of white powder that fell. A quick spring thaw would be particularly disastrous in light of the high snow accumulation in the state and in those up north.

Through bitter experience, the headmaster had learned to keep the dates of the Academy's spring vacation flexible so that it could be made to fit in with the weather and the prophesied levels of the Connecticut River which now lay frozen at the foot of the ridge below him. Twice in the past the Academy had been caught off guard by the flooding river that had suddenly overflowed its banks, surrounded the ridge and cut it and its three hundred inhabitants off from Wyndham Locks. The boys had considered it a lark, but to the headmaster and his beleaguered kitchen staff, the five days of isolation had been a nightmare. And if they should ever be forced to open the dams up river for flood control, God help the Talbot Academy. James Harrothwait shook his head, hoping the spring thaw would be a slow and gentle one. It was in the hands of the Almighty.

The severity of the weather had a reverse effect on the social life at the Academy. Faculty wives, trapped inside, turned their energies to cocktail and dinner parties even though it meant drinking and eating with the same "dull" faces over and over again. Christopher had attended his first such faculty party with misgivings because of the problems he knew his blindness would present, but after his initiation—spilling several drinks, tripping over an undetected end table and getting his fingers uncomfortably sticky with onion and cheese dips—he had learned to be amused rather than annoyed by his mistakes and the overly solicitous attitudes toward them by his hostesses. This Saturday night, Neil and Marcia Logan were throwing the party and he was rather looking forward to it.

Being the coach, Neil could get away with a lot more than the more tight-collared teachers at the Academy and so his gatherings were usually far more boozy and boisterous than the others.

Christopher spent the afternoon working in his room with Lucas Howe who, thanks to a pulled ankle tendon, was unable to join a ski club trip. In the last three weeks, Christopher and Lucas had become close friends, and the two often put aside their work to indulge in long, pleasant conversations. They would sit before the fireplace enjoying its cozy warmth, feeling secure from the snow falling outside. They had learned to share the intimacy of touch without embarrassment. Lucas's hands often guided Christopher's over the keys of the Braille typewriter he was teaching himself to use, and Christopher had allowed himself to explore the boy's face with his fingers so that he would know better how his friend looked. This had been the first time Christopher had overcome his inhibitions about violating another person's privacy in this way.

"I wish I were going with you tonight," Lucas sighed wistfully. "I've heard Coach Logan's parties usually turn into orgies."

Christopher laughed. "You heard wrong. It's not that I couldn't use a good orgy now. It's been a long . . ." His voice trailed off as he thought of Susanne and their last fumbled attempts at lovemaking. Lately he had thought more and more of Susanne, wondering if they could really make things work again. "Anyway, the booze will be good and Marcia is a great cook."

"Don't stick your fingers in the mustard this time," Lucas giggled.

"Boy, did that ever sting." Christopher smiled at himself. "When I put that potato chip in my mouth loaded with yellow dynamite instead of cheese dip? God, I couldn't talk, just sputter. I must have looked like a fish gasping for air, and my eyes ran tears for ten minutes." Christopher laughed again, thinking of the debacle of the first party. "And that end table. Mrs. Harrothwait's sherry splattered all over Jim Willoughby's fly, and they say when she tried to wipe it off, he almost went through the floor." Christopher was howling now. "Jerry Fowler told me the expression on Willoughby's face was priceless, particularly when Harrothwait saw his wife with her hand on his crotch." He doubled up. "Poor Mrs. H, she really is a naive old thing."

Through his laughter, Lucas asked, "Do you want the rep red or blue tie, or the one with crests on it?"

"The rep blue, thanks," Christopher answered, taking the tie from his friend and working it under his collar. "I've got to maintain my conservative image around this place; can't be a longhair like you. How does it look?"

"A little to the left," the boy replied, adjusting the tie for him. "There, you look like hot shit." Without thinking, Lucas brushed a lock of Christopher's hair back in place and stood back to look at him proudly.

Pulling on his blazer, Christopher asked, "Still snowing?"

"Like hell."

"Damn. Why do the Logans have to live way down at the end of the lane? Why couldn't they have a nice place on the quad?"

"I guess coaches aren't very high up on the social ladder," Lucas said, thinking of his late father who had been coach of a small college basketball team.

Sensing what was in the boy's mind, Christopher countered cheerfully, "That's all right, sport; at least coaches always seem to end up with the sexiest wives."

"With the exception of heads of English departments," Lucas commented offhandedly.

Christopher paused. "Is . . . is she really that . . .?"

"Yes, she's built. I'm surprised you don't know yet. She sure has the hots for you."

He turned away from his young friend. "You're out of your mind, Lucas. We haven't said more than a few words to each other in the last three weeks. We're about as friendly right now as two of those rattlers."

"That's not what the grapevine says. Do you know she goes to the gym to watch you?"

That startled him. Christopher hesitated with one arm in his topcoat before words came. "Oh, cut it out, Lucas, you know what you can do with your grapevine on this one. Shove it." Before the other had a chance for rebuttal, Christopher pulled on the rest of his coat and started for the door. "I don't want to talk about Mrs. Catterby and what the boys think about her. It's none of their business. And it's none of yours." The vehemence of his defense of Karen Catterby startled him. He lowered his voice. "Come on, are you going back to your dorm or are you on dining hall duty tonight?"

"Back to the dorm," Lucas replied, chastened. "I'll walk you part way. You taking Milton?"

"Yep, he needs some exercise." Christopher pulled open the door, took a few steps into the hall and knelt down to put on the dog's harness.

"You've had a little visitor," Lucas said.

"I have? Who?"

"Simon. His tricycle is just to your left on the other side of Milton's basket."

Reaching over, Christopher touched the cold metal of the red tricycle. His fingers moved along its frame, the rubber handle grips, the rusty bell. "This thing is really beat up, isn't it?"

"How can you tell?"

"Hell, I can feel it. The paint's all chipped off and that bell feels like sandpaper. Wonder where he is? His mother says he never lets it out of his sight." Christopher raised his voice. "Simon?"

"Simon," Lucas joined in. "Come on, Simon, we know you're here."

A head popped out from a door farther down the hall. "You call, Mr. Hennick?" Fat Jack asked.

"Have you seen Simon Catterby up here?"

"No, sir, why?"

"Nothing, Jack, forget it."

The boy's head popped back into his room.

Only a few dim bulbs lit the third floor hall, and so it was not surprising that Lucas and Jack failed to see the small boy pressed back against the wall, squatting in the shadows behind a large communal trash bin. Milton looked toward the boy and whined as Christopher strapped on the harness.

"What's the matter, boy?" he asked, patting the dog's side affectionately. "You all right?"

Stopping his noise, Milton nuzzled Christopher's hand.

"Come on, boy, we've got to get moving or we'll be late for Lucas's orgy." The two young men and the dog walked down the creaking old staircase, casting long shadows against the dark walls.

Simon crept out from his hiding place and stood silently at the top watching them as they descended. Then he turned and tiptoed to Christopher's door. The knob turned slowly in his small hand.

"Come on in, fella," Neil Logan bellowed with his customary exuberance. He slapped Christopher on the back and knelt down briefly to give Milton a fond scratch under the ears. "Those were some mighty fancy turns you were doing on the trampoline this afternoon. Tom says the boys are learning a lot from your technique," Logan commented, pulling him in through the door. "By the way, Marcia hasn't moved the furniture around since you were last here, so you've got no excuse for throwing sherry on Willoughby tonight." He jabbed Christopher in the ribs and gave a howl of glee. "That was something for the books. The bar is set up on the dining room table, help

yourself." The coach had guided Christopher halfway
across the room when his wife, Marcia, intercepted
them.

"Chris," she said, giving him an affectionate kiss on
the cheek. "Where is my favorite dog? You haven't
left the poor thing out in this weather, have you?"

"He's fine out on the porch, Marcia," he replied.
"Besides, he's not much on martinis."

"Well, you go easy on them, young man." Marcia
restrained him as he started to leave. "Have you met
Sally Benton?"

"Yes, indeed," Christopher answered, extending his
hand forward and waiting for the cold, thin hand of the
science teacher's wife to take it. "We had a nice long
chat several nights ago at the Shepards'. Hello, Sally."

"Christopher," she said in her pinched voice, "I'm
so glad you're here. I want to talk to you about this
literary group I'm pulling together for the faculty
wives. As you know, I want—"

"Give the poor boy a chance to get a drink before
you take him over," Marcia interrupted with a slight
bite. Taking his arm, she guided Christopher the rest of
the way across the room through the other guests.
"Honestly," she mumbled in an aside, "that woman
actually *could* squeeze blood out of a stone. Don't let
her get hold of you or she'll have you lecturing at one
of her clubs every night of the week. She tried to get
Neil to set up exercise classes last year," Marcia said.
"Her group could have used it."

"Hi, there, Chris," James Willoughby's voice broke
in.

"Don't worry, James," Christopher said with a
smile, "I promise, no sherry tonight."

"Good, then I won't need this apron any longer," he
laughed. "What's your poison?"

"How about one of Neil's martinis? I do hear ice
clinking in that pitcher, don't I?"

"You sure do, and a martini it is just as soon as I can

pry it away from Jerry." He said the name with a trace of disdain as he reached for the pitcher in the hands of the tall, intellectual French teacher.

"We bachelors are always the ones accused of every sin in the books from lechery to alcoholism," Jerry Fowler rebutted with good humor, "but it's you married types who get into all the mischief." Handing the pitcher to James Willoughby, he turned to Christopher. "Hello there, were all the babies quiet on the third floor when you left?"

"At my end, they were. I can't speak for yours. Thanks," he said to the hand that deposited an icy glass in his.

"Ah, you've got the advantage of your guard dog. Have you had to call Milton into action to quell the monsters?"

"Not yet," Christopher laughed, "and I'm afraid Milton has been too spoiled by them to attack even if the need should arise. Say, maybe you could help me there. They all swear innocence, but one or more of the boys have been feeding Milton at night. They just don't seem to understand he's a working dog and has to stick to a strict diet and, for that matter, to me."

"I'll nose around," Jerry said. "How is Lucas Howe working out for you? He's a sweet kid, isn't he?"

"There's my wife beckoning," Willoughby broke in. "See you later." As he left the two men, he gave Jerry Fowler a strange look.

"He's been a great help. Funny, but I can't think of him as a kid. He's not that much younger than I."

"I guess not. As senior bachelor around here"—Jerry Fowler was in his late thirties—"they all seem young to me. Why don't you drop down and have a nightcap with me some evening. My door's always open."

"Okay, I will."

"Good. Whoops, here comes Sally Benton, and there I go. Good luck."

Sally swept down upon Christopher and was soon followed by Carol Willoughby, James's large, blowsy-looking wife. The women at Talbot liked Christopher, or perhaps it would be more accurate to say they liked to be seen in his company as proof to their rivals that they were fascinating enough to captivate this handsome young man. For his part, Christopher tried to erase the images of them he carried in his mind from his student days by dreaming up new and more flattering ones for them. He pretended Sally looked like Deborah Kerr and Carol like Anne Baxter in *All About Eve*. He had to admit that one of the advantages of blindness was always being able to surround himself with good-looking women. Soon Helen Engel, who sounded like Jane Fonda, and Linda Shepard, who could only be Bette Davis, joined them. After a few words of triviality to him and with refilled glasses, the four women degenerated into a gossip session.

Christopher stood at the edge of the group listening to them belittling friends and institutions with happy abandon almost as if he were not there. He was fascinated by the fact that so many people talked openly in front of him almost as if they thought that because he could not see, he also could not hear. Or perhaps they felt that his blindness gave them some kind of anonymity, that he would not associate the slander with the person voicing it. Would, he wondered, the conversations at Harvard parties be so trivial? If he were there, would he be eavesdropping in on some profound pronouncement or theory at this very moment, or was all cocktail party banter the same everywhere in the world? Who, he wondered, was Susanne with this evening?

"Well, will you look who just walked in," Carol Willoughby commented acidly. "Since when has Karen Catterby deigned to come down from Valhalla to visit us mere mortals?"

This was the first time Christopher had been at a party with the Catterbys. The image of Susanne faded and in his mind he once again felt the compelling touch of Karen's hands on his arms.

"Probably Neil," Helen Engel replied. "I understand the two of them used to have something going. She spends a lot of time at the gym." Christopher's ears perked up. "Poor Marcia."

"Poor Arthur, you mean." This was Sally Benton's contribution. "Can you imagine marrying someone like that?"

"She probably tricked him into it. He's not the most clever man when it comes to women, you know. Have you counted how old Simon is, and how long they've been married? Well, do that little exercise some day," Carol said. "According to my calculations, there's a month or two missing."

"Premature, darling?" Linda Sheppard suggested.

"You're being kind."

"You know Arthur's mother won't even talk to her," Sally confided. "Confidentially, she has hardly laid eyes on Karen since the day he brought her back."

"Well, you can't blame her," Carol countered. "A woman with absolutely no background. What could Mrs. Catterby possibly say to her? She's quite a grand lady, very social in Boston. I also understand that she is James Harrothwait's first cousin."

"I wouldn't voice that around too much, dear," Linda said cattily, "or people might begin to wonder how Arthur got his job here."

"Oh, Linda, you don't think . . ."

"Well, let's face it, he's no bargain either. Personally, I find him quite a bore."

Christopher had inched back out of the group, but his curiosity held him within earshot of their conversation.

"Look what she's wearing," Carol whispered as Karen and Arthur began to slowly move through the crowd in the direction of the bar.

Linda Sheppard's eyes darted quickly over Carol Willoughby's ample frame, a look that Carol was meant to catch. "Well, you have to admit she has the figure to pull it off. And your husband doesn't seem to be minding too much, darling."

Carol glowered at James Willoughby. "I don't care what you say, Linda, slacks and that blouse don't belong at the Academy. The thing's open practically to her navel." Carol Willoughby turned her back on the object of their conversation. "She's not wearing a bra."

"So Jim's noticed," Linda smiled. "Darling," she called, waving her hand. "Over here."

Karen waved back. She, too, forced a smile.

"Of course you know Christopher," Sally Benton said after the women had exchanged effusive greetings.

"Certainly. Chris," Karen said, extending her hand to take his. "I haven't seen you in weeks." Her hand felt warm and soft.

"Really?" Carol Willoughby asked. "The boys tell me you're always down at the gymnasium. Chris, you're helping Neil now, aren't you?"

"As best I can," he said. Lucas Howe's earlier comment about Karen was in his mind. "But sometimes I think they help me more than I do them."

"Simon enjoys watching the swimmers and gymnasts," Karen replied coolly to Carol Willoughby.

"How is he?" Carol asked. "Just how old *is* Simon now?" Her eyes smiled at the other women.

"He's well. And Peter? How is his arm? Mending?"

Carol Willoughby's smile faded. She had always suspected that somehow Simon Catterby was responsible for Peter's fall on the ice and his broken arm. "Pete's doing fine. The cast should be off in a few more weeks." She moved gradually from the group and blended into the other party guests. So, too, did the other women, leaving Christopher and Karen standing together at the dining room table.

"Another drink?" she asked, pouring herself a double Scotch.

"Thanks," he replied, holding out his glass to her. "Martinis are in the pitcher."

"And how is Mr. Hennick faring these days?" Karen returned his glass.

"Very well, I think."

"Very well, period," she contradicted. "The headmaster tells me you've won over the boys and are a first-rate teacher. Congratulations."

"You helped a lot. That day we—"

"I think we'd better forget about that day."

"But why? You made me see things that—"

"Arthur," Karen interrupted, "come over here and talk to your star teacher." Christopher noted the tension in her voice. "We don't get much of a chance to see him now that he's turned back into an athlete."

"Oh?" Arthur asked, somewhat incredulous. "Well, well done, my boy," he said generously. "I must admit you constantly surprise me. First you go around telling the boys that Shakespeare was a literary thief"—Arthur Catterby chuckled—"and then . . ." He sobered. "Then those snakes. A nasty business."

A chill ran through Christopher at the mention. "Please, don't remind me."

Arthur looked at the young English teacher and then his wife. "Makes you realize how careful Christopher has to be. Why, even a simple, childish slip could—"

"Arthur!" she cut in, "I don't think Chris needs a lecture on taking care of himself right now."

"I was just . . . I was merely pointing out that in a conflict of some sort, even our Simon, small as he is, is better equipped to handle himself than—"

"Damn it!" Karen spat out sharply. Several of the

guests turned in their direction. She lowered her voice. "For Christ's sake, will you get me another drink?"

"Well, just be careful, Chris," Arthur ended, patting his arm. "You keep out of mischief." He took Karen's glass, looking at her with hurt innocence.

"A double," she ordered, glaring at him.

"Hey, you two are monopolizing this poor guy," Neil Logan exclaimed, breaking into the threesome and taking Christopher by the arm. "If you don't come over here and flirt with Marcia, there'll be no living with her for months."

Left alone briefly, Karen turned on Arthur. "Just what are you trying to say?" she demanded in a low voice.

He handed her her drink. "Absolutely nothing," he replied. "What is the matter with you this evening?"

"Simon. You implied that Simon—"

"I implied nothing," Arthur interrupted with a long sigh. "You are always reading things into what I say. What on earth do you think I was trying to say about Simon? I adore him, you know that. Ever since the fires, you've become paranoid about—"

"Please, Arthur, don't. Don't say another word."

"Darling," he implored, "if you're so worried, why don't we simply take him to a psycholo—"

"Stop it," Karen snapped. "I won't hear about it."

Arthur Catterby reached forward and took the glass from her hand. "Come along, darling," he said gently, "let's go home, you're upset. As long as we're together—you, me, our son—you won't have to worry. I promise I won't let anything happen to him. Everything will be fine, believe me."

The gaiety and life she had shown when they first entered the room seemed to drain from Karen as she looked at her husband. "All right, Arthur," she said wearily, "let's go home."

She averted her eyes as they passed Christopher.

He heard Neil Logan call, "Karen, Arthur, leaving so soon?" and turned to face the door. His blind eyes could not see the quiet desperation in her face.

Watching them depart, James Willoughby shook his head. "How does Arthur do it?" he asked Mark Shepard, the Academy's history professor. "How does he keep that hot ticket under his thumb?"

"There must be more to Arthur than meets the eye," Mark replied.

"There sure must be."

Chapter 8

CHRISTOPHER PULLED HIMSELF FROM THE WATER after completing his fiftieth lap and sat on the edge of the pool. The gymnasium was off limits to all the students on Sunday mornings. They had chapel and various housekeeping chores to attend to before lunch. Reaching for his towel, he balled it up into a pillow for his head and lay back on the tiles in the welcome silence of the vast room to catch his breath, folding his hands over his heaving chest. One foot moved slowly back and forth in the water creating massaging currents lazily about his ankles.

"Do you come here every Sunday?"

Christopher shot up into a sitting position, turning his head from side to side to locate the voice.

Although spoken quietly, Karen Catterby's words had a shattering effect in the place as they reverberated hollowly within the high glass and tile-covered walls.

"Mrs. Catterby?"

"Up here in the balcony. I've been watching you. I hope you don't mind. You swim so well, so easily, so . . ."

"Thank you," he called, embarrassed at her compliment. "How long have you been there?" He could think of nothing else to say.

"Does it matter?" Karen laughed. "I'm all alone today. How about getting dressed and taking pity on a Sunday widow? I feel in the mood for one of those old-fashioned ice cream sodas at Wyndham Locks. Can I tempt you into a walk?"

The invitation in her voice was obvious. Christopher instinctively reached for his towel and wrapped it around his waist to cover the thin black bathing suit he wore. "Sure, I guess so," he stammered. "Where are Arthur and Simon?"

"Visiting Arthur's mother in Boston. Their bimonthly pilgrimage."

Remembering Sally Benton's comments concerning Karen's relationship with her mother-in-law, Christopher did not press the subject. "Okay, I'll get dressed and pick up Milton." He started toward the door to the locker room.

"Why bother with Milton?" Karen called down to him. "I make a pretty good guide dog," she laughed, "and I talk a lot more."

He waved toward the balcony. "See you in the lobby in a few minutes."

Slipping out of his wet trunks, Christopher was keenly aware of the tingling excitement within his body. He moved a hand slowly down across his chest to his lower belly and felt that excitement grow within his grasp.

What the hell am I thinking, he demanded, releasing himself and reaching into the locker for his clothes. Remembering the gossip about Karen Catterby and his fragile position here at the Academy, he dressed slowly. He knew that she liked him, he sensed it. And Lucas said she had been watching him work out. With Arthur and Simon gone, would she try to put the make on him today?

He had not slept with a woman for many months. The last times with Susanne had been embarrassing disasters. How would he react if Karen Catterby did try? Quickly pulling on his old, multicolored lumber jacket, he slammed the metal locker door and walked toward the gymnasium lobby. Why take the chance? Play it cool, he repeated over and over, play it cool.

"Well, I don't make such a bad dog, do I?" Karen asked, giving Christopher's arm a small squeeze as they walked slowly back along the snow-rutted River Road from Wyndham Locks.

"I'm turning in Milton tomorrow," he laughed. "Gosh, I don't know when an ice cream soda has ever tasted so good. Do you know, I haven't been off the campus since I got here over a month ago." He was relaxed and in a happy mood. He enjoyed being with her; his earlier nervousness had disappeared. It had been an innocent excursion filled with laughter and silly chatter. Although he knew her to be far older than he, Karen was like a girl. They seemed to understand each other, even flirted a bit.

"Will you teach me to swim?" she asked.

"You mean the blind teaching the blind?"

"No, you fool, the talented teaching the novice. I've never learned. Strange, isn't it? Surrounded by the river and all these ponds, yet I never bothered to learn."

"It's easy."

"Maybe I never had a teacher I trusted"—she paused—"or an incentive."

The implication of her last words slipped by Christopher. "What about Arthur? Anyone who spent summers as a kid on Cape Cod should be a fantastic swimmer."

He noted the coolness in her voice. "Arthur doesn't swim."

"But that's impossi—"

"Arthur's not much of an athlete," Karen said, cutting him off. "As he explains it, Arthur is a scholar, he always was a scholar, and he'll always be one. There is no need for him to dissipate his talents."

"When did he decide that?"

"He didn't, his mother decided for him." Karen had lost her earlier light-hearted spirits. Her words were tinged with bitterness.

"Hey," he asked, "are we getting serious?"

"No, never," she laughed, brightening. "Come on, let me show you my 'retreat.' You need one at Talbot, you know. I spend hours there all by myself, reading, thinking, dreaming."

"Is it a cave, a nest, a cloud that you've got anchored somewhere up there in the sky?"

Karen stopped and looked at him. "I love you for that." She suddenly leaned forward and kissed the young English master's cheek. "Oh, how I wish it were. I'd pull up the anchor and . . ." Her daydream returned to reality. "No," she sighed, "it's just a simple old boathouse. But it's beautiful. In the spring I love to sit and listen to the river as it flows past. It's angry and violent. In summer it's lazy and calm, you can hear the fish leaping, see the splash in the smooth water, the rings spreading out."

"And in the fall?"

"Autumn is cool, full of the colors of the trees. Leaves float past like small boats on the way to some distant place. I wonder where the leaves do go. All the way to the sea?"

"Why not, it's a nice place to go." Christopher's mind was filled with the images of the seasons; he had seen them so clearly as Karen spoke. The tug of her arm led him off River Road toward the clapboard boathouse. It sat hidden from the buildings on the ridge by a cluster of large willows whose screening branches were held captive in the ice covering the Connecticut River.

Karen led him down an uneven, slippery path. The side door of the boathouse opened inward and Christopher followed her up the steps.

"A description, please," he asked, smelling the varnish and paint that hung heavy in the air.

"It's basically a large square. Showers and a locker room at the rear, the rest one big room with boat racks to your left, a couple of long benches on your right and paint cans all over the floor." He heard her moving about the room, moving the cans left by the student maintenance crew. "The whole front is a series of doors opening out onto a wide platform that slopes down to the river. You mean you've never been in here before?"

"Never."

"I'm surprised." Her voice softened with suggestion. "It has a rather unsavory reputation. I thought you'd know."

"Why should I?" Christopher's throat felt suddenly tight and dry.

"No reason," she replied casually, closing the side door. "There, now I'm just as blind as you are; there's no electricity down here in winter. We're equal." Christopher heard her move toward him, felt her presence. "I can't see you, you can't see me. All we can do is feel." He felt her hands brush across his cheeks to the back of his head. They pulled him forward to her lips. Her kiss was light, gentle, lingering. He did not return it.

"I've wanted to do that ever since that first evening. Is it wrong to take what you want?" Her lips were a fraction of an inch from his; her breath warmed them as she spoke. He stood rigid, his hands at his sides.

"But you and . . . you're . . . I have no right." He could barely get the words out.

"I've given you the right." Karen's hands moved slowly across his broad shoulders and down over his arms, feeling his body under the thick wool of his jacket, feeling the body she had seen so many times in the Talbot pool. "We need each other, Chris, we have since the first night."

Panic welled up within him, not excitement. It was happening so fast. He felt paralyzed from the waist down as her hands moved around him and then under the jacket to his hips. "I . . . I can't," he stammered. "I . . ."

"Relax, darling, relax." Karen's soft words were warm against his neck. "It's just you and me—out of time—just you and me, Chris." Her hand moved slowly across the front of his leg. "I've thought of no one but you since the day you came, thought of nothing but this."

"No," he cried, suddenly grabbing her arms and holding her immobile. He heard her sharp intake of breath. Releasing her, he turned away and buried his head in his hands in humiliation. "I'm sorry, I'm sorry," he nearly sobbed. "I . . . I . . ."

Karen stood back from him and spoke to his back, the coolness in her voice betraying the hurt and anger she felt at his rejection. "Is it Susanne?"

"No, it's . . . I just can't . . ."

"You want a woman, don't you?" A touch of cruelty entered her voice. "You sleep with women, don't you?" she demanded, waiting for his answer. "Or has Jerry Fowler got to you? Lucas? You and Lucas?"

"No," Christopher cried, "oh, my God, no. What are you saying. He's just a friend, a—"

"Friends can be lovers," she shot back mercilessly.

"No!" In desperation he struck out angrily at her accusation. "Just because I don't want to fuck my boss's wife doesn't mean I'm . . ." His voice choked. ". . . I'm queer." Silence fell between them, each waiting. "Oh, God, I didn't mean that," he said miserably. "Please understand, please. I'm not ready, not for you, not for anybody. I want to, I so desperately want to, but I just can't seem . . . It doesn't work for me any more. I don't know why."

Karen's voice softened at his obvious distress. "A woman scorned says terrible things. I didn't mean them either." She moved to him, putting her hand on his shoulder. "Is it because you can't see?" she asked gently.

"I don't know, maybe."

"And it's why you and Susanne parted?"

"One of them."

Turning him to her, she took his hand, her voice brightening for his benefit. "You know what I think? I think I've got a real macho man here who can't stand being on the bottom. After the accident, when you and Susanne were together, did she make love to you, or you to her?"

Christopher remained silent.

Karen kissed him lightly on the cheek. "Think about it. And when you want me, I'll be there. But it's your move now." He felt a gust of cold air across his face as she opened the door. "Let's head for home." As she took his arm, he covered her hand with his.

"I'm sorry. Honestly. I was afraid something like this would happen."

"Maybe that's why it didn't."

"Still friends?"

"Or lovers. It's up to you."

As the two of them moved slowly out from behind the willows and up the path to River Road, Simon sat on his tricycle like a sentinel looking down from the ridge. To his left a gray squirrel hopped through the snow and came to a halt, staring up at the motionless boy quizzically. Turning suddenly, Simon hurled the rock he had been clutching tightly at the startled creature. Its squeal of fright seemed very loud as it was carried by the wind through the barren trees.

*   *   *

"Must we go through this all over again?" Arthur sighed, taking off his glasses and rubbing the sides of his nose. "You are blowing it all out of proportion."

Karen stood in the door of his study, an after-dinner whiskey in her hand. "But you said you were going to Boston, there were no if's about it. You and Simon were going."

"I told you, when we heard the weather report, we decided to turn back."

"Weather's never kept you from your 'dear' mother before," she accused.

"Karen," Arthur said patiently, "would you rather have had us drive all the way back in a blizzard?" His hand absently touched Simon's shoulder. The little boy sat cross-legged beside Arthur's desk chair glaring up angrily at his mother. "Well, look out the window. Would you prefer we were out in that?"

Crossing the study, Karen pulled back the heavy draperies and looked out into thick snow swirling through the blackness between the dormitories on the ridge. "What time did you get back?" she asked quietly, her back to her husband.

"Oh, around lunchtime, I guess," he answered vaguely.

"When 'around lunchtime'?" she persisted.

"I don't know, is it so important?"

"It's just because you're always so infuriatingly vague. Can't you just once—"

"All right, all right," Arthur interrupted testily. "It was about twelve-thirty. I made Simon a hamburger when we found you weren't at home." There was a trace of accusation in his voice.

She turned to look at her husband and then down at Simon beside him; his large brown eyes held hers.

"By the way," Arthur asked casually, as he opened a book, "where were you?"

Watching Simon's face, Karen replied equally casually, "I went for a walk. It was a beautiful day earlier this morning."

"Alone?"

"No." She had rehearsed the answer should the question come up. "With Christopher Hennick. I played guide dog and took him over to Wyndham Locks for an ice cream soda." Simon's eyes continued to bore uncomfortably into hers. "You know, it's the first time that poor boy's been off this campus since he arrived. We really ought to do more for him."

"Quite right, my dear, we really should," he replied vaguely, riffling a few pages of the book. Arthur looked up. "Anyway, I'm glad you weren't alone. I was a bit concerned, you know, coming back and not finding you here."

"I'm perfectly capable of taking care of myself," she bristled, looking back at him. "I was taking care of myself long before I met you."

"Yes, I know all that. But now that you have us, Simon and me, those terrible days are over. It's a husband's duty and," he smiled down at Simon, "a son's. Isn't it, Simon? We'll take care of Mommy, won't we? Keep her safe, huh? Keep her from getting hurt by bad people?"

"Stop that!" Karen cried. "Don't keep telling him that, Arthur, I won't have it." She moved to the boy and held out her hand to lift him up. He shrank back from her. "Simon."

"Let the boy be," Arthur insisted, putting his hand on Simon's shoulder to hold him there. "He's upset about something, probably about not being able to see his grandmother. I don't know what else could have disturbed him so, do you?"

Pulling back, Karen walked to the door without looking at her husband. "All right, Simon, stay with daddy for a while. But remember, bed in thirty minutes."

"Close the door, dear," Arthur directed. "It's good for us men to have a little time together, just the two of us." He smiled sweetly at her. She glared her answer and left, the door still open. Simon scrambled to his feet and pushed it shut.

"That's a good boy," Arthur said, patting his backside when he returned to stand by his chair. "You love your dad, don't you?" Simon nodded enthusiastically. "And your mommy, too." The little boy's face clouded. "We won't ever let anything happen to Mommy, will we?" Simon's face slowly moved into a smile. "Of course we won't. Now, there's Daddy's son." Arthur leaned over and kissed the top of the boy's head. "Now, find something to amuse yourself with while Daddy works on his book."

Simon moved off a few paces and leaned on the desk watching his father as he arranged various volumes before him and began recording passages from them on the tape machine that sat on the corner of the desk. Sometimes his father let him talk into the microphone and then would play it back. He liked that game. Simon knew that his father was the smartest man at the Talbot Academy no matter what Peter Willoughby and Tom said. His father was the smartest man in all the world.

Walking to the fireplace, Simon lay down before it and stared into the flames and glowing coals beneath. They made beautiful pictures in his mind. He saw castles glowing before him, statues, marvelous windows from great churches rippling in the intense heat. And he saw the place where Satan came from. His dad had explained it all to him. Simon reached out and took the cardboard tube of long matches that stood beside the fireplace. It was decorated with beautiful Chinese patterns. Twisting off the top, he withdrew one of the long sticks with the blue tip. As he had seen his father do, he struck it on the rough black paper on the bottom of the tube.

Arthur looked up at the noise and watched his son as the little boy stared into the flame slowly creeping along the wooden stick. "Be careful, Simon."

Without looking at his dad, Simon nodded. The flame neared his fingers and he felt the heat. Simon waited until the hurt was too much before throwing the rest of the burning stick into the fireplace and watched as the major conflagration consumed it. It's all gone, he thought. All gone. He wished mean people could be all gone the same way.

Rolling over on his back, Simon looked around his father's study, his most favorite room in the whole house. There was no other room like it anywhere in the school, of that Simon was sure. All his friends thought it dark and gloomy; not he. Simon felt safe and cozy there.

The other walls were painted the same color as the velvet draperies, deep, rich red. And so was the ceiling. Like a cave way down underground, thought Simon. He knew another cave way down underground, but his parents wouldn't let him play there. It was in the cellar.

Simon looked up at his father's back as Arthur Catterby pored over the novel that lay open before him. Hanging in the corner facing him was Simon's favorite picture. It was a painting of Bael. His father said that Bael was the first king of hell, that place where you go if you're bad. He had three heads. One was shaped like a frog's, another like a man's and the third like a cat's. His father said Bael's voice was raspy and harsh and would try to talk like him. It made Simon laugh, but it frightened him a little, too. Bael was a good fighter and he had seventy legions under his command in hell. That was a lot of soldiers. He made those people who prayed to him more alert and cunning—that meant smart and sort of sneaky. And Bael could teach people how to make themselves invisible so other people couldn't see them. How nice it would be to be invisible, Simon thought; he could go wherever he wanted and no one would know, not even his mother.

His eyes moved on to the framed photographs of those black natives dancing and doing funny things on the ground. His father said they were voodoo and stuck pins in little dolls to make people they didn't like get sick. He thought for a long time about that as he studied the strange people, some with eyes turned back into their heads, dancing in a circle.

The other picture in the study was a painting of the man his dad was writing about, Mr. Faust. He was a very handsome young man and was standing in some kind of laboratory with a beautiful girl. Behind him, in a dark corner, was the devil with his horns and a deep, red cape. He was smiling and holding up a rolled piece of paper. His father told him that Mr. Faust had given the devil his soul so he could be young and smart. Simon wondered exactly what a soul looked like. His father said that we all had souls. He felt his body all over and wondered what part of it was his soul.

Arthur Catterby's voice broke into Simon's thoughts. His father had turned in his chair to look across the room at him. "Come on over here, Simon. Shall we play with the tape recorder again?"

Simon's face broke into a wide grin. Jumping up eagerly, he hopped to the desk. "Can I hold it?" His father held out the microphone. "What shall I say?" Simon asked breathlessly.

Arthur Catterby thought a moment and was about to answer when the sound of approaching footsteps stopped him. "Too late, we don't have time now. We'll play the game tomorrow," he whispered, patting Simon's shoulder and taking the microphone back.

The little boy moved away just as the door opened. "Come on, Simon, time for bed," Karen Catterby said, crossing the room to him. He stared down at his shoes. "Simon?" He moved his foot in a little circle on the carpet, avoiding her eyes.

Karen glanced over at Arthur. "You two look like the cats who swallowed the canary. What have you been up to?"

"Men talk," Simon said softly to the carpet, parroting his father's words.

"Oh, God," Karen sighed in exasperation, "save me from all this." She grasped Simon's shoulder and turned him around to face the door. "March," she ordered, swatting him none too gently on the seat of the pants.

The little boy looked back over his shoulder at her and then at his father.

"Go along now, Simon," his father said. He winked at his son.

Simon's face burst into a broad grin and he skipped from the study. They heard him hopping up the stairs one at a time.

"I'll be there in a minute," Karen called after him. She was about to follow when her eyes caught sight of the long tube of matches lying near the fireplace. Its top was off.

"Arthur," she cried, turning to face him. "You sat there and let him play with those matches? Are you mad? How many times have I warned you about—"

"I'm sorry, I'm sorry," he said wearily, holding up his hands to fend off her words. "Nothing could have happened. I was here. You do so overreact, my dear."

"Overreact?" she almost shouted.

"Can't you ever forget those fires in Heidelberg?" His words were like a blow to her stomach. "And those poor people your brother killed?" Arthur continued. "Must you heap all that tragedy on Simon? He's just a curious little boy. All boys are fascinated by matches, by—"

"Stop it, Arthur," Karen gasped. "I won't—"

"Once and for all, Simon had nothing to do with the boys who died here. The fires had nothing to do with Simon." Karen slumped against the bookcases. "Or do you know something I don't? Do you?"

Finding herself suddenly on the defensive, she shook her head violently. "No." She thought of the match gun she had taken from her son's pocket. "No, of course not."

"Then stop worrying. I know some people believe tendencies of that type can be passed through the blood. I don't. Yet if in some way Simon were . . ." He paused, looking deeply into his wife's troubled face. "We wouldn't want to have to send Simon away, now would we?" She stared mutely at him. "Of course not. Now stop all this business. You'll make yourself and the boy sick."

Arthur Catterby turned from her and looked down at the open book before him. Karen slowly moved toward the door. Her hands were like ice. Arthur's words stopped her. "Did you spend much time at the gymnasium today?" he asked casually, not taking his eyes from the book.

She stood with her hand on the doorknob. "I beg your pardon?" she asked the wood before her.

"Were you down at the gymnasium today? Neil Logan says you're very interested in sports, that you spend a lot of time watching the boys. I was just curious, that's all."

"No, I wasn't there today," Karen lied, sure that no one could have seen her and Christopher that morning at the pool. "And I only go down there because there's nothing else to do in this boring hole." She turned to him. "Besides, Neil is exaggerating." Karen studied Arthur's reaction.

"Good." He looked up and across the room at her. "It isn't wise to get too close to the boys, particularly an attractive woman like yourself. Rumors start so easily in a small school." He smiled at her. "We can't afford a breath of scandal, you must certainly know why."

"Your appointment to Amherst." She spoke the name of the college in a bored, I've-heard-this-all-before tone.

"Exactly, Amherst." He smiled sympathetically. "Don't for a minute think I don't know how hard it's been for you here after your . . ." Arthur paused, searching for the right word. ". . . more *liberal* days in—"

"What the hell are you implying, Arthur?" Karen cut in, her voice hard, filled with challenge.

"Nothing. Absolutely nothing," he replied, retreating before the cold anger in her eyes. "I was merely saying how much better, how much more interesting and stimulating your life will be at Amherst. That's why we should all make sure that everything we do now is . . ." His voice tapered off.

"Are you blaming me for your not getting the appointment last year?" she demanded. "Is it because I'm German, Arthur? That's what your mother says. Or do you think there's another reason?"

"No, nothing of the sort. Of course not," he stammered.

"Perhaps they're waiting for that piece of scholarly research you're doing, Arthur. Perhaps they're waiting to read the definitive Faust."

"There's no need to—"

"Well, they'll have a long wait because you're never going to finish it. And do you know why?" Karen's eyes locked into his. "Because it's your prop, Arthur, the only thing that makes you stand out from all the other failures in this place. You'll never finish it because if you ever do, you'll have to face reality and admit you're a failure, too. And, Arthur, you are a failure."

"At least I fathered a son," he shouted. "That's more than those other German bastards."

"Did you?" Karen sneered. "Did you really?"

"I've got the papers, Karen," he challenged, his entire body shaking in anger, "don't ever forget that. Simon is *my* son. He is my American son. You'll never take my son, not if—"

"He makes you feel like a man, doesn't he, Arthur," she broke in, her voice cruel and even, not betraying the frightening effect of his implied threat on her. He could never know the power of his hold on her, never know how helpless she felt. "That little boy, that poor, plain, little boy is the only thing that proves you a man." Her hand tightened on the doorknob. "I feel sorry for you, Arthur. My life is terrible, but yours"— she looked around the study—"yours is hell."

Karen Catterby closed the door behind her, leaving her husband alone. The three heads of Bael looked down upon him as he buried his face in his hands and wept.

Chapter 9

THE BLIZZARD THAT STARTED ON THE DAY OF AR-
thur and Simon Catterby's abortive trip to Boston
raged throughout all New England for most of the next
two weeks. Snow drifted high around the buildings on
the ridge, cutting the Academy off from Wyndham
Locks for days at a time.

During this period, Christopher Hennick did his best
to avoid Karen, concentrating on his class work and
training in the school's Olympic-sized swimming pool.
He drove Karen and the events at the boathouse far
from his mind during the days, but at night he relived
her touch, her kiss, over and over, tossing and turning
feverishly, smothered within the confines of the narrow bed and heavy blankets covering him. He tried to
divert his thoughts to Susanne and their gentle lovemaking of the pre-accident days, but the promised
passion of Arthur Catterby's wife was ever-present,
overwhelming them. He awoke night after night
drenched in sweat and hard. What Karen had so
briefly unlocked in the boathouse was becoming an
obsession.

And his relations with Lucas had become strained. Karen's innuendo concerning their friendship had made him overly aware of the boy's maleness and his emotions toward him.

One Tuesday afternoon in early March, Lucas walked with a brooding Christopher back toward the young master's room. They had been exercising Milton and now planned to go over the class assignments for the next day. Lucas chattered happily about the challenge snowball fight to be held in the quadrangle that evening. Where once the grip of Lucas's steadying hand on his arm had felt friendly and reassuring, today it seemed too intimate, too possessive. Christopher had shaken it off as soon as they reached the hall of the administration building.

"Hey, it's freezing in here," Lucas commented as he entered the third-floor room and unzipped his ski jacket. "Gosh, Chris, you left your window open. You trying to turn us into Jack Londons?"

Christopher frowned as he heard the boy pull down the window. He could not remember having opened it again after getting up that morning, certainly not on a day as cold as this one. "I must be getting senile in my old age."

"Ah," Lucas smiled, "but it's a good excuse to have a fire." He knelt down and pulled the screen aside. Lighting a match, he watched as the flame caught the balled-up paper underneath the kindling and spread slowly up through the logs. Lucas loved fires; they reminded him of home and his parents. He held his hands out before him to feel the welcome warmth.

Tossing his checkered lumber jacket aside, Christopher crossed the room and dropped into the chair to the left of the fireplace. "What the . . . ?" he exclaimed, jumping up. Startled, Lucas looked up as the young master reached down to grasp the object lying beneath him on the cushion. Christopher turned it over in his hands, feeling the strangeness of . . . "It's a doll," he said, puzzled, "a little doll. What in hell is this thing doing here?" He sat back down and ran his fingers slowly over the small figure.

"Let's see." Lucas kneeled next to him to take it. "Hey, it's a Barbie doll." He shook his head. "But someone's really fucked it up."

"What do you mean?"

"Her hair's been cut off short like a man's and this rag tied around her. It's been painted in red and black squares." Lucas looked down at the smudges of red paint on his fingers. "Sort of like your lumber jacket, Chris." He turned it over. "Yuck!"

"What's the matter?"

"There's a nail hammered into the back of its head."

Wrinkling up his nose in disgust, Christopher held out his hand for the doll. "Sick, real sick." He felt the rusty nail protruding from the head of the small figure.

It fascinated Lucas. He leaned his arms on Christopher's knee and stared at the mutilated Barbie doll, oblivious to the sudden tensing of Christopher's body under his touch.

"Don't do that, Lucas." Christopher's voice was taut.

"Do what?" the other asked.

"Your hands."

"What about them?"

"Take them off me, God damn it," Christopher nearly shouted. "Stop pawing me! All day you've been—" He cut himself short.

Lucas sat back, startled, a puzzled and hurt expression on his face. "Gee, Chris, I . . . what's the matter? I didn't . . ."

"Forget it," the young master said shortly. "Forget it, it's me. It's . . . come on, let's get some work done." He tossed the doll aside, its existence forgotten in the aftermath of his emotional outburst.

"Chris, I didn't mean anything, honest," Lucas said miserably. He was flushed with embarrassment at what he suddenly suspected his friend was thinking. "I'm not . . . I mean . . ."

Lucas did not have the chance to finish his confused thought. The explosion and burst of flame that engulfed him as he sat before the fireplace turned his words into a horrified scream. Christopher felt the rush of heat and instinctively lunged forward to grab for the boy. "I'm burning," Lucas cried, beating frantically at himself as he rolled about the floor. Shouting for help, Christopher found and embraced him, using his own body to smother the flames, pressing Lucas's face tight into his sweater. Milton's desperate barking in the hall outside joined their cries. Within an instant the room was filled with yelling freshmen tearing blankets from the bed to wrap around Lucas and beating at the cinders and flaming bits of wood scattered about the room.

Lucas was rushed off to the infirmary in a state of shock while Christopher sat dazed in his desk chair. Jerry Fowler stood beside him, his hand gripping the young master's shoulder as he watched the last of the boys leave the room after cleaning up the mess. The door stood open to vent the place.

"You sure you're all right?" he asked.

Christopher nodded dully. "My hands hurt a bit, that's all. Lucas will be okay? He wasn't too badly burned?"

"He's in a lot of pain, but I don't think it's too serious. It could have been a lot worse; you saved his face."

"I don't understand what happened, I just don't understand how it—"

"You've got to be more careful, Chris," Jerry Fowler said softly, interrupting him. "Hold out your hand."

"What's this?" he asked, feeling the twisted, blackened object the older man dropped into the palm of his outstretched hand.

"The remains of your can of lighter fluid. It must have fallen in the fireplace when you were laying the fire."

"But I don't have any lighter fluid," Christopher said, "and Lucas always lays the fire."

Fowler looked at him sympathetically. "Chris, it was an accident. No one is blaming you."

"I don't *have* any lighter fluid," he repeated vehemently.

"That's your gold cigarette lighter on the mantle, isn't it?" Jerry asked.

"Yes, Susanne gave it to me. But I threw everything else out after the fire in my waste basket the first night. I don't smoke anymore. Go ahead, try to light the damn thing; it's been empty for weeks."

Jerry Fowler crossed the room and took the lighter. Christopher heard the rasp of its flint. "Well?"

"You're right, it's empty," Jerry said, looking down at the flame flickering from the gold rectangle in his hand. "Let's forget . . . ."

"Jerry," Christopher interrupted, holding up his hand, "do you hear that?"

The other man cocked his head. "What?"

"It sounds like squeaking somewhere out in the hall." Christopher suddenly remembered. "The doll, Jerry. Where is it?"

"Doll? What doll? I don't see any doll." His eyes moved across the floor and over the furniture in the room.

"It's a mucked-up Barbie doll. It has to be around somewhere." He paused as his mind shifted gears. "Simon Catterby! Was Simon around during the fire? Jerry, was he?"

The French teacher looked back at him strangely as

he shook out the pile of tousled blankets in his search for Christopher's doll. "Yeh," he said offhandedly, "I think I saw him when the boys were running around, but I'm not sure. That crazy kid and his tricycle always seem to be around somewhere."

"Was he in the room?" Christopher insisted. "Did you see him in here?"

"No, I don't think so. I really can't remember." He dropped the blankets back onto the bed. "Chris, I can't find any Barbie doll. If it were here, maybe one of the boys threw it out."

Christopher sat silently, thinking. "Forget it, it's not important." But somehow, he thought, it was very important.

"Okay," Jerry Fowler said, affecting a false cheeriness. "I'm off." He started for the door.

"Will you take me over to see Lucas later tonight? I have trouble navigating on those icy paths."

Jerry turned and smiled down at the handsome young master. "Sure." A slow smile crossed his face. "He's a nice kid, isn't he? A real nice kid."

James Harrothwait stood on the Catterby doorstep early the next morning impatiently ringing the bell. He frowned at the gray sky from under the umbrella he clutched in his hand. His concern over the burned boy he had just visited was made all the worse by his concern over the turn in the weather. Heavy rain fell around him and mist swirled low over the snow. Wednesday, March sixth, he thought; the thaw's right on time. He prayed to God that it not be too severe. The headmaster remembered the Connecticut River now slumbering under its cover of ice below the ridge and the devastation it could wreak when wakened by a sudden and prolonged thaw, particularly after such a winter as New England had just endured.

Arthur Catterby, coffee cup in hand, opened the door. "Good Lord, James, how long have you been standing out here? With all the commotion in the kitchen, I barely heard the bell."

"No mind, Arthur," James Harrothwait said, patting his cousin on the shoulder as he pushed past him into the house. "Is your charming wife about? I have a favor to ask of you both."

Following Arthur into the kitchen, the headmaster nodded graciously to Karen, who stood somewhat embarrassed by her state of careless dress. He accepted a morning cup of coffee.

"Let me come right to the point," Harrothwait said, sitting down at the littered kitchen table and making space for his cup and saucer. "There was a terrible accident yesterday afternoon. Poor Lucas Howe was injured. Oh nothing too serious," he added quickly as he saw their concern, "but, nonetheless, painful. The boy will be in the infirmary for at least three or four days. Now that leaves Christopher Hennick without his second pair of eyes, a pair that he has come to rather rely upon. Karen, will you work with him for the next few days until Lucas is up and about?"

His question was answered by silence. She looked at Arthur and then back to the headmaster. "Does Chris know about this?"

"No, but I'm sure he must agree. Why? Do you see any problem on his part?" He looked at her questioningly. "*You* have no problems doing it, do you?"

"Simon," she said. "You see, we—"

"Of course," he interrupted, "but I'm sure Eleanor Sanders or Carol Willoughby will be only too happy to look after the boy. They have children about the same age."

Karen looked doubtfully at Arthur.

"James," Arthur laughed, "of course Karen will help out. We are both very fond of Christopher, aren't we, dear?"

"Yes," she answered, forcing a smile. "When would you want me to start?"

"Why, this very afternoon," Harrothwait replied in somewhat better humor over the eagerness of his faculty to help each other in times of need. "I will go at once to tell Christopher. The poor young man is very shaken about Lucas's injury and the fire."

"Fire!" Karen gasped.

"What happened?" Arthur asked.

"Why, haven't you heard?" The old man was surprised. "It seems a can of lighter fluid fell into Christopher's fireplace and exploded. A nasty business." Seeing the horror in her eyes, he took Karen's hand and patted it paternally. "There, there, my dear. It could have been a lot worse. Fortunately Christopher had his senses about him and was able to save Lucas from serious burns." James Harrothwait stood up, taking a last gulp of his coffee. "Well, I must be off. Christopher will be expecting you at three."

"Let me see you out, James," Arthur said, following him from the room.

"Let's hope this rain doesn't continue," Harrothwait said as he stood in the front door. "I don't trust that river." Raising his umbrella, he strode out into the mist and, without turning around, lifted his left hand in a gesture of farewell.

Karen passed Arthur in the hall as he closed the door. "You don't mind reading for Christopher, do you?" he asked. "I thought we owed it to James."

"No, no, it will be all right," she replied quietly.

"Besides, you may find it entertaining," he continued. "Get you out of the house, give you a purpose." His voice followed her up the stairs.

Quietly opening the door to Simon's room, Karen looked down at the little boy as he lay sleeping. "You didn't do it, Simon," her thoughts spoke to him. "You didn't do it, did you?"

As if summoned from his sleep, the boy's eyes slowly opened. He stretched his little body and then lay back, smiling up at her.

Chapter 10

THE RHYTHM OF KAREN'S VOICE WAS BROKEN ONLY
briefly as she turned the page and glanced at Christopher across from her next to the now empty fireplace. Their initial embarrassment with each other had soon dissolved with the beauty of Hemingway's prose. They now sat relaxed but very much aware of the other's sensuality in the small room.

Trying to concentrate on the classic love story taking place among the rubble of the Spanish Civil War, Christopher felt as if he were floating in limbo surrounded only by the dark softness of Karen's voice. The tragic characters in *For Whom The Bell Tolls* did not exist for him. Karen was the only reality in the room, Karen and he.

For nearly two hours she had spoken only the words of Hemingway, her own remained trapped within her heart. How could she reach this young man? Every time she looked at him, Karen willed the sensations that moved through her body to cross the distance between them and enter his. She looked down to the page before her.

So now they were in the robe again together and it was late in the last night. Maria lay close against him and he felt the long smoothness of her thighs against his and her breasts like two small hills that rise out of the long plain where there is a well, and the far country beyond the hills was the valley of her throat where his lips were. He lay very quiet and did not think and she stroked his head with her hands.

Karen stopped. "That's beautiful," she said softly, speaking to herself, "so very beautiful."

"What?" Christopher asked, the change in her voice abruptly calling him back from his thoughts. "You said something?"

"What a beautiful description of Maria's body," she replied, "of two people being together. It's so tender. 'The valley of her throat where his lips were,' " she repeated.

Unconsciously Christopher raised his hand and touched his throat, moving his fingers gently down over the muscles to the bony indentation of the sternum. Suddenly aware of his action, he dropped his hand. "Not much of a valley here," he smiled in embarrassment.

"You're a man," she said reasonably and casually. "Feel mine." Putting aside the book, Karen stood up. "We women aren't so muscle bound." She took a step forward, paused, and then, making a quick decision, took hold of the cashmere turtleneck sweater she wore and silently yanked it up and over her head. Her rumpled hair swirled about her face and fell back down in place. Karen knelt before Christopher and reached out to take his hand.

He could sense her presence close to him. The warmth of her body seemed to engulf him. He felt the touch of her hand and did not pull away.

Karen directed the tips of Christopher's fingers to

her throat, placing them gently in the hollow of soft flesh. "You see?" she said softly, "we're frail little people, frail and vulnerable." During the silence that followed, Karen gradually loosened her hold on Christopher's hand, finally releasing it completely. His fingertips remained on her skin, moving ever so slightly over it, feeling its smooth warmth. Her back straight, head tilted back, she knelt before him as a slave before her master. She waited motionless.

Slowly, hesitantly, Christopher's fingers moved from the hollow of her throat across the thin satin of her neck. They stopped with the realization that the body they touched was bare. His heart pounded, his throat felt tight. His sleepless fantasies crowded his blind eyes. He could not take his hand away, could not break the intimate contact between them. For what seemed an eternity, he sat immobile. Then, swallowing, he slowly, tentatively lowered his hand over the flesh before him, feeling the unspoken permission in Karen's body, feeling the gradual swell of her breast under his touch. His other hand moved forward to cover the soft, waiting mound before it. Desire flooded through his body, and he slid from the chair to kneel facing her. He leaned forward, his lips gently reaching for hers. Karen met his kiss, lightly at first, then intensely. His arm suddenly locked her body tightly to his, she opened her mouth for his entrance. Christopher's sob was lost in the almost animal lust that swept them away.

Lying beside him in the narrow bed, Karen listened to the rain pelting down upon the slate of the dormer roof. She curled contentedly against him, pressing her cheek to his shoulder, entwining her fingers gently through the curly blond hair covering his chest. They had now been lovers for three days, three long afternoons in which each had committed himself physically and emotionally to the other.

Christopher smiled dreamily as he felt her body move in his arms, a beautiful and insatiable body that drained him completely. "I love you," he murmured softly, stroking her cheek.

"And I you," Karen answered against his skin, "since the day I first saw you, since the day you were born."

"That's a long time. Can anyone really love another person before they've met?"

Karen did not reply.

He lay thinking for some time and then asked, "Do I remind you of someone else?"

Karen sat up and looked down at him. "Why do you ask that?"

He paused before speaking. "Sometimes—when we make love—sometimes you call me Kurt. Do you, I mean, did you . . ." Christopher's voice trailed off, not wanting to verbalize the possible existence of a rival.

Karen's eyes moved from the face below her to the window. Through the gloom of the rainy afternoon she traveled back in time. "Kurt was my twin brother. He's dead," she said dully. "You look very much like him."

"I'm sorry." Christopher sat up and encircled her with his arms from behind, pulling her back into the protection of his body.

She continued staring through the rain to the life that his question had reopened. "We were born in Berlin just after the war. My father was killed on the Russian front, my mother was always very ill. Before they took her away she left us with the family next door; they had children our age. We never saw her again."

Christopher squeezed her more tightly as if to absorb the pain and loneliness she must have felt so long ago.

"Things were very hard, there wasn't enough food, wasn't enough of anything. The Gronauers loved us but they couldn't keep us any longer. I understand now; then I hated them. They put us in an orphanage. There were dozens of them in Berlin in those days. Kurt was so small. He cried for days. He needed someone to take care of him, to protect him. I tried." Karen fell silent as her mind carried her through the terrible years in one institution after another, how she was teased and abused, how the others taunted her, taunted the "little mother." She had worked in kitchens, stolen food for her brother, begged clothing for him, comforted him. Kurt had become everything to her. He was her reason for clawing and climbing through life.

Karen saw her brother growing into a young man, strong, tall, a beautiful blond god. And like a god, he was selfish and demanding; life centered around him. The other boys no longer bullied them. They were afraid of Kurt, of his mercurial and violent temperament. She told Christopher of some of the hardship. She did not tell him of the afternoon when she was nearly fifteen. The older boys—eight of them—had pulled her into the alley as she returned from work. Muffling her cries, they held her down on the garbage-littered cobblestones and tore away her clothing, forced her legs apart. She saw again their hungry, leering faces, felt their filthy hands as they pawed her virgin body.

Kurt had found her later that night curled up in the small room they shared in a deserted tenement by the Berlin Wall. In the light of a single candle, he washed the blood from her violated body, soothed the bruised skin with his hands, tried to kiss away the pain. His touch and soft murmurings gradually awakened new sensations in her body, sensations that blended strangely with the pain she felt. She had looked up at the handsome face of her brother above her in the flickering light. A smile slowly crossed it as he stared down at his hands moving over her young breasts,

moving down between her thighs, stroking life back
into her. "How does it feel to really be a woman?" he
had whispered as his lips bent to hers. She still remembered the taste of whiskey on them. The pain Karen
had felt minutes later when he entered her was a new
kind of pain. It excited her, it was a pain mixed with
passion. Through it she gave herself more completely
to him. Karen had felt Kurt's strength swell deep
within her. She had wanted it, she wanted more and
more of it. From the "little mother," she became her
brother's slave and sometime mistress.

"We left Berlin when I was seventeen and moved to
Heidelberg. I got a job at the University so I could
study there. That's where I met Arthur."

"And your twin brother?"

Karen remained silent for a minute. While she had
worked, Kurt occupied himself with the women of the
city, drifting from one minor scrape with the police to
the next as he sank deeper and deeper into the dark
world. Like Dorian Gray, the more violent his temper,
the more he bullied others, the more beautiful and
desirable he seemed to become. He had turned to
arson for money, torching decaying buildings along the
riverfront. She had pleaded with him; he had struck
her. There were other fires. People had been burned to
death. But fire fascinated him, fascinated him as much
as it horrified her. "Flames are in my blood," he had
once jeered at her, "the flames of death and the flames
of passion. Come feel my flame, little sister." He had
laughed as he pushed her hand between his thighs.

One night he killed a man in a brawl at one of the
bars on the docks. There were witnesses. While fleeing
the police he had been shot. Kurt died in Karen's
arms, his lips against her breast, his eyes staring into
the flame of the candle he had begged her to light. "It
beckons to me, little sister," he murmured softly. "It
calls me home."

Karen turned in Christopher's arms and embraced him tightly. "My brother died just before I married Arthur. Simon was born nine months later."

"And I remind you of him?" Christopher's voice betrayed the jealousy he felt.

"Oh, darling," Karen cried, "only in looks. You are so much more gentle, so much more . . ." She paused. "You give of yourself, Kurt only took. Of course I loved him, he was my life for so many years. But you—there can't be an evil bone in your body." She clung to him, pressing his goodness into her body. "Kurt is the past, he must be."

Karen's body suddenly stiffened. From far down the hall outside, the faint sound of a squeaking tricycle axle came to them. The blood drained from her face. She pushed herself violently from her young lover. "Oh, God," she cried in anguish to some force hidden in the mist swirling outside the window, "won't you ever give me peace?" Fleeing the bed in confusion, Karen snatched up her clothes and clutched them to her to shield her nakedness.

"Simon?" Christopher asked.

"No . . . I mean yes. Oh, I don't know anymore. I've got to get away, I've got to get out of this place, it's . . ."

Feeling his way across the room toward her voice, Christopher took her by the shoulders. "Hey, it's all right," he said soothingly. "Don't get so excited. Just be quiet. Simon won't know you're in here. It's long past the time you usually leave." He pulled her to him, feeling the tenseness in her body.

She nodded. "Can you lock the door?"

"There's a wooden wedge that Lucas made for me on the mantel. Just slip . . ." Karen had the wedge and was kneeling at the door before he could finish. She pushed it under as quietly and firmly as she could, her ears alert for the noise of her son's tricycle. None came. Could she have been mistaken? Could guilt have made her misinterpret a squeaking door, a window being lowered?

Rising, Karen crossed to the bed and, sitting on the edge, began to slowly pull on her clothes, waiting, listening. Christopher joined her and put his arm around her reassuringly. She leaned her head back into his shoulder, comforted by the warmth of his skin. They said nothing. The only sounds that intruded into their separate thoughts were those of boys calling to each other somewhere down in the quadrangle. The hall remained silent.

After half an hour, Karen finally stood, her decision made. Christopher rose with her. "Tomorrow afternoon?" he asked softly.

She shook her head. "Chris, we can't see each other anymore. It's too dangerous."

"Don't say that," he whispered sharply, turning her around to face him. "Just because—"

Karen pressed her fingers to his lips. "It won't work, it can't work, believe me. I should have known. We can't keep it secret, not in this place. I love you too much to risk—" She stopped herself.

"But you're helping me with my work," he argued desperately, "everybody knows that. Our being together is perfectly understandable. Why would there be any gossip?"

"I'm not talking about gossip."

"Then what?" he demanded. "What's the risk?"

"Lucas is being discharged from the infirmary tomorrow morning," Karen said flatly. "There's no more excuse for us to . . . to . . ." Her voice trailed off.

"Don't leave me," Christopher begged, "please, not now. Please."

She looked at the tortured face, the face of her brother, and buried her head in her hands as she leaned weakly against him. "Don't ask me, oh, darling, don't." Helplessly torn between memory, love and fear, the inevitability of her actions and the consequences were so clear to Karen.

"If not here, then the boathouse," Christopher pleaded. "No one will ever know. After Lucas leaves. Karen, just tomorrow. Just one more time, please. We'll arrange something."

Pressed against his chest, Karen could hear and feel the beat of his heart, the strength of his arms. Slowly, reluctantly, she nodded her acquiescence. Then, as if fleeing from some fearful result of her decision, she pushed away from him and ran to the door, stooping to pull out the wedge.

Christopher stood pathetically alone in the dim light of the room. "Tomorrow," he called softly.

Slowly opening the door, Karen peered down the shadowy hall and then looked back at him. She did not answer.

He stood thinking for some time after. The possibility that Karen might leave him had strangely never come into Christopher's mind. His dark, private world that now included her had seemed so separate, so insulated from that of the Talbot Academy that the thought the two might come into collision had never really occurred to him. But the fright of discovery had put everything back into perspective. Simply stated, the junior master of English was sleeping with the wife of the head of his department. And that just was not done. Arthur Catterby himself appeared too affable, too naive and preoccupied to even suspect their liaison, but the school was filled with hundreds of eyes eager and willing to put the wrong interpretation on whatever they saw. What could he be thinking of, why the risk? He absently touched his shoulder. The touch of his hand brought back the touch of Karen's lips. He stood in the center of the room feeling her hands everywhere on his body, her warmth, her lingering smell—the fragrance of her perfume still clung to him.

He would not give her up no matter the risk, no matter the consequences. He was a whole man again. Just the thought of her brought a stirring in his loins.

"Never," he said aloud to the shadows of the room. An involuntary shiver suddenly made him aware of the cold and his nakedness. Pulling on a pair of jeans, his running shoes and a sweater, he snatched up his checkered lumber jacket. He needed air, needed to breathe. Christopher yanked open the door and knelt down to pat Milton. "There's my favorite friend," he said, ruffling the fur behind the dog's ears. With deft fingers, he strapped on the harness. "How about a nice run in the rain, huh?"

Milton nuzzled his hand affectionately and licked the face of his blind master.

Straightening up, Christopher urged the dog ahead of him toward the staircase. He now found it easier to use the handrail and to meet Milton at the bottom. He heard the sound of the dog's paws heading down before him and strode confidently ahead, his hand reaching out for the balustrade to the right. Too late he felt the taut cord bite into the skin above his ankle, too late to stop his plunge forward into space. Arms flailing in air, Christopher crashed down the shadowed staircase, somersaulting and tumbling from one sharp, bone-crushing blow to the next until consciousness left him.

Christopher's twisted body was found by a group of freshmen returning from intramural basketball practice. Distant voices seemed to be calling to him through miles of thick, black gauze. His left wrist ached. Opening his eyes to his world of darkness, he turned his head slightly toward those calling voices. "He's coming out of it," someone said. He felt a hand on his forehead.

"Where am I?" he asked groggily.

"In your room." The voice was that of Arthur

Catterby. "The doctor is here. You had a nasty fall, young man."

Christopher lay still, his mind slowly reconstructing the afternoon. "What time is it?"

"A little after six. How do you feel? Does it hurt anywhere?"

"My wrist." As soon as he spoke, Christopher felt gentle hands take hold of his wrist and move it back and forth slowly. The pain was agonizing. He cried out. The hands remained still, just the fingers probing the bones and muscles beneath the skin.

"Only a sprain, thank God," a strange voice said. Christopher felt a wet bandage being wrapped firmly around the wrist. "How does your head feel, Mr. Hennick?" the doctor asked. "Can you count backward from one hundred for me?"

Still dazed, the young English master began the count. "Ninety-nine, ninety-eight, ninety—" He stopped. "There was a rope across the stairs, I tripped over a rope," Christopher exclaimed. "Someone tried to—"

"There, there, Chris," Arthur Catterby broke in, his hand once more on Christopher's forehead. "Just rest." The head of the English department whispered to someone and Christopher heard footsteps leave the room and cross the hall to the head of the staircase. They returned almost immediately and after a whispered conversation, Arthur spoke once more. "Christopher, you've had a bad accident, you're confused. Perhaps you tripped over your dog's leash." His voice became more positive. "That's it, you must have stumbled over Milton. There is no rope, string or anything across the head of the staircase. Besides," he continued reasonably, "who would want to do such a terribly dangerous thing? Why, it could kill someone."

"But I felt it," Christopher protested, "just above my ankle. Milton doesn't have a leash. . . ."

"Chris, Chris, just lie back and relax. We think you

have a minor concussion, you can't think straight now. Later we'll talk."

"Here, drink this down," the doctor's voice said. Christopher felt a hand lift his head and the cold rim of a glass against his lips. Almost reluctantly he opened his mouth to drink the cool liquid. "That should relax you. Aside from your wrist, some bruises and the shaking up your head took, there's been no real damage done. You're a very lucky young man. I'll drop by first thing in the morning to see you on my way to the infirmary."

Christopher felt the mattress beneath him lift up as the doctor rose. After another whispered conversation, he heard the man leave the room and close the door. Everything had happened so fast. Could he be sure? Was there really a cord? Yes, yes, of that he was sure. "Arthur?" he asked the darkness.

"Yes."

"There was a cord. I know it."

After a considerable silence, Arthur replied. "Chris, you're very popular. Why would one of the boys, why would anyone want to hurt you? Can you tell me that?" He paused. "Have you hurt anyone, are you flunking one of your students? Is there any bad feeling?"

"No, not that I'm aware—"

"Are you afraid, Chris?" Arthur interrupted.

His words were rather a shock. Christopher had never thought of being afraid, it was not in his nature. He had been puzzled, curious, but he was not frightened.

"You know, you're very vulnerable," Arthur Catterby continued, "not being able to see. Things that hold no danger for the rest of us can be deadly to you. You'd be a very easy person for someone to hurt. You have a long term ahead of you. If you really think there is someone, tell us who. But if you have only suspicions, unfounded accusations, the school is helpless."

Christopher lay silent, thinking of what Arthur had just said. In his mind he heard the squeak in the deserted hall earlier that afternoon that had so alarmed Karen. "The only person I can think of . . ." He hesitated. How could he accuse Simon to his own father? "No," he said finally, "there's no one."

"Are you certain?"

The young master nodded.

Arthur's tone brightened. "Come now, Chris, admit it. You're not really sure what happened. You just had an accident, nothing more. Am I right?"

The draught the doctor had given him was taking effect. The events of the afternoon swam before him in a gentle haze. "I guess so, Arthur," Christopher sighed lazily. He felt he was floating.

Arthur Catterby's words came to him from far away. They seemed strangely menacing. "On the other hand, Christopher, you, not I, may be right. You may have real reason to be afraid."

Chapter 11

Anxiously looking at her watch, Karen Catterby paced the uneven floorboards of the boathouse. The entire school would be at the Saturday afternoon swimming and wrestling matches, the basketball team had an away game at Choate. No one would be anywhere near the river in this weather, but she could not shake the terrible feeling of watching eyes. After his fall down the staircase in the administration building yesterday, her attempts to reach Christopher and call off their meeting had been in vain. He had been surrounded by boys and she dared not leave a message with Lucas. This would have to be their farewell. It had to be for his sake. And yet could she bring herself to break it off? She was in love with Christopher, she needed him. Like Kurt, he was in her blood, his touch ignited life in her. She could not bear the sterile world here at Talbot without him. Flight was her only salvation and yet Arthur's chains held her. She was prisoner in the personal hell of her own making.

Looking up at the slanting roof of the old boathouse, she shivered. The rain drummed ceaselessly on its shingles. Its noise covered the squashing sound of approaching feet along the snow and mud path and the click of the latch. Behind her back, the door slowly opened. A gust of wind pulled it from his hands, banging it loudly against the side of the building. Karen's breath caught in her throat. She whirled about.

His hair plastered wet across his broad forehead, Christopher stood in the rain staring blankly ahead with Milton at his side. "Is this the place?" he asked with a sheepish grin.

Her heart went out to her beautiful man-boy. Everything else was forgotten. "This is the place," Karen replied softly, moving forward to take his hand and lead him in to her.

Their lone sentinel, Milton settled down before the closed door as Christopher drew her into his arms and pressed his lips to hers. They clung together for minutes, the beat of the monotonous rain on the roof enveloping them in their own special cocoon of anonymity and security. As they kissed, drops of cool water from his face ran down hers, bathing her with his youthful freshness and innocence. She pressed Christopher closer. It was the only way she could express her love and need for him at that moment. Then gently, slowly moving from his embrace, she unbuttoned his soggy lumber jacket and let it fall to the floor as she led him to the storage room at the rear of the boathouse where a pile of worn canvas had been smoothed into a resting place. Sinking into it, Karen pulled him down beside her.

"Never," she whispered. "Never will I let you go."

The next days passed in great contentment for Christopher. Everything, even the weather, seemed to conspire with them to keep their secret. Rain and heavy mist swirled around the school on the ridge, blotting out the boathouse below. The thoughts of the headmaster and his faculty were centered not upon listening for gossip, but upon the sudden and devastating thaw. The Connecticut River was already clogged with great ice chunks floating down from the north; several bridges upriver had been torn away by the force of the water piling up behind the ice dams that had wedged beneath them.

But the threat of the river was far from the lovers' world. Lucas was back with Christopher, his burns healing well. The most noticeable effects of the fire were his missing eyebrows and singed hair. They worked together in perfect harmony and friendship, a friendship no longer strained by Christopher's self-doubts about his own sexuality. It was a friendship more strongly forged for having shared the brief terror of the explosion. His classes went well, the students eager in both their work and discussions. Every afternoon after his last class, Christopher and Milton lost themselves in the mist to arrive minutes later at the boathouse where Karen always waited.

Sometimes they made love, sometimes they just lay in each other's arms talking and dreaming of the next day, the one after that and all those to come. Christopher came to accept the explosion and his near-fatal fall as accidents, carelessness on his part. Gone was the paranoia Arthur's menacing words had briefly raised within him. For her part, Karen's relationship with Simon had become more gentle and relaxed. The little boy no longer seemed to dog her steps if, indeed, he ever had. Perhaps she had attributed things to him because of the guilt she had felt. The squeak in the hall outside Christopher's room—certainly, she had imagined it. She *had* to have imagined it.

Karen completely replaced Susanne in Christopher's thoughts and her driving personality dominated his entire world. Together they talked of Europe and the wonderful, beautiful and romantic places they would visit. It no longer pained him to think he would see them through another's eyes. And together they began to work out his ambitions, his future. As she had been unable to do with Kurt, she pushed him to see the greater and greater levels of his potential. He now saw the Talbot Academy as a jumping off place for bigger and better things rather than a goal in itself. And as one day led to the next, Karen actually began to permit herself to believe she would play a greater and greater role in Christopher's dreams for the future. Somehow she would escape Talbot. Somehow everything would work itself out.

Leaving her, Christopher would make his way to the gymnasium to spend an hour or so practicing in the pool and on the trampoline. He had gotten to know every inch of the building, even better than those with sight who took every corridor, door and wall for granted. Later he would join Lucas in his room.

To the faculty and students around him, Christopher was a highly visible person; he always seemed to be around. No one could have possibly suspected that two hours of every day were missing, those in which he lay in the arms of Arthur Catterby's wife.

It was Friday when Karen picked her way slowly through the mist toward the boathouse carrying a thermos of rum punch. She had come early to arrange a surprise picnic for Christopher. And why not, she had thought; the rain had stopped briefly and it was the warmest day of the year so far. A flimsy excuse, but enough of one to enable her to please him.

The river fog had settled more thickly than ever, so thick that she could barely see the muddy path and trees ahead of her. Nearby she heard the painful groan of the ice as it was forced slowly, one great slab atop the other, along and over the banks of the river.

Reaching the boathouse, Karen found the door already open. Christopher, bare to the waist, knelt with his back to her in the center of the room by one of the sculls, his familiar red, black and white checked lumber jacket tossed to one side. Two of the wide doors to the river were also open and a lantern burned at the back of the room. In her eagerness, Karen did not take in the incongruity of the situation. Smiling, she moved silently forward to surprise him and tossle his blond hair.

Sensing someone close to him, Frank Cannel suddenly turned, ready to pounce upon one of his fellow classmates. Karen froze, her hand extended toward him. The two stared at each other, not knowing what to say. Frank was the first to break the silence. A smile spread across the brawny youth's face as he began to understand her presence. He rose to his feet. "Why, Mrs. C," he said sarcastically, "fancy meeting you here. Long time no see."

Karen backed off a few steps. "You're getting the boats ready for spring, Frank?" she asked, taking pains to keep her voice even and formal.

The young football player paid no attention to her question, his eyes moving up and down her body. "Planning a little party?" he asked, looking at the thermos in her hand.

"I was just passing on my way to the village and—"

"Oh, come on, now, Mrs. C, you can do better than that. It's old Frank you're talking to." He circled her and stood between Karen and the door. "I've missed you, our little . . ." He paused and then went on, emphasizing the word he knew from experience turned her on. ". . . *fuck* sessions. Who have you got today? Anyone I—"

"Don't be vulgar, Frank," Karen snapped, trying to retain an outward appearance of calm. "I'm going now."

"Look who's talking about vulgar," he laughed. "If our dear headmaster knew about your vocabulary, more than his hair would turn white. As long as you're here"—Frank reached behind him and closed the boathouse door as he had often done in the past year— "why not say hello the way you used to." Karen

Catterby's sexual fantasies about rape excited him, excited him far more than those casual, bored whores he and some of his teammates dared each other to visit in New York while on their way home for Christmas vacation. He took the thermos from her unprotesting hand as she backed away. Opening it, he drained half its contents while staring deep into her eyes. The rum spread warmth through his gut.

"Frank, don't be stupid," Karen said firmly. "I'm going, and I'm going to forget this ever happened. If you've got a brain in that thick head of yours, you'll forget about it, too." She started for the door.

His powerful, naked arm flashed out, grabbing her about the waist and pulling her to him. "Come on, Mrs. C," he coaxed, his lips trying to meet hers as she fought against him. Grabbing the back of her head, he forced her resisting mouth to his. She beat her fists against his back, finally bringing her knee sharply up between his legs. Frank gasped, releasing her as he bent over in agony. Karen's hands were on the door latch when he pulled her roughly back. "Just like old times, eh?" he rasped into her ear as his hand sought her breast beneath the heavy wool of her sweater.

Not daring to call out for help, Karen struggled impotently against the strength of her young assailant, all the while feeling his hands hard against her skin, probing her body, his mouth uttering the filth of the German alley against her neck, over her eyes, her face, devouring her, overwhelming her with vivid memories. Her breath came hard. She tasted the salt of his skin, inhaled the rancid sweat of the bare arms that moved over her and, without realizing, her body began to move with his as she struggled with him. They moved in a harmony that sent flames through her.

Not encumbered with sight, Christopher and Milton moved easily through the heavy mist. He smiled in anticipation of Karen, her soft warmth and the stolen two hours they would share together. His life had become beautiful. A hesitancy on Milton's part made him pull his hand back from the boathouse door. He stood listening. Christopher's now sensitive ears picked up the sounds of movement within . . . and voices—rasping, ugly, mumbled voices.

"Fuck me," Frank Cannel murmured urgently against her ear as his tongue flicked over and around it, "Fuck, baby, fuck." Reaching down, he lifted Karen violently from the floor and carried her back to the pile of canvas. Falling upon her, he tore at her clothing. She struck and kicked back at him, but there was little power in her blows, little resistance in her fight. Her only cries were those of passion.

Christopher stood stunned and helpless; his chest felt as if a steel band gripped it. He recognized Karen's voice. The other was also familiar, someone on campus. And he recognized the sounds of love. He stood, betrayed. How could she? he demanded over and over. How could she do it here, do it knowing he would be coming? His shock and hurt suddenly turned to anger. All those not-so-subtle innuendos about her he had heard from the faculty wives, the innuendos he had dismissed along with the growls and pokes in the ribs from their husbands when Karen was in the room. "Bitch," he cursed under his breath as he backed away from the door. Bitch, he wanted to shout aloud at the house, fucking bitch, fucking, nympho bitch!

He fled up the path, his booted feet twisting and sliding in the mud, tripping and bumping against Milton. He had to get away, as far away as he could. Careless and oblivious to everything about him in his flight, the young English master slipped on the path and fell headlong onto the cold, sodden mat of last year's leaves. Pushing himself up, Christopher clung trembling to the trunk of a willow as he tried to fill his lungs with air, tried to control himself. He could not.

He leaned back against the wet bark and uttered an agonizing wail to the swirling mist about him and, burying his face in his mud-spattered hands, wept helplessly.

Frank Cannel stood fastening the buckle of his jeans as he looked down at the crumpled figure, her half-open eyes still clouded with lust. For her benefit, he made an elaborate show of adjusting his considerable manhood within the cramped confines of the tight blue denim. "See you soon, Mrs. C," he said, smiling. He pulled on his t-shirt and slipped into his lumber jacket as he crossed the boathouse and walked out through the open river doors onto the deck slanting down into the river. Ice had piled high against it on the upriver side and across most of the front, but had left a small gap, perhaps six feet square, open to the dark water that flowed swiftly beneath. Kneeling down, Frank scooped up a handful of the icy water and splashed his face. When he heard a slight noise behind him, he smiled to himself. "Still hot to trot, Mrs. C?" he asked suggestively without turning. He cupped more water in his hands, waiting for her reply. "Well, I always say, one good fuck deserves an—"

The shock and force with which the long steel point of the dart plunged into Frank Cannel's back cut off his words. His hands grasped frantically behind him for the object. Still kneeling, he swiveled around wordlessly in time to see the glint of the second dart as it was driven up into his face, driven viciously again and again until it struck deep behind the bone. His mouth gaping open in horrified disbelief and shock, the boy toppled backward into the green-black water.

The sound of the splash roused Karen from her lethargy. Christopher flashed into her mind. Oh, God, what time was it? He would be there soon. She hurriedly pulled on her skirt and sweater, quickly trying to repair the ravage wrought by her young rapist. Her long blond hair smoothed as best she could, Karen slipped into her trenchcoat and walked out into the boathouse. The place was deserted. Thank goodness Frank was gone. She had time. It would be all right.

Karen was jerked up short by a squeaking sound coming from outside the side door. She went cold. Moving quietly forward, she pulled the door open suddenly, hoping to confront Simon once and for all. He was not there. Instead she saw three narrow tire tracks in the mud of the path. Following them with her eyes, she caught sight of the battered red tricycle and the hand pulling it just as they dissolved into the thick mist.

In a state of confusion, Karen pulled the door quickly shut and leaned back against it, trying to think. What was going on? Her mind raced back over the events of the last months. And then a movement by the boat deck caught her attention. Pulled by some terrible force she feared but could not resist, she moved reluctantly forward out through the doors toward the dark shape that slowly rose up from the swirling mist of the river. It seemed to be trying to claw its way up onto the decaying old deck. Karen stared at it in horrified fascination as she moved ahead, her mind refusing to accept what she saw.

The ghastly, torn face she vaguely recognized as Frank Cannel looked up at her, whimpering, guttural sounds coming from its gaping mouth. One glazed blue eye stared at her, imploring her for help. Everything seemed in slow motion. It wasn't real, it was a terrible, terrible nightmare. Karen numbly watched her hand reach forward and slowly, purposefully pull her son's steel dart out from the jellylike hole of Frank Cannel's other eye. As if she had wrested away the key to his life, the mutilated boy slid silently back down into the dark water and disappeared under the ice.

Clutching the dart, Karen backed away, her eyes wide in terror, the back of her hand pressed to her mouth. The steel tip bit into her skin, bringing reality with its prick of pain. "Oh, my God," she gasped. "Frank. He's killed Frank!" She wanted to scream, to throw up. Nausea surged into her throat. She fought to swallow it back down. She had been right; none of them had been accidents. She saw everything so clearly now. Karen stared down at the dart in her hand, saw in her mind the tricycle tracks in the mud outside. Simon. They would come for Simon. She had to get to him, get him away from Talbot before it was too late.

Thrusting the incriminating evidence into her pocket, Karen turned and ran back across the deck, through the boathouse and up the slippery path to River Road and the ridge above. She fell, picked herself up, fell, scrambled forward, running in panic through the mist to her son. The few students she passed in her desperate run failed to notice her muddy disarray. They looked back at her and smiled. "Old Lady Catterby's probably just found out they're swimming nude at the gym this afternoon," one junior snickered to the other with a wink.

Karen burst through the front door of their house and closed it behind her, slipped the lock and fastened the chain. She looked down at her blood-stained hand. Closing her eyes, she wiped it on the arm of her coat. "Simon," she called. There was no answer. Karen hurried across the living room and through the dining room to the kitchen. He was not there. The double doors to Arthur's study were ajar. She peered in hesitantly. No one. She crossed back to the hall and started up the stairs. "Simon," she called. "Simon, are you in your room?" She was halfway up when she heard her son's distant voice.

"Here I am, Mommy."

Karen ran quickly back down and headed once more toward the kitchen. "Simon, I want you to come here," she said as calmly as she could, pushing in the swinging door to the room. There was no one there. The door to the cellar stood open. She had not noticed it before. "Simon," she called, "are you down there?" Silence was her only answer. Karen stood at the top of the stairs, unable to control her panic and frustration. "Come up here this instant," she demanded. "You know you're not ever supposed to be down there. Simon? Simon, do you hear me?" Craning her head, Karen listened intently. A faint noise came to her ears.

She looked at her watch impatiently. She had to get Simon away from the Talbot Academy as fast as possible and that meant catching the late afternoon train south. They would have to hurry. She would have taken the car, but Arthur always kept the keys with him. "Stop playing games," Karen snapped, starting down the stairs. "Come here this instant."

In the light of a single light bulb hanging from the ceiling, her eyes searched the piles of dust-covered boxes and old furniture stored about her. "Simon."

"Here I am, Mommy."

Whirling, Karen looked into the gloom behind her.

"Here I am." His voice sounded so far away.

Her heart jumped as she saw the open door into the old pump room under the dormitory. No one, *no one* was allowed in there; it was too dangerous. The only way into it was through the door in the Catterbys' cellar and it was always kept locked. Again she heard a noise. Karen threaded her way between the cartons to the entrance of the pump room. Groping to her right, she switched on the electricity. Only two old bulbs flickered on, casting weird shadows among the confused jumble of unused pipes and machinery.

When the Academy was built originally, a deep shaft was drilled down through the ridge into the domed roof of a large subterranean cistern into which flowed fresh, cool water, filtered and purified by nature through layers of rock and soil. To facilitate repairs, a wide stone ledge had been carved around the circular walls of the cistern, which was reached by a narrow iron ladder set into one side of the shaft. Two heavy pipes ran up the other side from the water to the pumps above. It had once supplied all the needs of the Academy. Abandoned in favor of the daily tested water from the Wyndham Locks reservoir, the old pump room had once proved a fascinating hiding place for Simon until his parents had discovered it and locked it.

Karen's eyes tried to penetrate the shadows. She had never liked the place. "Simon," she called, "don't tease Mommy. Please, dear." She waited for his reply. "I've got a surprise for you. If you hurry, we're going to take the train to Hartford. Maybe all the way to New York. You'd like that, wouldn't you?"

All she heard was the sound of scuffling feet. Tracing it, Karen's eyes came to rest on the great, round, iron manhole cover of the shaft. It had always been down, but now it stood up on edge, raised by the heavy chain wrapped around the old electric-powered winch above. A new panic swept Karen. "Simon," she cried, "are you hiding down there? Simon, answer me." Karen ducked under overhead pipes, and moved out across the room toward the open shaft.

"Mommy," Simon's voice called to her, "here I am." The faint words reverberated in the stone chamber below.

"Oh, my God," she wailed, "you are down there." Karen stood holding on to the great iron cover and looking down. The shaft itself was dark, but a dim glow came from far below. Obviously several bulbs still burned in the dome of the cistern. She stared at the water rippling in the light below her. "Simon, you come up here," she shouted.

"Mommy," came the echoing answer. "Help me, Mommy."

Karen did not hesitate. Swallowing her fear, she sat down on the cement floor at the edge of the shaft and gingerly lowered her feet onto the rungs of the old ladder. She started down slowly, hand over hand toward the water and the ledge of the cistern where Simon must somehow be caught. "Don't worry, darling," she called, "Mother's coming." Her voice sounded unnaturally loud in the confines of the stone shaft.

Halfway down, another sound came to her ears, that of metal grating on metal, chain link slipping over link. Looking up, Karen saw the circle of light formed by the round entrance of the shaft above slowly getting smaller as the great iron cover began to lower. "No!" she shrieked, climbing upward. "Don't. I won't tell about Frank and the others, you know I won't. I swear. No, no!"

The final crash of the heavy cover as it fell into place drowned out her terrified scream.

Chapter 12

CHRISTOPHER WALKED SLOWLY DOWN THE HALL OF the administration building to his last class Saturday morning trying to decide how to act when he and Karen met again. He still couldn't place the familiar voice he had heard with hers. It had been gnawing at him all night.

"What happened to you yesterday?" Lucas's question broke into his thoughts as the younger boy fell in beside him. "I waited all afternoon."

"Then you waited in vain," Christopher replied, trying to treat the subject lightly. His head throbbed miserably and his empty stomach churned. The Station Grill in Wyndham Locks and its sympathetic bartender, Grim Grace, had been a beacon of comfort to Christopher after his betrayal at the boathouse. Seeing his despair but asking no questions, Grim Grace had bundled him into the last booth in the sleazy bar and, making motherly clucking sounds, wiped his face and smoothed his hair. He had been a favorite of hers ever since his illicit ventures into manhood during his student days at Talbot. She had spent much of yesterday with her plump arm draped around Christopher's shoulders, ordering beer after beer for him as he denounced life in general and women in particular—all except Susanne. He had felt the urgent need for the reassuring sound of her voice and phoned her. There had been no answer. Later that evening, during her break, Grace Corrigan had driven Christopher and Milton back to the Academy.

"Jeez, you look terrible."

"Thanks, Lucas," he replied sarcastically, "I needed that."

"Sorry." The boy was silent, but for only seconds. "But you really do look—"

"Lucas," Christopher sighed wearily, "I'm sure I do look terrible, about as terrible as I feel. Now can we let the matter drop? Okay?"

As he looked at him, the boy's curiosity mounted. "I didn't know there was a party last night. At Coach Logan's?" he asked casually, hoping to lure the English master into some dreadful admission of faculty debauchery.

They had reached the open classroom door. "Nice try, my friend, but I'm afraid my whereabouts of Friday afternoon and evening shall forever remain shrouded in mystery." He smiled at the frustrated and inquisitive expression he knew must be spread across Lucas Howe's face. "After you, Mr. Rosencrantz," he said formally, extending his hand to the classroom.

"Thank you, Mr. Gildenstern," Lucas replied sourly.

"Good morning, gentlemen," Christopher called with forced gaiety as he crossed to his desk. "Let's finish off Hamlet today. Frank," he asked, turning, "does the play have any parallels to the politics of the current administration in Washington?"

He was answered only by whispered conversations between the others in the class.

"Frank?" He frowned. "Okay, you guys, are you going to let me in on the secret?"

Alan Fleischer was the first to speak. "Frank's not here, sir. Didn't you know? The headmaster told us all at breakfast this morning."

"He didn't show up for wrestling practice yesterday afternoon or for supper," Tony Arnacella interrupted. "Or last night, he—"

"Mr. Harrothwait called his parents this morning," David Roon broke in. "Everyone's real worried."

Alan Fleischer recaptured the floor. "The police were in the dining hall. They wanted to talk to anyone who saw Frank yesterday. And they want us to help search the entire school and woods this afternoon."

"Except the guys playing basketball," David corrected.

The freshmen in his first class had not mentioned Frank Cannel's disappearance to him. Christopher stood silent as the class broke up into a series of jumbled conversations between the boys. Each had his own idea of what had happened to their classmate, each speculated upon his whereabouts, including the strong probability that he was "shacked up" with one of the whores living on the outskirts of Wyndham Locks who serviced the migrant tobacco workers in the summer. "Frank's a real ass man," Christopher heard one of the boys say to another, "but he wouldn't—"

"All right, gentlemen," Christopher broke in, "let's leave the mystery of Frank Cannel and his activities, innocent or not so innocent, till after class. Hamlet needs you right now."

The missing captain of the wrestling team and the police search were the only topics of interest that day during lunch, an interest to which Christopher was not immune. His thoughts kept returning to the voice behind the boathouse door, the voice making gutter love to Karen. Could it have been Frank Cannel's? He tried to remember how Frank sounded in class but could not recreate it. Why had he called upon him first that morning? Was it a coincidence or an unconscious recognition of the voice that had plagued him all night long?

Much later that afternoon, Christopher pulled himself from the Academy's pool and walked to the locker room, casually toweling his dripping body. He flexed his muscles, feeling cool and refreshed from the strenuous physical exertion, yesterday's alcohol and sleeplessness worked out of his system. As he rubbed the towel vigorously back and forth over his back, enjoying the abrading sensation of the coarse damp cotton against his skin, he heard the distant wail of an ambulance siren. His hands froze as the siren grew louder and louder and stopped. Well, he thought, slowly lowering the towel to the bench beside him, the mystery of Frank Cannel has been solved for better or for worse. He began pulling on his clothes.

By the time Christopher had dressed, dozens of students had gathered on the west side of the ridge by the gymnasium. They stood in small groups talking quietly with hoods pulled up against the light rain, looking at the ambulance and the two police cars sitting before the dormitory at the southwest corner of the quadrangle. When he emerged from the gym and started to walk up to his room in the administration building, Lucas joined him. His voice was filled with both sadness and excitement. "Steve Van Buren found him. Frank's dead."

"Where was he?"

"Down at the boathouse." Christopher stopped and turned toward the boy. He had half expected Lucas's answer. "Gave Steve a real scare. At first he thought it was you."

"Me!" Christopher was jolted. "Why me?"

Frank was floating face down, partly under the ice, caught on the barbed wire under the deck. He had on a lumber jacket just like the one you always wear, and with his blond hair . . . well, Steve thought it was you, that you'd slipped and fallen in."

"Did he drown?" Christopher asked, resuming the walk up the path to the quadrangle.

"They don't know; I guess so. His face was all cut up, Steve said. Probably from the current knocking him into that wire. They found a thermos with rum in it. Knowing Frank, he could have got drunk and fallen in. The police are at the Catterbys' now."

Christopher's heart jumped at the mention of the name. He now knew it had been Frank Cannel's voice he had heard with Karen, but how could the police have possibly linked her to him? Had she . . .

"They wanted to talk to Simple Simon," Lucas said.

"Simon?" Lucas's last words left him at a loss. "Why Simon?"

"They found tricycle tracks in the mud under the roof overhang down there, and everybody knows Simon's the most tricycle-riding kid on campus. Besides, the little creep seems to know just about everything that goes on in this place. I wonder if he knows about Frank and his mother?"

Again Christopher's heart leapt. "What the hell are you talking about?" he scoffed, trying to ridicule the implication in the boy's statement, an implication he now knew to be true.

"Mrs. Catterby and Frank used to play house together, or at least that's what Frank said. And he's not the only one. She's supposed to be a real hot num—"

"Shut up, Lucas," Christopher snapped angrily.

"But—"

"I said, shut up!" The two walked on in silence, the younger feeling a quiet sense of injustice for being attacked for what he thought was common knowledge.

But he guessed he could understand Christopher's reaction. After all, he was faculty and the faculty had to stick together.

The afternoon did not prove productive. Finally, Christopher closed the Braille book he was reading. "Lucas," he asked casually, "what exactly did Frank Cannel look like?"

Putting aside his papers, the boy tapped his head with a pencil as he looked across the room and groped for a description. "Well, he was blond, tall, kind of handsome, I guess, and really well built. He was on the football team and captain of wrestling, and . . ." Lucas shook his head at the inadequacy of the picture his words painted. He smiled as his eyes moved over the face of his teacher. "Gee, Chris, I guess the best way to describe Frank is that he really looked like you."

The seemingly innocent words shook the young master. But he continued along his line of inquiry with apparent casualness. "The day I got here, there was a memorial service going on for one of the boys who died in a fire."

"Right, Alan Rivkin," Lucas confirmed.

"What did *he* look like?"

Again Lucas Howe tried to come up with a true description of one of his lost comrades. "He was blond, a real good runner, he was . . ." Lucas paused and smiled. "It's not a cop-out, but he looked a lot like you, too."

"And the boy who died when his room caught fire. You told us about him the first day we were here?" Christopher's voice was tight.

Slowly the pattern began to occur to Lucas just as it had to Christopher. "Just like you," he answered dully, not fully understanding the import of his words. "Hugh Snyder looked just like you. Chris, it's really spooky, isn't it? I mean it's weird, it's . . ."

"They were all accidents?"

"Yeah."

"All of them? There was never any doubt?"

"No. Why?"

"How long did Hugh Snyder have his hot plate?"

"I don't know. He kept it hidden, none of us knew he had one. It was a real surprise."

"Particularly in a place with such an active grapevine," Christopher commented wryly. "Did Rivkin smoke?"

"We can't smoke, it's against Mr. Harrothwait's rules."

"Come on, Lucas," he said, disparaging the statement, "I was a student here, remember?" Lucas smiled. "Well, did he smoke?"

"I don't think so. He was a real jock; so was Hugh. They trained all the time." He smiled again. "Real studs, too. Rivkin told me once that 'fast fucks made fleet feet.' "

"Any rumors about either of them and any faculty wives?" Christopher asked the question so innocently that Lucas did not appear to make the connection.

"Rivkin was having it off with someone. He never said who."

"In Wyndham Locks?"

Lucas's imagination and interest slowly began to involve themselves in the puzzle. He shook his head. "No, couldn't have been. Alan seldom went over there. If what his roommate said were true, she'd have to be here. I wonder . . ."

"Wonder no more, my friend," Christopher said, feigning gaiety to interrupt the boy's train of thought. "I was just catching up on the past gossip of the Talbot Academy. That's it for today. I'll go over the tapes by myself. Have a good Sunday."

The abrupt termination of their afternoon session only partially diverted Lucas Howe from the questions raised by their conversation. He left, but his mind remained. Why was Chris asking about the other boys? Was it just idle curiosity, or did he really suspect something? He hurried on to his dormitory. There were an awful lot of coincidences, he had to admit, but his friends had been victims of accidents, of that he was sure. Like today, the police had investigated and confirmed it. And that's what the headmaster had said in his reassuring letters to all the parents of the students. They had to be accidents. After all, this *was* the Talbot Academy. But there sure were an awful lot of coincidences.

Too many coincidences, Christopher reasoned as he sat in the blackness surrounding him, his mind conjuring up ghastly pictures of the three dead boys who looked exactly like him. Had no one before made any connection? The more he thought about it, the more uneasy he became. The first two had died in fires. Christopher had now been involved in two "accidental" fires, either of which might have proved fatal.

"Hold on, let's not get overly dramatic," he said aloud. There were perfectly reasonable explanations, innocent explanations if you took each death separately. But because of his personal involvement, because of *his* "accidents," Christopher could only see them joined in the context of what he now suspected. Frank Cannel was a powerful athlete. A fall into icy water should not have been enough to kill him. He would have been up and out in a flash no matter how great the shock. Of course, everyone would think he drowned because he got tangled in the barbed wire. Everyone thought Christopher had tripped over his own feet when he took the fall down the stairs, but in his mind he still felt the rope biting into his ankle. If what he suspected were true, then incredible as it seemed, there had to be a murderer running about the halls of the Talbot Academy. But who? And why? He inspected his hypothesis from all angles.

Rivkin was having sex with a faculty wife. So, too, was Frank Cannel—with Karen. "Karen," he repeated aloud. Was Rivkin's faculty wife also Karen? Had Hugh Snyder slept with her? All three and Christopher looked alike—all looked like her dead brother Kurt, the twin she idolized. Could she be the common denominator that linked the deaths of all three boys? Were they threatening to expose her, blackmail her? She was strong-willed, passionate. Could she have struck the fatal matches, pushed Cannel into the river, held him under? He remembered her embrace, felt her arms entwined about him, her hands roving over his skin. No. Karen's body was too greedy, too possessive for her to deprive it of its pleasures, and she was not strong enough to fight Frank. Besides, what student would want to give up a campus mistress as well as risk expulsion from the school by exposing her? No, he was way out in left field. Yet he could not shake the growing fear that somehow through her he was marked as the fourth in the chain of death.

Did only he know of the passion-filled voices behind the boathouse door yesterday? The tracks in the mud! The police were talking to Simon. Simon! His stomach tightened. Karen appeared afraid of Simon for some reason; she seemed to freeze whenever he was near. He remembered her reaction to him the day he found them together in the quadrangle, her panic, and her cry in Christopher's room when she thought she heard his tricycle outside in the hall—that was the day he had been tripped on the stairs. The Barbie doll! The missing doll with the nail driven into its head. It was a kid's sick little voodoo doll. And Jerry Fowler had seen Simon around just after the lighter fluid exploded in the fireplace. He remembered Susanne's description of Simon's hate-filled face when they had first met. Of course, he looked just like the other boys; he would have represented a threat to Simon. And he remembered Arthur's words about Simon's attachment to his mother and the jealous "little things" he sometimes did.

That weird little boy. Was it possible? Could he actually be killing off his mother's young lovers? Was he physically capable of creating all those supposed accidents? Christopher slowly nodded his head. Clever little boys could light matches, push people into rivers, stretch ropes across stairs. Oh, God, they could even open snake cages and classroom doors. Arthur Catterby's prophetic warning came back to him. "You are very vulnerable. Things that hold no danger for the rest of us can be deadly to you." Christopher realized for the first time how really vulnerable he was, realized that a little boy, one who really hated him, could be very deadly. And if Simon knew he was sleeping with his mother? But of course, he *must* know!

He was right, he had to be. It *was* Simon. What a joke, what a terrible, sick joke. He, Christopher Hennick, at one time big man on campus, was at the mercy of a little five-year-old. Fear gripped him. It was all so very simple, so logical, so inevitable. Simon was going to keep trying to kill him until he succeeded. Sooner or later he would succeed. He had to; he had eyes.

The police! They were at the Catterbys' now. He had to tell them. Not bothering to put on a jacket, Christopher headed for the door. They would believe him; he would make them believe him.

Moving as quickly as he could beside Milton, he heard footsteps coming toward him down the hall of the administration building. He called out. "Hello." Someone stopped. "Are the police still over at the Catterbys'?"

"Gosh, sir," the student replied, "I'm not sure. They were the last time I looked."

Christopher rushed ahead. He had to get Simon before Simon got him.

Reaching the Catterbys' door, he pushed the bell,

suddenly realizing he could not just barge into their home hurling accusations at their son. He'd have to have a reason. And then he'd get the police off to one side. His mind whirled as he heard the lock on the door pull back.

"Christopher," Arthur Catterby's voice boomed affably. "Come in, come in. Don't stand out there in the drizzle."

"Arthur, sorry . . ." he stammered, "sorry to bother you, but . . ."

"Good Lord, you're soaking wet," the head of the department said. "Come over here by the fire."

"No . . . no, thank you, I'll just stay a second. I know this is a bad time for you." He hesitated. "I was concerned about Frank Cannel. He was in my class, you know. Are the police here?"

"Why? Do you want to talk to them about something?" Arthur asked. "You don't know anything about that terrible accident, do you?"

"No, no." He groped for words. "I . . . I thought they could tell me what to say to the other boys to explain Frank's death."

"Just tell them it was an accident," Arthur replied. "Frank slipped and drowned in the river. The shock of that icy water must have been terrible. And as for the police, I'm afraid you're a little late, Chris. They left nearly an hour ago." Christopher stood ashen and helpless, not knowing what to do next. "I'd invite you to dine with us, but Karen's gone as well," Arthur continued. "Dashed off to New York yesterday afternoon to do some shopping, left a note with Simon. Looks like we're all bachelors for a while—you, me, and little Simon here."

The boy looked up smiling as Christopher backed away from them, feeling behind him for the doorknob. In his mind he pictured malevolence emanating from the child's eyes. He found the knob and tried to turn it. It would not move.

"Chris," Arthur asked, "are you all right? You're white as a sheet."

It's locked, the young master's mind screamed. I'm locked in. Losing all composure, Christopher turned to tug again and again at the knob.

Looking at him strangely, Arthur stepped forward and pulled his hands away. "Here, let me help you with that; sometimes it sticks in weather like this." Christopher heard him bang the door with his fist and then the click of the latch as he opened it. "Are you sure something's not the matter with you?"

"Nothing, nothing, Arthur, I'm fine," he replied in a choked voice, "just fine." Christopher grabbed desperately for the door.

Simon's foot pressed down on the pedal of his tricycle and moved slowly forward. Christopher turned, and as he fled through the mist and rain to his room, he heard the squeak of its rusty rear axle.

Chapter 13

DYNAMITED HIGH INTO THE AIR, THE EXPLOSION OF thousands of tons of shimmering, green-white ice filled the picture tube of James Harrothwait's television. He watched the surge of dark water breaking through the now ruptured ice dam that had blocked the Connecticut River. Uprooted trees and jagged fragments of buildings torn from the riverbanks swirled downstream in the thundering currents that threatened him and the Academy he had spent his life creating.

In his mind the headmaster traced the crest surging down through Vermont and Massachusetts toward the Connecticut River Valley, swelling as one town after another in acts of self-preservation was forced to open the sluice gates of their overflowing reservoirs to save the restraining dams.

James Harrothwait crossed the room and switched off the late Saturday night news. He returned to stare out through the window at the rain-filled darkness. Wyndham Locks and the Academy stood directly in the path of the overflowing river. The ridge would be safe, but the low-lying buildings and the gymnasium would be inundated. He turned as his wife entered the room bearing a tray with two mugs of cocoa and a plate of cookies.

"Is it very bad?" Mrs. Harrothwait asked gently.

"Very. The low areas to the south of us are being evacuated. Hartford is preparing to close the entrances through the dike. They estimate the last train through will be some time tomorrow afternoon."

"We're going?"

He sat wearily on the couch beside her. "I'm afraid we must."

"Oh, James," she said softly, putting her hand over his. "Everybody?"

He nodded, taking a sip of the steaming chocolate. "This is the worst we've had to face since we've been here, old girl. Aside from the damage, Talbot could be an island cut off from help for I don't know how long. The electricity will most certainly go, we wouldn't be able to keep much food."

"We've used boats before."

"Not this time, I'm afraid. It's too dangerous. Only Emil Croucher will stay to look after things—he volunteered."

"But Charles, he's so old."

"Talbot is his life."

Mrs. Harrothwait looked at her husband sadly. "It's yours as well." He made no reply. She tried vainly to put some enthusiasm in her voice. "Very well, when do we go?"

"Tomorrow afternoon. I've contacted most of the parents to alert them that their sons will be starting spring vacation eight days early. Many are driving here to pick them up. The rest of the boys should be able to either catch the last train through the dike south to New York or get the bus across to Bradley Airport. I hope the planes will be flying in this weather. If not, we'll just have to stay in the Wyndham Locks elementary school until they do."

She picked up a cookie and placed it in his hand. "Poor James, it has been a difficult day, hasn't it?"

"One of the worst I've ever known," he sighed. "The Cannel boy's death was very upsetting to me. He was a fine young man."

"They say he had been drinking."

"They may say what they like. Frank was a fine boy, he would not break the rules of the Academy. A deplorable accident."

"You are sure, aren't you? It comes so soon after the Rivkin boy that I . . ."

He reached over and patted her hand. "My dear, I am very sure. They were popular boys, no one would want to harm them." Putting down his mug, the headmaster pushed himself up from the sofa. "Now, not another word. I think I'll take a last look at the river before bed." He walked toward the hall closet.

"But you were down there only an hour ago," she protested gently.

"Just checking. I'll sleep better for it."

"James Harrothwait, I doubt you'll get a minute's sleep this night."

Smiling at her from the door, he pulled on his raincoat and picked up an umbrella. "And knowing you, my dear, neither will you."

Nor would Christopher. He sat tensely at his desk facing the door under which he had crammed the wooden wedge as a primitive lock. Milton lay peacefully at his feet. Christopher reached down to stroke the animal from time to time, more to assure himself of its protection than to comfort it.

He had toyed with the idea of just taking Milton and fleeing the school that very night, or telephoning the police from the public phone down on the first floor of the building, or going to the headmaster. But how could he explain his fears? How could he accuse a five-year-old child of being a killer? Who would believe him, take him seriously? And what about his own relationship with Karen Catterby? Surely they would be found out. He would only bring to an end his short teaching career at Talbot. And he desperately needed the salary and a favorable recommendation from the headmaster if he were to go after the fellowship at Harvard again.

Karen would be back from New York tomorrow night. She already suspected the truth, of that he was sure. She alone would understand the danger Simon represented to him; she would control Simon. Until then, Christopher decided he would have to protect himself as best he could from that little devil, would have to keep out of his way. He would either stay holed up in his room or keep in the company of the boys. He tried to put aside his panic and think rationally. There were only eight more days until spring vacation. If he were careful, alert, he could last it out until then. The vacation would give them all time to work things out.

Sometime later that night, a small noise in the hall jerked Christopher from a fitful sleep. He sat up in his chair, listening, waiting for some sound at the door.

"Chris-to-pher," a small voice whispered through the door in a singsong rhythm. "I am here, Chris-to-pher. Chris-to-pher, here I am."

The young master's hand reached down for Milton.

The little voice giggled. After some minutes of silence, Christopher heard the faint squeak of the tricycle fading away down the dimly lit hall on the top floor of the administration building. His whole body trembled as he tried to bring himself under control. Tomorrow, he thought, tomorrow Karen will be back. She'll stop him.

*   *   *

The water that had been slowly moving up the sides of the cistern crept across the ledge toward Karen Catterby as she lay exhausted in sleep. She had spent most of Friday night and Saturday clinging to the top of the rusted iron ladder hammering uselessly at the heavy cover that sealed her in and calling to Simon, calling to anyone who might hear. Through the small holes in the round iron cover, she had twice seen her captor kneel to look down smiling at her face. Her hands were scraped raw and bleeding.

Karen's eyes opened with a jerk as icy water touched her leg. She lay for several seconds staring up at the brick dome above her, trying to place this strange, alien environment in which she found herself. The water reached her hand. She jerked it away. Everything flashed back to her. Sitting up, Karen looked about her. Tiny waterfalls flowed freely from the brick-lined walls. "Oh, my God," she gasped, huddling back against the wall, watching in terrified fascination as the water inched closer and closer toward her. She knew exactly what was happening. Pressure from the rising Connecticut River nearby was raising the water table and forcing water into the cistern. Soon it would be completely flooded. There would be no refuge from it except the narrow old ladder up the shaft. Her back pressed against the wall, Karen moved through the now ankle-deep water to the ladder and pulled her stiff, sore body upward. *Somebody* had to hear her call for help.

Reaching the top, Karen once again removed her shoe and beat frantically upward against the iron cover, her voice so hoarse that her rasped cries were barely audible in the pump room above. As her body heaved back and forth on the ladder, she failed to notice its rusted mounts moving back and forth in the crumbling mortar of the shaft wall. Chunks as large as her bleeding fist fell down into the rising water below.

Hurling down her shoe, Karen pushed up with all her might against the heavy cover above her in a futile act of frustration. The added pressure was too much for the ladder. Its loosened mounts wrenched free of the rotten mortar and the top ten feet bent back away from the wall, snapping one of its vertical sides. It twisted in air, throwing her off balance as it struck the pipes running up the other side of the shaft. Karen hung on desperately by one hand, her scream unheard. She stared down at the water far below and at the remaining sidepiece of the ladder bent to the point of breaking. How long would it hold?

Hardly daring to breathe, she slowly, ever so slowly reached forward with her free hand and took hold of the rusted, iron rung below the one to which she now clung and gradually lowered her weight downward. She dangled in space, waiting. And then, her eyes glued to the bend in the ladder, slowly reached for the next rung, lowering herself bit by bit down across the shaft toward the relative safety of the ladder below the break. She had nearly reached it when the ladder twisted once more. Karen swung her feet forward and grabbed desperately with both hands for a secure rung as the second sidepiece snapped and the top ten feet of iron plunged down the shaft. She clung to the remaining ladder, sobbing with relief. She was safe, but for how long? She didn't think the water could reach her this far up, but for how long could her exhausted body cling to the ladder? How long before she fell back down into the icy water rippling below? "Won't somebody come?" she moaned, looking up at the iron cover ten feet above. "Why won't somebody come?"

Sunday morning found the Talbot Academy in organized chaos. The headmaster's announcement at breakfast of the immediate evacuation had been greeted with cheers, which soon subsided when he also announced that the spring vacation, although starting eight days early, would correspondingly end eight days sooner. But excitement gripped the students as they carried out their assigned chores in preparing the school for closure while watching the water spreading across the playing fields and moving up toward the ridge. The main surge of flood water was not expected until evening. Chains of boys emptied the low-lying buildings of furniture and athletic equipment, carrying it up to be stacked in the dining hall and the dormitories. The entire quadrangle was a beehive of activity, filled with shouts and running students, their hands full of suitcases, rucksacks slung over their backs.

His packing finished, Lucas Howe pushed his way to Christopher's room through the freshmen running back and forth on the third floor. The blind master stood outside in the hall answering questions and issuing orders, thankful for the security the boys' presence gave him and relieved at being able to get away so soon from the Academy and Simon. The oncoming flood was heaven sent. He had arranged to stay with Susanne in Boston. At last they'd have the chance to put their lives back together again. While he was there, he'd contact Karen by phone and settle the Simon matter once and for all. If she would do nothing, he would go to the police regardless of the consequences.

"You look happy," Lucas commented, "but the bags under your eyes stretch to your knees."

"Right on both counts," Christopher laughed. "How are the boys coming along?"

"Okay," Lucas replied, looking around him. "I thought you might like some help packing. Mine's all done."

Christopher felt for and put his hand on the younger boy's shoulder. "You know, you're quite a guy. Thanks, I could use some help." As the freshmen started down with their bags, Christopher pulled out his suitcase and Lucas began to fill it under his instructions.

Around noon, parents living nearby started arriving in their cars, driving slowly along River Road over which several inches of water already flowed. The buses soon followed and the evacuation started in earnest. Each boy whose name was read off took a box lunch and climbed aboard the appropriate vehicle destined for the train station or airport. Christopher and Lucas joined the students milling in the rain by the buses.

"Ah, there you are, Christopher," Arthur Catterby called as he threaded his way through the lines of waiting students.

"Hello, Arthur," Christopher replied to the man who grasped him by the arm. "Has Karen returned from New York yet?"

"No. She called this morning while I was out. Simon took the message. She plans to meet us at my mother's home this evening. I'm glad she's not messed up in all this," he said, shaking his head at the activity around them. "Would you mind giving me your grade book. I want to review it over the vacation."

"I didn't think you'd . . ." A chill went through Christopher. "It's back in my room."

"I'll get it," Lucas broke in.

"Not so fast, young man. The headmaster has been looking for you," Arthur said. "Have you seen him?"

"No, sir."

"Then hop to it." He turned back to Christopher. "Sorry to ask you, but I really would like that book."

"That's okay, Arthur, no trouble."

Arthur reached down and picked up Christopher's suitcase. "Here, Steve," he called to Steven Van Buren, "put Mr. Hennick's bag in the lead bus. You are going to the station, aren't you, Chris?"

"Right."

"Good. I'll watch for you; I have to help pass out the lunches."

"Come on, man's faithful friend," Christopher said to the dog beside him. Gripping Milton's harness, they turned and started back for the quadrangle.

In contrast to the noise and chaos going on below, the colonnade running around the quad seemed deathly still and deserted as he and Milton walked toward the administration building. They mounted the creaking staircase to the third floor and moved down the dimly lit hall. In the silence, his footsteps reverberated through the old building. Christopher released Milton in front of the open door of his room and crossed to his closet. Reaching up to the top shelf, he groped for the several grade books that he and Lucas kept well hidden from the curious eyes of the freshmen. As his hands found them, he heard a key softly turning in the lock behind him. The books dropped from his hands. Christopher whirled about, bumping into the closed door. Fumbling for the knob, he turned it and pushed. The door did not budge. Panic exploded within him. It was happening; the nightmare he had feared was happening!

He threw himself desperately against the door again and again. "Simon," he shouted, banging the heavy wood panels, "open this thing. Simon! I'll tell your mother. Simon? Simon, do you hear me?"

Instead of an answer he heard Milton bark. It was the first time he had ever heard him bark inside the building. Christopher stood back, listening. The dog's low growl came to him, and then a yelp. The young master beat on the door. "Simon!" He heard only Milton's snarling mixed with yelps . . . then screeches, horrible screeches . . . and then silence. "No, no, no," he moaned, sliding down to the floor of the closet. Christopher buried his head in his hands. "Simon, please. Simon."

*   * — *

Emil Croucher stood at the northern end of the ridge, shoulders hunched against the rain, watching the last of the evacuation vehicles creep cautiously away through the muddy water that now swirled freely over River Road. The buses crowded with laughing, jostling boys moved more confidently, their axles well above the flood, but the hubcaps of the headmaster's ancient station wagon bringing up the rear were nearly submerged. Emil tried to picture the road in his mind. Were there any dips in it where deeper water would threaten James Harrothwait's car? He thought not.

As the rear lights of the station wagon faded from sight in the rain, the old custodian turned his attention to the broiling river down to his right. The boathouse roof showed through the dripping trees along the bank. The structure was almost completely under water. That was where the Cannel boy had drowned. He had never liked him. A smart aleck, he thought, not like most of the other boys. Well, they were all gone now; everyone was gone. The Academy was deserted. He alone was in charge and that was a great responsibility. The first thing he must do was make an inspection of all the buildings to be sure lights were off and windows closed. The boys were careless about things like that.

Turning, he walked slowly back toward the administration building. He might as well start there and then work in a circle around the quadrangle. In the wet gray of the afternoon he could see lights in some of the windows on the top floor where the freshmen lived. Typical, he thought. Emil first checked the main door to the building; it was locked. He walked to the west wing and pushed through the door into the locker room used by the day students. That door secured, he continued on into the main hall. What on earth was that, he wondered, squinting at something sitting in the shadows by the west staircase. As he approached it, Emil Croucher smiled in recognition. It was Simon Catterby's red tricycle. Lord, he thought, how that boy loved his tricycle; he was always with it. Best get it out of harm's way.

Emil leaned down to take hold of the favored toy. He hardly felt the blow from the hammer that crushed in the back of his skull.

The faint click of the bolt in the door cut into Christopher's numbed brain. How long had it been, he wondered. He felt for the face of his watch, but his earlier attack on the closet door had broken it. Had thirty minutes gone by, or an hour? Hesitantly, he reached for the knob and turned it. Under slight pressure, the door swung open, a rush of welcome cool air hit his sweat-streaked face.

Christopher slowly stood but stayed in the closet, almost reluctant to leave its confining safety. "Simon?" he asked tentatively. "Simon, are you there?"

There was no answer.

"Simon?" He raised his voice. He could not hear a sound in the room out there. Christopher inched ahead, his ears alert to any noise, any movement, that might herald attack. "Simon?"

The room was empty; all his senses told him so. He moved a few steps farther. The buses, he had to get down to the buses, had to get past that evil little bastard. Something heavy and soft stopped his foot. Christopher pushed against it with his shoe. It lay reluctant, blocking his path.

With dread, he slowly crouched down, reaching out tentatively to touch the silver-gray fur of his dog. "Oh, baby," he mumbled softly, "what has he done to you?" Christopher's fingers moved along Milton's sleek coat until . . . his stomach retched as vomit rose in his throat. He felt the still sticky blood clotting the fur around the deep, jagged gashes hacked into the poor animal's torn belly. Christopher turned his sightless eyes away, swallowing to keep from being sick.

He would have wept, mourned Milton, but there was no time now. He had to get to those buses.

With blood-smeared hands, he groped about the floor for his stick. Finding it, Christopher rose and felt his way around the butchered animal to the door. He so desperately wanted to run, but his brain shouted caution. Simon was somewhere out there. Stay close to the walls, he warned himself, hold onto railings with both hands, feel ahead for ropes. Tapping the stick before him, he felt his way to the head of the staircase and began a slow, cautious descent, pausing every so often to listen for some sound of impending danger from the little boy. Had he left, or was he silently standing nearby watching and waiting for the right time to strike? Christopher heard nothing.

Reaching the lower hall, Christopher covered its length as fast as he dared and pushed open the door to the colonnade around the quadrangle. The rain had stopped and a cold wind blew from the north. It had been raining when he was last outside. How long *had* he been held prisoner in that closet? The buses!

Throwing caution to the winds, Christopher ran forward, flailing his stick furiously against the pavement before him, running down the path leading to the gymnasium where the evacuation was taking place. "Hello," he called as he ran, "hello, wait for me." They had to still be there—or at least a car. Surely they would have waited; someone would have missed him.

He came to a breathless halt when he felt the tar road under his feet. "Hello," he shouted. "Is anyone here? Hello?"

The campus was silent. He heard only the gurgling flow of the rising flood water nearby. Turning back to face the buildings around the quadrangle above him, Christopher cupped his hands to his mouth and shouted at the top of his lungs. He waited and called again. The fear gripping his stomach told him he cried for help in vain. They had all gone. All but the weird little bastard who had locked him in the closet and hacked his dog to death. How had Simon managed to elude the evacuation, slip out from under the watchful eyes of his father? It did not really matter how; all that mattered was that he was trapped on an island with a vicious little killer and he had to get off. He was desperate. Swim! Simon would not have counted on his doing that. He was a powerful swimmer and the water could not be that deep. He could do it. He *had* to do it before that demented child struck again.

Quickly feeling his way forward with his white stick, Christopher moved northward along the road toward Wyndham Locks. In less than a minute he felt the icy water splashing over his shoes. He hesitated only briefly before pushing slowly ahead, using the firm tar surface of the road under his feet as his guide to safety. A curtain in one of the windows on the ridge above was silently drawn back. A pair of large brown eyes scowled as Christopher waded deeper and deeper into the frigid water swirling around him.

The current was strong, much stronger than he had anticipated—and deeper. As he pushed slowly ahead, he found it difficult to keep his footing and began to realize the extreme danger he faced in his sightless fight with the river to reach Wyndham Locks. Yet he preferred to fight something tangible, pit his strength and skill against the water rather than wait helplessly at the mercy of the deadly caprices of the little demon who waited for him back on the ridge.

As if to punish the young English master for the boldness of his decision, a sudden surge of water sucked his feet out from under him and rolled him over and over, forcing him up and then down beneath its surface. Holding tightly to his stick, Christopher fought panic-stricken against the current to regain his footing as he was swept off the road toward the submerged playing fields that had been turned into a great, fast-moving lake by the rampaging river. Somersaulted and tumbled roughly ahead in the icy water, he felt the branches of a bush and grabbed out desperately for them with his free hand. Catching hold, Christopher braced himself against the current and pulled himself up, shivering and gasping for air. He had lost. He could never make it. He would have to return to the ridge. But where was it? Christopher had lost all sense of direction in his world of blackness as he had been rolled and tumbled by the river. The water was over two feet deep where he stood, but which way was the deeper water, which way the dry land of the Academy?

Then almost like a beacon, over the rushing water floated several faint chords from the Talbot Academy organ. Christopher's heart jumped and he shouted aloud with joy and relief. There *was* someone else up there on the ridge, someone who knew how to play the organ. Jerry Fowler! He played the organ at chapel services. He must have stayed behind when they discovered Christopher was missing. Of course, the buses had to leave before the water rose too high. They knew he and Jerry could fend for themselves until a boat could get through to them. And Jerry could protect him from that little bastard, Simon. He would have to believe Christopher when he saw Milton's bloody, mutilated body. *That* was no accident. Jerry must be playing the organ as a way to attract him to the chapel rather than having to search the entire school.

The music came from Christopher's right. Leaning into the current, he moved slowly in that direction, making sure his footholds were secure before committing his weight to them. He had not gone far when he felt the ground under him slope upward and the current slacken to form a sort of backwash from the main flood. Pieces of wood and other debris carried downriver by the flood bumped against his legs as they circled slowly in the gentle whirlpool in which he

found himself. As Christopher moved through the
water toward the sound of the organ, a large object
floated up against him. Without thinking, he reached
down and pushed the waterlogged bundle aside. The
body of Emil Croucher turned in lazy circles and
floated out into the main current, where it was swept
swiftly away.

Chapter 14

CHRISTOPHER REACHED THE WESTERN SLOPE OF THE ridge by pulling himself along the chain-link fence surrounding the submerged tennis courts. It took him several minutes to locate the path and follow it up to the quadrangle.

As he pushed through the door of the administration building, a welcome blast of discordant sound from the organ overwhelmed him. Christopher used his stick to feel his way up the steps toward the second floor and the double doors leading into the choir loft high over the chapel's rows of hard, straight-backed pews.

"Jerry," he called. His voice was lost in the harsh chords. Continuing on up, he made for the partially open loft doors and flung them back.

The organ stopped abruptly.

He stood at the top of the loft stairs, dripping wet and shivering from the cold. "Jerry?" he asked, facing the organ down to his right. He moved forward.

The great musical instrument played the first three simple notes of "Three Blind Mice" just before Christopher's feet slipped out from under him on the scattered marbles laid carefully in wait for him. He plunged forward into air down the several steps of the narrow loft. The wind knocked out of his body, Christopher fell back on the bottom step, dazed. The only sound besides his painful gasps was that of several marbles rolling over the hard wood and dropping from one step down to the next, the noise multiplied in the empty chapel. A hand slowly reached down and picked up Christopher's white stick. The young English master heard it snap and the pieces drop hollowly onto the wood beside him. And he heard a child's giggle as the loft doors above him closed.

Ice-cold, wet and trembling, Christopher pushed himself up into a sitting position. So this was how it was to end, he thought stoically; a cat-and-mouse game on a deserted island with a sadistic little killer. There would be one trap, one attempt on his life after another. One would kill him, of that he was certain. But did it have to end this way? Was he just going to sit there and wait? The stubborn, competitive will of the once champion athlete slowly came into play, refusing to give up, refusing to be beaten by a child. No, God damn it, he answered himself. There had to be some way to fight back. If only he could get close enough to that little bastard to grab him, if only . . .

The sound of a tricycle's squeaking back axle echoed mockingly in the distance.

Simon knelt on the heavy iron manhole cover in the pump room. "Daddy said you wanted to go to New York and would never come back. He said you didn't want to live with us anymore." He peered through one of the holes in the iron cover down into the shaft at his mother. She clung exhausted to the ladder about ten feet below him. Her face drawn and haggard, Karen looked sick. He had never seen his mother look so ugly.

"Darling, that's not true. Now open the cover," she pleaded in a rasping voice. "Please."

"No."

"Why?"

"You'll go away."

"I promise I won't. Simon, please. Mommy's so very tired. If you don't open it, I'll fall down into all that water. Please, darling."

He looked beyond her at the water that had now completely filled the cistern and rose several feet up into the shaft itself.

"I'll tell you what," his mother begged desperately. "Bring Cousin James here and I'll tell him right in front of you that I'll never go away."

"He left," Simon said matter-of-factly. "They all left because of the water."

Karen's heart fell. She looked at her watch. It read nearly eight-thirty. They must have evacuated the school that afternoon, eight days before schedule. What could she do?

"Christopher's here," Simon said. "He tried to swim away." Simon smiled. "But he almost got drowned."

A desperate ray of hope flashed through her. "Simon, you like to keep secrets, don't you? Daddy was wrong. I wasn't going to New York at all. I was going to go to Disney World. And guess what. I was going to take you."

Simon remained skeptical.

"I was going to take you last night. It was a surprise. I wasn't going to tell Daddy or anyone. Just the two of us, our secret."

He stared down at her silently.

"We could go tonight. But we can't, not if I'm down here." Karen paused as she saw her son get up.

"You promise?" Simon asked. "You promise we are really going? I can see Mickey and Donald Duck? I can—"

"You can see it all," she said eagerly. "We'll sleep on the train. Won't that be fun?"

"I like trains."

"I know you do, darling. Do you know how to lift the cover?"

"You promise? It won't be like the other times?"

He sounded so skeptical to Karen that she wondered briefly if she had been that terrible a mother. "I promise. I love you, Simon. I'll never fib to you, never again."

Through the design of holes in the cover above her, she could see Simon move away. A few seconds later an old motor groaned into motion and creaking chains slowly began to raise the heavy iron cover. It was up no more than a foot when Simon's face peered under it.

"We'll go tonight," he confirmed. "On the train."

"Yes, darling, tonight." The relief that flooded through Karen's mind as more and more light shone in from above was almost dizzying to her. She held more tightly than ever to the ladder as her escape came closer and closer. But she quickly sobered as she looked up into the small face ten feet above her. The top of the ladder was gone. A rope, she needed a rope.

"Darling, is there a rope up there? Go look for a rope."

Simon disappeared. Within minutes he was back carrying a coil of clothesline in his hands.

"Tie it around the machinery up there and throw the other end down to me," she ordered. "Tie it real tight, now."

Having given in to his mother and their shared secret, Simon was eager to obey. It was almost like a game. Returning to the shaft, he threw Karen the line and knelt to watch. It looked pathetically thin to her as she reached out to pull it close. Would it hold her weight? It had to. She looked once more down the shaft at the black water below.

Still holding onto the top rung of the ladder, Karen tested her strength on the line. "Oh, God," she groaned. Exhausted from clinging to the ladder for more than a day, she would never be able to pull herself up to freedom. It would be impossible, her strength was almost completely gone. And Simon was much too small. Christopher was her only hope.

"Where is Christopher?" she asked.

"I hate Christopher." Simon's face wrinkled up into an angry frown. "He looks like the man in your picture. He hurt you."

"No, darling, he didn't. He loves us both—you and me."

"I heard him."

"He really does love you, Simon. He told me. I promise."

The little boy made no reply.

There was no time to argue. "All right, then, if you want, I'll never see Christopher again, not if you'll just bring him here, just this once. Mommy needs him to pull her out."

Simon stared down at her impassively, evading her request. "Milton's dead. He's all bloody." A bolt of ice shot through Karen. "I put him in the ground next to my mouse."

Perhaps she was too late. "Simon, Christopher's all right, isn't he?" she asked desperately.

The boy did not answer.

"He's not hurt?" she begged. "You can find him?"

He nodded reluctantly.

"Bring him here as fast as you can. And . . . and Simon, do you know where Daddy keeps his gun in the desk?" She knew he did. "Quick, go get it and take it to Christopher."

Simon looked at her suspiciously. "No. No, he'll shoot me."

"He won't, darling. I told you, Christopher likes you. Believe me."

Simon read the desperation in her voice. It disturbed him. "Yes, he will. He's mad at me."

"For God's sake, Simon," Karen exploded angrily, "do as I tell you."

His little face clouded darkly and he moved back from the opening of the shaft.

"Simon," Karen called, "Simon, I'm sorry. I didn't mean to shout at you. Mommy's just tired. Simon? Simon? Get the gun, Simon. For Mommy."

Christopher was moving slowly along the second floor corridor unscrewing the bulbs in the wall sconces when the electricity was cut off. He felt the heat of the bulbs fade as he touched them and realized that the power lines must finally have been knocked out. At least, he thought, fate had given him one weapon in his fight against his little adversary. They would be equal in the darkness. He held his second weapon in his right hand, the heavy handle of a push broom found in the janitor's closet. Creeping silently along the hall, he pressed himself back into the deep door frame of the science lab directly across from the head of the west staircase. He stood rigid, waiting. Sooner or later Simon would pass that way hunting for him.

He did not have long to wait. Somewhere in the hall above on the top floor he heard the squeaking of Simon's tricycle. The sound faded as it moved to the other end of the building where his room was. Christopher heard the bump of its tires as the tricycle was pulled down the far staircase by little hands. After a silence, the squeak of the faulty rear axle once again reverberated down the long second-floor corridor, growing louder and louder as it approached him. Christopher held his breath and pressed back into the doorway, wondering what deadly new form Simon's next attack would take. The sound was practically upon him, he would have little time in which to defend himself. It slowed and stopped directly in front of him. Simon looked up at the English master. A smile slowly spread across his face.

Unknown to Christopher, fate had taken back his first weapon. The sky had cleared and cold, blue moonlight streamed through the laboratory windows to clearly silhouette him against the glass-paned door. The little boy took the gun out of his pocket and pointed it at him. He had the chance only to say "Christo—" before the terrified young man's foot found the tricycle upon which he sat and, with one great shove, sent the machine and the child on it skidding across the hall and looping down the staircase. Simon's scream ended abruptly as his head smashed against the floor of the landing below, the gun he had come to give Christopher spinning from his hand over the boards into a dark corner, the tricycle clattering end over end down on top of him. Its front wheel turned slowly in the air and stopped.

Christopher stood breathing deeply in the doorway, listening for a sound from the little boy. He stood for what seemed an eternity. Was he dead? Unconscious? Or just lying down there waiting for him? He moved slowly to the head of the stairs. He had to find out. He had to kill Simon before the boy had another chance at him. Oh, God, he thought to himself, I'm about to kill a five-year-old boy with my bare hands. I can't, I just . . . But then a picture of what Milton's blood-clotted body must look like came to him. And the bodies of Frank Cannel floating in the river, the burned corpse of Alan Rivkin.

Christopher took a deep breath and started down the stairs to where the boy must be when a sound froze him. It was the squeak of the tricycle. It was coming from the far end of the hall. But that was impossible.

"Chris-to-pher." He heard his name called in Simon's singsong voice. It was slowly coming closer along the second floor corridor, the voice and the squeaking tricycle. "Chris-to-pher."

There was no sound on the landing where he was sure Simon lay, but now Simon somehow was pedaling his tricycle toward him down that hall in the administration building. What was happening to him? He was going mad. In his own personal blackness, had he fantasized it all? Was Simon really down there waiting for him or coming down the hall on his tricycle? Christopher backed up the two steps into the hall and grabbed hold of the railing leading up to the third floor. In his confusion he knew only that he had to get away.

"Chris-to-pher," called the little voice. "Here I am, Chris-to-pher." There was no mistaking the menace in that voice.

Using the broom handle as his eyes, Christopher climbed up to the third floor as fast as he could and fled down the hallway to his room. Halfway there he paused to listen. He heard the bumping of tricycle wheels as hands pulled it up the stairs behind him.

"Leave me alone," he shouted at the sound. "Don't come any closer. I'll hurt you. I've got a club." He smashed the broom handle loudly against the wall.

The small voice seemed cold and emotionless. "Chris-to-pher." It floated through the air to him. "Here I am, Chris-to-pher."

Turning, the terrified young master ran down the rest of the dark hall to his room, slamming the door behind him. He searched desperately for the wedge, crawling about the floor, his hands sweeping across the carpet, his brain in such panic and turmoil that he failed to realize Milton's torn body no longer lay where it had been. Not long before, a sensitive little boy with tears running down his cheeks had discovered it and dragged his lifeless dog friend off to the heaven place where, with loving care, he and his mother had from time to time buried the other lost animals from his bedroom zoo.

The knob of the door turned slowly and it swung in. "Chris-to-pher." The voice was almost on top of him. Christopher scuttled across the floor crablike, pushing his back into the corner of the room behind his desk. He held the broom handle, ready to lash out.

He heard a faint metallic click followed by his name. "Chris-to-pher." But the voice he heard now was not that of a small five-year-old boy, it was the deep voice of a man. "Are you ready? You're going to die now."

"Arthur," Christopher gasped.

"That's right, Christopher, Arthur Catterby." He spoke softly and rationally. "The man with whose wife you slept, the man of whom you and the others made a cuckold. Didn't you think I knew? Did you think 'good old Arthur' was blind—as blind as you?" No longer needed in his deception, he slipped the small tape recorder onto which he had captured Simon's voice during their "games" back into his overcoat pocket. It was the same type that had lured Karen into her own private hell in the cistern. Arthur pulled out a clothespin contraption. "Well, they are all dead, Christopher. All dead but you."

"Arthur, I—"

"Two of them died in fires," Arthur Catterby pressed on smoothly, oblivious to the interruption. "You don't like fires, do you, Christopher? They can be very dangerous for a blind man, can't they?" A flaming match sprang across the room from the clothespin gun in his hand, striking Christopher on the cheek. He slapped at it with his free hand.

"I . . . I thought it was . . ."

"You thought it was my little watchdog, you thought it was Simon." Arthur chuckled. "So did his mother; I made sure of that. She was afraid our little boy was a killer, that he'd have to be sent away to an asylum. And Simon could still be sent away; he could have killed those poor, unfortunate boys. Instead of mine, they could have been his matches, his darts. All I have to do is say the word and people will think him unbalanced, dangerously unbalanced. That's why she's afraid of me. Do you understand, Christopher? That's why Karen will never leave me for scum like you." Arthur smiled. "Poor Simon, poor innocent little pawn. He thought we were just playing our spy game to protect his mommy. And poor not-so-innocent Christopher. You got caught." Another match shot across the room to Christopher's face.

"Please, Arthur," he cried desperately, "don't. I'll leave; I'll never—"

"Too late, Christopher, too late for pleas, too late for tears," he said evenly. "You can't take back what's done. I wonder how many of the faculty know what you did with my wife. Did you brag about it, huh?" Snap, still another flaming match struck the young master's face. He brushed at it. "Did you brag about it in that sweaty locker room of yours with Neil Logan? Did you snap his jock and flick him on the ass with your towel and laugh about me? Did you?" His voice began to rise. "Poor cuckolded Arthur? Did they all laugh, Christopher?"

"No, believe me, it was noth—"

"Nothing?" Arthur interrupted. "Is that what you were going to say? Nothing?" His voice suddenly grew cold with rage. "Nothing that you seduced my wife, rolled naked with her? Oh, we knew you, Simon and I. We could smell you out the minute you arrived, you and all the other long cocks on the . . ." He broke off. Christopher could hear him panting from the emotion seething within him. Arthur Catterby slowly brought himself back under control. His voice returned to taunting his blind captive. He was the master now, not the frightened young man cringing before him, his golden hair clotted with mud, his face streaked, wet clothing clinging to his body. That body! Arthur could see its contours through the wet cloth in the shaft of moonlight coming through the window. He hated that body and all the others like it. He hated them just as much as his wife wanted them, craved them. "Tell me, Christopher, what did it feel like, you and Karen?"

"Please, Arthur." Christopher slowly stood. "We didn't—"

Snap. Another match flamed through the air at the hand holding the broom handle. Christopher jerked it away, stepping back against the wall, his foot sweeping the carpet to find and smother it. "Are you afraid of me? Were you afraid of me when my wife's hands were moving over your body, when she spread her legs to you? Were you afraid as she thrust up and cried out? Were you?" Arthur taunted.

Christopher said nothing.

"Well?" Snap, a match flew into the waste basket beside the trembling young man.

Flames began to dance across the papers there, began to reach up and illuminate the room. Panic swept through Christopher as he felt the heat. Snap. Snap. He knew other matches must be leaping across the room, leaping where? A slow flame began to crawl up the curtains near him. Snap. The papers on his desk began to curl as fire danced across them. This was to be his flaming tomb, just as the old tobacco barn had been Alan Rivkin's. As soon as that door shut him in. "No!" he shouted, lunging forward, swinging the heavy broom handle as the desperate will to live exploded within him. "No!"

Taken by surprise at the suddenness of his victim's charge, Arthur fell back and to the side, the flailing pole catching his shoulder painfully as Christopher crashed out of the burning room into the hall. He scrambled to his feet and followed, watching the blind man as he stumbled down the staircase into the darkness below. He shouted after him. "It's only a matter of time, Christopher. You can't escape me." Smoke billowed out of the room behind him and a Satanic red glow silhouetted Arthur Catterby's dark figure. "Wherever you go, poor, blind Christopher, I'll come for you." His laugh echoed through the deserted building. "You sold your soul to me for my wife," he called after the young master. "Now I'm coming to collect, Christopher. I'm coming for you."

With Arthur's crazed laugh ringing in his ears, Christopher fled along the lower hallway past the library, the study hall, banging the broom handle from side to side in front of him as he ran. But where could he run to escape the madman coming after him? Where? Arthur's demented words jumbled through his brain. He pushed through the door out into the colonnade around the quadrangle and stood in the cold wind not knowing in which direction safety lay. He could lose himself in the rooms of the dormitories, there were over a hundred of them and . . .

Arthur's taunting call from across the quadrangle stopped him. "I'm coming, Christopher. Oh, yes, try the dorm on your right. Why don't you hide in there. That's where Hugh Snyder burned up. He paid his debt to me just the way you're going to pay your debt, Christopher." Arthur's laugh filled the empty quadrangle.

The gymnasium was down the ridge to his right. He remembered what Arthur had said—"your sweaty locker room." Arthur hated sports, Karen had told him so. Arthur wouldn't know the layout of the gym, and there were no lights, the flood had taken them out. Christopher was sure he could lose him in the blackness of the maze of halls and lockers that he knew like the palm of his hand. Christopher turned and ran down the path, stumbling on the steps, picking himself up and running on only to fall again. He could not know that his flight was clearly visible to Arthur in the moonlight. Arthur followed, his ears ringing with grotesque and mysterious voices.

Much sooner than he expected, Christopher splashed into the rising waters of the flood swirling around the Talbot Academy. He waded on down, the swift current tugging at his legs, threatening once more to sweep him away. A piece of wood slammed into him, nearly knocking him down. Moving to his right, he felt for and found the chain-link fence by the tennis courts and pulled himself along as the ice-filled water moved higher and higher around his body.

Watching him carefully, Arthur followed slowly by the same route. He smiled with the knowledge of how easy the boy was making it for him to exact his just vengeance for the humility he had been caused. It would be an "accidental death by drowning."

The water was nearly to his armpits when Christopher felt the double metal verticals of the door in the middle of the fence. It was just across the path from the side door into the gym's main locker room. The current was particularly strong at that point as the angry water was forced to divide its flow to sweep around the large brick structure barring its way. Judging the current, Christopher threw himself diagonally against it and swam as hard as he could until it carried him across into the rough wall of the gymnasium. He pressed himself to the bricks and edged back against the swift-moving water until he felt the steps leading up to the locker room door. He grasped the knob, using it to help him up.

With great effort, Christopher slowly pulled the door out against the pressure of the water, but once open wide enough for him to slip in, the current tore it from his hands and flung it back wide open against the outside wall. Nearly a foot of muddy water already covered the gymnasium floor. The rush of the higher water outside swept Christopher before it through the door, smashing him into the first rows of lockers and the wooden benches floating between. Half crawling, half swimming, he slipped and scrambled through the room to the door leading into the main hall of the building. Even though the level of water in the locker room was now higher than that in the hall, he had little trouble pulling the door open and closing it behind him. Only a small, gurgling rush of water escaped as he passed through.

Although he could not swim, sight made Arthur's trip into the locker room one of relative ease. He was able to let the current do most of the work in carrying him across to the open gymnasium door and through. The rows of lockers and overturned benches were dimly lit by the moonlight. After a thorough search of the lockers, toilets and shower stalls, he waded toward the door that must lead into the main part of the building.

Christopher had already investigated the wrestling rooms and smaller storage rooms in search of a hiding place among the mats and other equipment. But everything not nailed down had been removed and taken up to the ridge for safekeeping. Most of the rooms were either locked or completely bare. He pushed on through the icy water back into the main hall and was contemplating what might afford him cover in the bleachers surrounding the basketball court and the swimming pool when he heard a gurgled rush of water into the far end of the hall by the locker rooms. Only human hands, not the rising water, could have opened that door. He stood frozen, his blind eyes staring in that direction at the shape of the man he knew must be there.

"Chris-to-pher." Arthur's voice mimicked that of his son. "I'm coming for you, Chris-to-pher."

Chapter 15

STANDING ATOP THE BLUFFS OF WYNDHAM LOCKS, James Harrothwait stared impotently across the vast gulf of seething water separating him from the ridge of his beloved school. The moonlight rippled sparkling over the swift, undulating currents silhouetting the dark, broken trees and debris they carried with them. In the eerie, blue-white light, the Talbot Academy looked skeletal and deserted. He knew it was not.

How could Christopher have failed to board the evacuation buses? He had seen the blind boy with Lucas Howe minutes before they pulled out. And Arthur? Why had he disobeyed his direct orders and remained at the school with his son? Well, perhaps it was for the best. At least he could look after Christopher, he and Emil Croucher. The four would be uncomfortable but safe.

"James!" the headmaster's wife gasped, clutching his arm.

He and the others standing near them looked at her. "What is it, my dear?"

"The roof of the administration building," she replied, pointing to the ridge, "I thought I saw a light."

230

The group focused their attention on the building. "But there's no electricity," the headmaster assured her, "you know that." He patted her hand patronizingly. "Probably just the moonlight playing tricks."

"I know what I saw, James," she persisted. "It was not the moonlight playing tricks."

"Maybe someone over there is trying to signal us with a flashlight," the mayor, an old friend of the headmaster, suggested.

The head of the school peered through the thick lenses of his spectacles, his tired eyes trying to focus on the slate roof and the clock cupola that sat atop it. They moved slowly along the ridgepole searching for some figure, some sign of movement. But the distance was too great. From where they stood, anyone moving on the roof would be no larger than a flyspeck. The headmaster was about to turn back to his wife when something curious caught his attention. It looked like a low, thin white cloud moving in the wind away from the east end of the building. He frowned as he watched it, a continuous white line that actually seemed to be coming *from* the administration building. Slowly his body stiffened. A sudden, brief flare of light behind the eastern corner of the building confirmed what he feared. "Fire," he murmured under his breath. Only his wife heard; her grip tightened on his arm.

"That's where Christopher's room is," she said softly. "Remember what happened when he first arrived."

There was no mistaking it now. A red glow began to silhouette that corner of the building; several windows along the front of the top floor suddenly lit up. "Oh, God," James Harrothwait cried in anguish.

The others saw it, too. Flames began to shoot up through the old roof, fanned eastward by the wind.

"There's a sprinkler system," the mayor said. "James, there *is* a sprinkler system." His statement sounded more like a question.

"There will be little pressure in the tanks without the pumps," the headmaster replied as he slowly turned to meet the gaze of his old friend. "Hal, the pumps run on electricity."

The mayor looked from James Harrothwait back to the school. The flames now engulfing the top of the east side of the administration building were being reflected by the flood waters below.

"We've got to get men over there, Hal," the headmaster demanded.

"Impossible. Not through all that water. The fire trucks would be submerged."

"Then by boat." James Harrothwait's mind whirled desperately. "The Hartly yacht!" he cried.

"It's too early in the season, it's up out of the water."

"How long will it take to launch it?"

"But they're not here," the mayor protested.

"It's the only craft on these parts of the river big and strong enough to get us over there."

"But we can't just—"

"How long?" the headmaster demanded, his bushy white eyebrows forming a menacing line across his forehead.

"Maybe . . ." Hal Murdock replied uneasily, "maybe thirty minutes with help."

"We are all here," the headmaster said, indicating the others in the group who had crowded about to hear the verbal exchange, "all the volunteers you need. Hal, we've got to save that school." He paused to make his point. "And there are a child and three men over there. One of them is blind."

The mayor looked into his steel-blue eyes and seemed to take strength from them. "Frank," he barked, "ring the volunteer firemen and get those men down to the boatyard as fast as your ass can move. Take some men and pick up the pumps and hoses from the station. You've got thirty minutes, no more."

Frank Wingam, selectman, burst into a grin. It was the first real emergency he had known since being in office and he and the men of Wyndham Locks would prove they were up to it. Turning abruptly, he ran to his car and sped off.

"The rest of you follow me," the mayor ordered. "It's not going to be easy to launch that big bastard into all that shit." The men in the group ran after him.

"James," Helen Harrothwait said, restraining her husband, "you're not a young man. Your heart."

"It's our school," he replied softly to her warning. "Would you have me—"

She put her fingers to his lips, silencing him. "Just be careful. We have come a long way, we have a longer way to go." Helen Harrothwait reached up and gently stroked his silver-white hair back into place. "Be careful."

Christopher slowly backed away from the taunting voice through the icy water that now reached his thighs. His hand groped behind him for the wall; instead he felt the railing of the stairs leading up to the spectators' balcony overlooking the end of the school's modern swimming pool. A sudden idea flashed through his mind as he recalled the marbles in the choir loft of the chapel.

"Chris-to-pher," Arthur mocked as he waded slowly toward his wife's young lover. His attention was diverted by the glass-enclosed trophy case fastened to the wall opposite the main doors of the building, its silver cups and plaques a lasting testimony to the athletic prowess of generations of Talbot students. One trophy in particular caught his eye and a slow smile crossed his face. Arthur smashed the glass with his elbow and reached in to pull out a long ebony javelin, its sterling silver tip honed to knife-edged sharpness. Weighing the spearlike object in his hands, he looked back to the young man up ahead of him.

"All it took to claim Alan Rivkin's soul was a single match, one small match. To claim Frank Cannel's, just a little dart," he bragged. "Simon's little steel dart. But Frank was only a boy; you're a man, Christopher." Arthur moved closer. "A big macho football player. It would take more than a little child's dart to kill you, wouldn't it?"

Arthur's voice grew louder, and Christopher could hear the splash of water as he approached. His hand tightened on the railing. Why had Arthur smashed the trophy case? Was he holding a sliver of glass like a knife as he neared? Christopher realized his only hope would be to wait until he could get Arthur near enough to use his superior strength to wrestle him down, hold his head under water, drown him.

"It would take a lot more than a dart, Christopher," Arthur repeated, closing the gap between them. The javelin flashed forward in his hands, its silver tip biting deep into Christopher's shoulder. Surprised by the blow and flash of pain, Christopher backed up a step, his hand instinctively going to the wound. "A lot more," Arthur said again. The silver tip jabbed forward again, tearing the skin of the young athlete's side.

Now he knew what Arthur had taken from the trophy case. It was ironic that he, himself, had been on the track team responsible for winning that javelin six years ago. Turning, Christopher fled up the stairs. He burst through the double doors into the balcony and threw his weight back against them. There were only eight rows of seats in the balcony, each two steps below the next to afford a good view of the Olympic-sized pool beneath. He heard Arthur's wet, slogging footsteps as he slowly mounted the stairs and stopped on the other side of the doors. The two men waited for the other to make the next move.

One door suddenly flew open from Arthur's vicious kick, knocking Christopher off balance. He fell backward, grabbing for the seat backs to regain his footing.

He knew Arthur now stood at the top of the balcony looking down at him. His mind saw the silver-tipped javelin in the other's hands. Slowly Christopher straightened and backed down the remaining steps, his hand trailing over the back of one seat to the next until he felt the balcony railing at his back.

Arthur stared down at his cornered prey. Behind and below him, the moonlight reflected off the muddy water that had flooded the entire auditorium, hiding the pool itself two feet below its rippling surface. "Well, Christopher, it's time for your payment," he said quietly. "No place left to hide." He walked down several steps, studying the young man before him. If he had not already been blind, Arthur would have enjoyed taking his revenge by plunging the javelin deep into those eyes as he had done to Frank Cannel.

Christopher stood motionless, his hands grasping the railing on either side of him, a suppliant to the caprice of the crazed teacher. He felt the sharp tip of the javelin touch his lower belly, felt the pressure against his skin slowly increase.

"How would you like to feel a great black shaft sticking up into your belly just the way you stuck your shaft up into my wife's belly?" he sneered. "Huh, how would you like it? An eye for an eye, a tooth for a tooth?" Arthur prodded Christopher with the javelin. "I asked you a question," he snarled, applying more pressure. "Answer me."

"I . . . I wouldn't like it, Arthur," the young English master mumbled. He could hardly get the words out. The javelin was too long, he'd never be able to reach Arthur.

"I didn't hear you, Christopher," Arthur shouted, prodding him painfully with the silver tip.

Christopher swallowed, moistening his dry throat. "I wouldn't like it," he repeated louder.

Arthur laughed viciously. "Of course you wouldn't, but that's just what you're going to get. This great

thing right up through your body like a giant phallus."
He laughed again at the analogy, enjoying prolonging
his victim's terror. "I wish you could see it, Christopher. But you can feel it, can't you?" Arthur moved
the tip lower. His voice rasped with years of pent-up
frustration and hatred. "It's only fair, isn't it? You
fucked my wife, now I'm going to fuck you. I'm going
to fuck you dead." His shrill laugh filled the flooded
auditorium, then he lowered his voice menacingly.
"And when they find your stinking, decayed body in
all that mud out there, they'll think poor Christopher
drowned. Just another accident."

The pressure of the silver tip eased slightly on
Christopher's groin, Arthur had committed himself to
his final move. "Welcome to hell, Christopher."

In the split second that Arthur pulled the javelin
back to get the momentum he needed to plunge it
forward again into him, Christopher grabbed the end
of the ebony shaft with both hands and, twisting aside,
tugged it toward him with all his strength, catching
Arthur off guard. Yanked off balance, the surprised
older man cried out and crashed forward down the
steps into Christopher. Shrieking with rage, Arthur
beat and tore at him as Christopher at last got his arms
around his tormentor. The two grappled, straining
against each other, muscle fighting muscle as they
teetered over the railing.

Christopher had to get him over and down into that
pool below. There in the deep water he would have the
advantage his blind eyes denied him up here. He drove
his fist hard into Arthur's gut, knocking out his breath,
and exerted all his strength to force his resisting adversary backward. Struggling, they seesawed back and
forth across the railing and, losing their balance,
started to slip over. Christopher broke away from
Arthur, trying desperately to get into some sort of
diving position before hitting the water. He knew the

submerged pool was at least eight feet out from under the balcony. He gave a last powerful kick against its side to thrust himself out over deep water. Arms flailing in air, Arthur fell headfirst straight down, his body crashing through the shallow flood water onto the tile just beneath its surface.

Coming up from his dive, Christopher treaded water silently, waiting for the thrashing sounds of water to lead him to Arthur. He would not flee this time. It was kill or be killed. He heard nothing. Slowly, Christopher swam to the edge of the pool and eased himself up. His hand touched the rough tweed fabric of Arthur's topcoat. He lunged forward in the shallow water reaching for his head. Arthur did not fight his grasp. His body floated limp.

Kneeling in the water, Christopher held him up. He put his ear to his heart, felt for his pulse. Thank God, he thought, the fall had taken Arthur's life for him. He got to his feet and waded wearily across to the bleachers, pulling Arthur's inert body with him. He lifted him up onto a seat above the muddy water and slumped down a few rows away, burying his head in his hands, exhausted both physically and mentally. His nightmare was over.

The gurgling water forcing under and around the doors and flowing through the gymnasium was the only sound in the now silent auditorium. It was strangely soothing to him. The violence and terror of the last days now seemed so unreal, seemed to have happened so long ago in the past. Only the fact that he sat there wet and shivering brought any reality to it. In his mind he saw Arthur and Karen, their frustrations and failures so magnified in the stagnant world of Talbot that she had been driven to perversion and he to murder. And caught in between, the only thing each really loved—Simon. "Simon!" Christopher gasped aloud, sitting bolt upright. The name reverberated across the water and about the high ceiling of the auditorium.

Flames roared unchecked through the entire length of the freshman corridor on the third floor of the administration building and up through the attic to the roof above. Glass panes shattered in the heat, their blackened shards exploding outward to let the fire escape up the old brick sides of the structure. Fanned by the wind, the conflagration leapt high into the sky, turning the night into a rosy glow that was reflected in the turbulent currents that fought to hold back the Hartly yacht. James Harrothwait and several dozen fire fighters stood on the deck looking up at the ridge as the boat rocked and twisted under them. The headmaster's eyes were rimmed with tears of agony.

Christopher's eyes, too, were filled with tears, tears caused by the smoke that swirled around him as he stood hesitantly holding open the west door from the colonnade into the burning building. He was terrified of fire. If only he could see, could know how bad it was, know where the flames were. The heat was intense. Was he walking blind into a furnace? Would his exit be cut off? But he was responsible for the life—or death—of the little boy. One way or the other, he had to find Simon and bring him out.

Moving slowly into the hall outside the chapel, Christopher felt along the paneled wall as he edged ahead toward the west staircase where the boy had fallen. The entire building shook and he retreated back a few steps and pressed against the wall as the top floor of the east end of the building collapsed. Caught by the draught, a rush of smoke and flame surged down both the second and first floor halls toward Christopher and the landing where Simon lay beneath his twisted tricycle. Burning bits of wood and embers from the floors above glowed beside his small, outstretched hand.

"Simon," Christopher shouted. "Simon, are you up

there?" A fit of coughing overtook him as the acrid smoke invaded his lungs. He tried to call to the boy again, but could not. He pulled a wet handkerchief from his pocket and tied it over his mouth and nose. Christopher inched forward toward the staircase.

As he moved across the main hall to the foot of the stairs, a blast of heat hit him. How close were the flames, he wondered as he started up. The burning railing leading to the third floor crashed down, flaming wood bouncing over the stairs. A piece hit Christopher on the shoulder, burning his neck and hair before he could knock it away. "Oh, God," he wept as he sank to his knees and began to crawl up, his hands searching for the body of the little boy. The glowing embers scattered about on the hardwood steps bit into the flesh of his fingers. Another violent crash at the east end of the building heralded another intense wave of heat. "Simon," he rasped in panic, choking in the smoke, "where the hell are you?"

He reached the landing and cried out as he knelt on a burning chunk of railing. Pulling back, Christopher slapped at his steaming trouser leg, still wet from the flood waters. Sitting back, he inched ahead using his feet to clear any debris from his path. His shoe tangled in something and, leaning forward tentatively to investigate, his fingers found the hot metal spokes of a wheel. His tricycle! "Simon," he coughed, throwing aside the once frightening machine. "Simon, are you there?" Christopher felt the small body and lifted him up in his arms. "Simon," he cried, shaking the boy. "Simon, come on. You can't be dead."

The little body convulsed, Simon coughed. Christopher clutched him to his chest. "Thank God. Simon."

The boy's eyes opened slowly seeing nothing at first, not knowing where he was. His head throbbed with pain, his swollen cheek and the large purple bump on his forehead witness to the terrible fall that had knocked him senseless. Pushing against the encircling arms, he looked for the first time into the face of the man holding him. He saw Christopher in the haze and began to struggle.

"Hey, Simon, it's all right. I'm not going to hurt you any more," he said, trying to calm him. "It's all right. I'm sorry about before. I thought you were going to hurt *me*." He felt the boy's body through his heavy coat. "Are you okay? Anything broken?"

"My head hurts," Simon mumbled. "I want my mommy." He coughed again, the smoke clearing the fuzz from his head. His brown eyes widened as they saw the flames over Christopher's shoulder. "Fire," he cried, scrambling around in the confining arms, nearly breaking free.

"Hold on," Christopher said, grasping the child's arm firmly. "We're going to go now, but slowly."

"No, no," the boy shouted, trying to tear himself away. "Mommy."

"She's okay, Simon. She's at your grandmother's. Now lead me down the stairs and let's get out of here." Christopher got to his feet, still holding the boy's arm. He reached out with his other hand, trying to locate himself on the landing.

Eyes wide with fear, Simon pulled ahead. A flaming mass of debris crashed down from above and he pulled back as it scattered on the stairs between them and the hall below. Christopher heard the noise and felt the staircase under them tremble with the impact.

"The stairs are burning," Simon cried.

"All of them?" Christopher demanded.

"I'm scared." The little boy tried to lose himself by burrowing his face into Christopher.

"All of them?" Christopher shouted, shaking the boy.

"Almost."

"Then we've got to run down fast. Take my hand," he ordered. "Simon, take my hand." Simon took it reluctantly and held on tight. "Now, you look for the places where the fire is smallest and run, run right down through it. I'll run after you. Now go." He braced himself, but the boy stood stone still. "Simon, run," he shouted.

"No, I'm scared," he sobbed.

Christopher felt the heat on his face; the air was filled with the sound of flames and crackling timbers. Reaching down, he scooped up the petrified boy in his arms and hugged him. "You're going to be all right. I won't let anything happen to you. Simon, trust me. Please." He felt the boy's grip tighten around his neck.

"Now, hold on," he ordered. Freeing one hand, he found the wall of the staircase. "You've got the eyes, I haven't. You tell me where to walk."

The boy shook his head, his face still buried deep against Christopher's damp jacket.

"Simon," the young English master shouted, "where?" Without waiting for an answer, he started down the stairs, coming almost at once upon a pile of burning wood. He could feel the intense heat and moved back up the steps.

A frightening crash of a falling floor somewhere down the hall shook the entire building under them. It startled Simon into action. "You won't leave me," he mumbled against Christopher's shoulder.

"You're damn right I won't. Now, come on, be brave."

Slowly turning his head from the welcome moisture of the jacket, Simon looked down through the swirling smoke and flames. "Go to the right," he said in a small, terrified voice. Christopher edged across the step. "Now down two."

"That's the boy, Simon," he said, coughing as he felt gingerly ahead with his foot and moved down two steps. "We're going to get out of here all right. We make a great team."

"Go over to the right again." Simon now leaned out from Christopher searching for the path to safety. He began to feel confident in the man's arms. "Stop. Now down four steps."

Christopher's clothing was steaming by the time they reached the foot of the staircase. Simon wriggled down to the floor and ran ahead through the smoke. Looking back, he saw Christopher standing hesitantly, his dark form outlined through the choking gray air by the fire roaring behind. The little boy scurried back and, taking his hand, led him out of the flaming building to the cold wind of the colonnade around the Talbot Academy quadrangle.

Christopher slumped down on his haunches against the brick wall of the first dormitory, gagging and gulping the fresh air into his aching lungs. But Simon tugged at his hand, urging him onward. "Steady there, Simon, let me catch my breath. I—"

"Mommy," the boy cried. "You've got to help Mommy."

"She's at your grandmother's," he repeated.

"No, no," Simon insisted urgently, "Mommy's down the deep hole in the cellar. It's filled with water."

Christopher's face snapped up in the direction of the boy's voice. He had to be telling the truth. Jesus, what on earth had Arthur done to Karen in his madness? Would this nightmare never end?

Rising, he let Simon pull him ahead down the colonnade, not hearing the muffled calls of the men from Wyndham Locks to each other as they struggled up the northern slope of the ridge under the burden of hoses and hand pumps. James Harrothwait led them toward the conflagration, his white hair blowing in the wind, a stark contrast to the flames before him.

Karen floated between delirium and consciousness caused by the complete exhaustion of her body. Her mind was a jumble of vague pictures: Arthur pulling the tricycle through the mud at the boathouse, his use of Simon's voice on the tape recorder to lure her into the cistern, the vicious, obscene words he had spit at her through the holes in the iron cover. The pain in her arms and shoulders had long since turned to numbness; she had wedged her arms over the top rung between the ladder and shaft wall to keep from losing her hold and falling back down into the icy water below.

"Mommy, Mommy."

Simon's voice seemed to be coming to her from a hundred miles away. With great effort, she raised her head slowly and opened her eyes. In the beam of the flashlight Simon had found in the kitchen, she saw her brother's face. "Kurt," she cried weakly. "Oh, Kurt, you've come." Vaguely, somewhere in the back of her mind, she knew she must be dead.

"Karen?" Christopher called. "Karen, what is this place? Where are we?"

"Kurt, help me."

"It's Christopher, Mommy," Simon called down. "It's Christopher. He saved me from the fire. I brought him just like you told me." Karen fought to clear her brain. "The big building is all burning down," Simon went on in a rush of excitement, "and . . ." Christopher, of course, it was Christopher. ". . . fell into the fire. I . . ."

"Help me," she wept. "Chris, please help me. I can't hold on any longer."

"Where are you?" His hands felt around the edge of the open shaft.

"About ten feet down. Right under you." She choked back her tears. "The ladder's gone. I can't get up. I'm so tired." She heard Christopher talking to Simon about the clothesline. He pulled it up. "I can't," she cried hopelessly. "We tried. I'm too weak, I can't hang on."

A minute later Christopher lowered the line back

down, its end tied into a loop. "Can you stand in the loop and hold on while I pull you up?"

She stared at the rope and then at the anxious faces above her. Simon's eyes glistened with excitement. "Christopher will get you out, Mommy."

Slowly pulling her right arm free, Karen almost fainted from the pain. She closed her eyes to keep from screaming. Flexing her arm and hand muscles, she reached out and took hold of the clothesline. "I've got it," she said dully.

"Simon," Christopher asked, "is the other end tied around something really strong? You can tie knots, can't you?"

The little boy nodded proudly. "My daddy taught me." Jumping up, Simon ran back to look at the knots he had made in the line around one of the steel supports of the pump. He returned to kneel by Christopher. "I tied it real tight," he promised. Together they were going to get his mommy out of the hole. That was good. And then they'd go off to Disney World. He guessed Christopher could come, too, if he wanted. He wasn't at all mean like he had first thought. Simon smiled at the young master.

Tugging at the rope until he was satisfied, Christopher called down to Karen. "Okay, now stand in the loop and hold on. Let me know when you're ready."

Painfully, she freed her other arm, hugging the ladder as the circulation slowly returned to it. Biting her lip and trembling, she put one foot into the thin loop. The rope started to swing out, threatening to topple her. Closing her eyes, she quickly released the ladder and clutched the line with both hands. It swung back against the side of the shaft.

"You all right?" Christopher asked, feeling the movement and stretch of the line in his hands.

"Yes, yes," she gasped, looking down and then up. "Hurry, Chris, please hurry."

The young athlete grasped the line in his strong

hands and leaned back, his boots digging into the rough concrete at the edge of the shaft. The muscles of his arms, back and shoulders knotted and bulged as they strained against her weight. The rope began to inch up. Simon looked from Christopher to his mother, his small hands beating together in his excitement.

Karen could no longer see Christopher's face. Instead she studied her hands on the line as they inched up past one brick after the next, one foot, two, three. The hopelessness of her situation began to fade as she realized that Christopher was going to get her out. And with that realization, her determination and some of her strength began to return.

"I saw Arthur," she said, "saw him at the boathouse. He killed those boys, not Simon. I thought all along . . ." She looked up at her son's puzzled face staring down at her and stopped. The rope jerked slightly every time Christopher released and grasped it anew with one hand and then the next. Four feet, five feet.

"I was trying to find Simon, take him away. I thought he was down here. Arthur used a tape recorder with Simon's voice."

"I know all about his tape recorders," Christopher rasped through clenched teeth. "Don't worry, you're safe now." Six feet, seven feet.

Now Karen could just see the top of his head, his tossled blond hair in the beam of the flashlight Simon had set down beside him on the cement floor. Eight feet. She reached up with one hand; her fingers could almost touch the rough lip of the shaft. "We can go away, Simon. You and me. Just like I promised." She looked back at Christopher. Suddenly another face emerged from the darkness behind him, an ugly, wet face with blood running down one side, a face insanely contorted with hate. Her eyes widened in horror. "No!"

"Daddy," Simon cried, looking up.

Bellowing with rage, Arthur Catterby lunged forward, locking his arms around the straining athlete's throat. "You'll never have her!" he shrieked. "Never!"

Stunned, Christopher held the line desperately, his thoughts solely on not letting Karen fall. Arthur tried to crush his throat, choke off all air, but he continued to pull at the line, one hand, then the next. He was becoming light-headed.

"You thought you killed me, did you?" Arthur shouted.

"Arthur," Karen cried, "for God's sake, don't, don't . . ."

"Stay with the devil where you belong," he screamed.

"Simon," she called.

The little boy leapt at his father, pulling at his arm, trying to pry it away from Christopher's throat. Arthur struck out at him viciously. The movement allowed a gasp of air into the younger man's lungs. He pulled back with all his might.

Karen reached up to catch hold of the edge with both hands to help pull herself up. Simon beat frantically at Arthur, screaming at him, in the confusion not seeing this man as his father. With one blow of his arm made more powerful by his rage, Arthur knocked the little boy across the cellar. He lay crumpled on the floor, watching in terror.

Straddling Christopher, Arthur beat his head against the cement over and over as he bellowed obscenities at the dazed youth who still clung desperately to the line. Karen wrenched herself over the edge, collapsing beside the struggling men. "Don't, Arthur, leave him alone," she cried. "Leave him . . ." Pulling herself up to her knees, she tried to wrench her husband off.

"So you can run off with your lover and take my son?" Arthur raged, still pounding Christopher, who tried feebly to fight back. "Simon stays here."

"No," Karen cried, beating at him and pulling his face back away from Christopher. "You can't keep us here any longer. We're free of you at last."

"No one will ever take my son away," he bellowed.

"Simon's not your son, you fool," she shouted viciously, "he's Kurt's! He's Kurt's and mine!"

Arthur's hands froze on Christopher's throat. Slowly he turned to his wife, her words confirming what he had feared to face for so many years. "You, you . . ."

Karen rose and backed away. "My brother is Simon's father. Simon is mine, all mine." Arthur released the throat of the semiconscious master and slowly stood, his eyes tearing into hers. "Kurt's." She hurled the name cruelly, inflicting another wound on the man she had detested for so long, not caring about the consequences.

Simon cringed in the corner, watching them and the grotesque shadows they cast against the brick wall as they moved together in the beam of the flashlight. Arthur lunged forward, grabbing Karen. The shadows merged and swayed back and forth as the two struggled, their curses filling the old pump room. It was like the pictures in the Faust book that his father had shown him so many times. She tore at his face as he slowly strangled the air from her. "Bitch! Drunken, whoring bitch," he screamed. She fought back frantically. One hand brushed her coat pocket, she felt the forgotten object. Thrusting her hand in, Karen's fingers closed over the steel dart she had pulled from Frank Cannel's eye. Raising it above her head, she plunged it over and over into her husband's back. "Kurt's! Kurt's! Kurt's!" Simon shrank against the wall, covering his eyes.

Rearing back, Arthur flailed at the pain. She broke away, but not fast enough. He caught one of her hands and whirled her around. Karen drove the dart home into his chest with the other. He screamed, wrapping his arms around her in a fierce bear hug that drove the dart even further into him. In that instant Arthur knew he was dead. "Satan's whore!" he howled, hurling his weight toward the open shaft, carrying Karen with him. It was her scream that last reverberated up from the bowels of the earth.

Simon stared wide-eyed at the circular hole in the cement floor for nearly an hour. He did not understand what had happened, or why. He waited for his mommy and daddy to climb back out of the hole and come to him as tears rolled silently down his cheeks. Christopher would help; he would pull them out. He crept over to where the young man lay unconscious and shook him gently. He did not move. As he had done with his lost sparrow, Simon smoothed the blood-clotted yellow hair away from Christopher's forehead and looked down at him. His face looked peaceful and asleep. Sighing, Simon snuggled down against the warmth of his body and pulled Christopher's arm around him. That was how James Harrothwait found them hours later.

Chapter 16

"FEELING BETTER?"

"Susanne?" Christopher asked at the sound of the familiar voice. "That you?"

"Yes." He felt her touch on his arm. "You've been out for several days. How do you feel?"

"Like my head was in a vise. Where am I?" He reached up and gingerly touched the bandages that swathed his head and eyes.

"The University of Connecticut Medical Center. Your skull was fractured in two places."

"I'm going to be all right?"

She squeezed his arm. "Nothing can hurt that thick head of yours. Besides, you're not getting out of our spring vacation together that easily." Her voice lost its playfulness. "Chris, what happened back there? They won't tell me anything."

Christopher lay silent for a long time, trying to sort things out in his mind. "What happened?" he said finally. "Something very tragic and something wonderful. Two very sick people died." He paused, searching for the right words. "And I guess you could say that in their dying, Christopher Hennick got re-

born." He covered her hand with his, feeling its softness and warmth, feeling gentleness, not the urgent,
demanding power of Karen's. "I've learned a lot
about me, Susanne. About us."

She said nothing, waiting.

"I found my world is a lot bigger than Talbot, than I
thought it could be. That I can do just about anything I
want."

"I always knew you could," she said softly, her eyes
filling with tears. Susanne brushed them away with her
free hand.

"And I found that my world won't be complete
without you, that I need and love you just as much if
not even more than I ever did." He felt her kiss.

"Oh, darling." Susanne made no attempt to hide her
emotions. The tears now flowed freely down her
cheeks and her next words were spoken through her
sobs. "I want to get right into this bed with you and
hug you so tight that I'll break every bone in that
beautiful body of yours."

He tried to joke, "Hey, crazy lady, don't you think
I'm broken up enough already?" but he knew he, too,
was crying. And for the first time he became acutely
aware of the gauze covering his eyes. He touched it.
"Why are these bandages on my eyes?" he asked. Her
hand tensed. "You said it was my skull."

"Chris, I . . ." she paused.

"Go on."

"I don't know if I should be talking about it."

"Look, nothing more can happen to them that
hasn't already happened."

She sighed. "They don't want to get your hopes up.
During the examination after the operation they saw
some slight reflex in your eyes toward light. You got
such a terrible pounding . . ."

He waited for her to finish, his fists clenched.

"Well, they had to get some bone fragments out that
were pressing against your brain. The surgeons don't

know for sure, but they think that something might have happened, that there might be a long chance you could get some of your sight back."

"How long is 'long'?"

"Very long," she answered honestly. "It happens so rarely that—"

"Then let's forget about it." His fists relaxed. "I can get along perfectly well without them."

Susanne looked down at him. She heard a far more confident and certain man than the one she had left standing alone in the snow several months ago. "I really do love you, Chris Hennick." She kissed him again and then stood up. "You have some friends waiting outside to see you. Okay?"

"Who?"

"A surprise." He heard her walk to the door and then return followed by others. She lowered her voice and whispered in his ear. "They couldn't tear him away from you. He was beside you all the way here in the ambulance. He was so upset they thought it best to let him come along."

Susanne moved away and in her place Christopher felt two small, cold hands take his. "Christopher," a little voice asked, "are you all right now?"

"Hey, sport," Christopher answered brightly, "I'm fine as long as you're around. We make a great team, remember?" Painful pictures of what he and the little boy had been through flashed before him as he held the small hands in his. He squeezed them.

Simon's voice was tentative. "You're not going to die, are you?"

"Look, little buddy, I . . ."

"You're not going away?" he persisted.

"No, Simon," Christopher's voice broke as he realized the agonizing reason behind the boy's question. "No, I'm not going away for a long while, I promise." He felt the little boy's lips on his cheek and heard his footsteps leave the room.

"You're very important to Simon right now," James Harrothwait said gently as he rose and approached the bed. "You're his only link between what happened in the past and his new future. You were there."

"Gosh, is the whole Academy here?" Christopher asked, trying to smile. His head throbbed mercilessly.

"No, just us, my boy." He felt the reassuring weight of the headmaster's hand on his shoulder. "Will you be coming back to Talbot?"

Christopher lay silent.

"There will be terrible memories, but remember, you are loved and admired by many. And that little boy—you saved his life."

"No," Christopher replied, "actually, I think Simon saved mine. He gave back a life I thought I'd lost."

"You've proved something to yourself," the old man stated bluntly.

"Yes."

"There will be no more Miltons."

"No, no more blind poets."

"Paradise regained?" he asked, alluding to their conversation on Christopher's first afternoon back at Talbot.

Christopher nodded slowly. "Regained."

"And will there be a Marston Fellowship in that paradise?"

"I think I can handle it now."

The headmaster smiled across the hospital room at Susanne. "I think you can. We'll miss you at Talbot."

"But I—"

"You've outgrown us, my boy. You are a competitor, a winner. You are one of those who needs an ever expanding world to conquer, new challenges. Others need stability, need the security of a smaller world . . ." He paused. ". . . like poor Arthur. Talbot was that world to him, one which grew smaller and smaller and finally trapped him because he refused to grow within it." The headmaster sighed. "And there are others, but fortunately not many. Like you, most use Talbot as a great learning experience, as a stepping stone in their evolution."

"But you've stayed at Talbot for as long as anyone can remember," Christopher said, "and yet you're certainly not small. You're the wisest, the most inspirational man I've ever known, and that includes all those grand professors at Harvard, every one."

"Thank you, Christopher." James Harrothwait smiled at the compliment. "I am sure there were times during your student days when you would not have been so generous. But you see, Talbot per se is not my world. My world is the minds of all the boys who pass through and go on to do great and wondrous things. You are part of my world, and I am proud of what I may have helped you become and what you will accomplish. My world has written books, built bridges, explored continents, and it continues to expand with every graduating class. If you remember that, Christopher, as a teacher you will lead a very rich and rewarding life." The headmaster lapsed into silence, thinking about some of the outstanding students he had sent out into the world.

"And Simon?" Christopher asked. "What will become of him?"

"He will be staying with Mrs. Harrothwait and me at the Academy. Under the circumstances, his grandmother felt it best." A gentleness spread across his craggy features. "It has been a long time since we have had a son of our own to bring up. Simon is a good little chap—inquisitive, smart as a whip. We are lucky, very lucky to have him. And you? You have obviously made plans."

"I want to finish out the year," Christopher said.

"Good. We—and the boy—need you."

"Hey, what about me?" Susanne asked. "Where do I fit into this paradise you two keep talking about?"

"What do you think, Mr. Harrothwait?" Christopher asked, extending his hand to meet hers. "Will she make a good Eve?"

The old man looked deep into her eyes and saw the love and concern he had seen so many times in the eyes of his wife. "She should do just fine, Christopher, just fine."

AN ODYSSEY INTO THE OCCULT

Novels Of Terror That May Frighten You Awake In The Night

Peter Straub
Ghost Story
44198/$3.95
Julia 49564/$3.95
If You Could
See Me Now
45193/$3.50

John Russo
The Awakening
45259/$2.95
Night Of The
Living Dead
43768/$2.50
Bloodsisters
41692/$2.95
Black Cat
41691/$2.50
Limb to Limb
41690/$2.75
Midnight
83432/$2.25

Judi Miller
Save The Last
Dance For Me
46502/$3.50
Hush Little Baby
43182/$2.95

Whitley Strieber
The Hunger
46785/$3.50

Bob Veder
Playing With Fire
43593/$2.95

Paul Walker
The Altar 42496/$2.95

Guy Smith
Satan's Snowdrop
45248/$2.95

Russell Rhodes
Tricycle 45893/$2.95

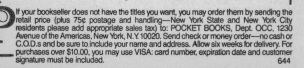
If your bookseller does not have the titles you want, you may order them by sending the retail price (plus 75¢ postage and handling—New York State and New York City residents please add appropriate sales tax) to: POCKET BOOKS, Dept. OCC, 1230 Avenue of the Americas, New York, N.Y. 10020. Send check or money order—no cash or C.O.D.s and be sure to include your name and address. Allow six weeks for delivery. For purchases over $10.00, you may use VISA: card number, expiration date and customer signature must be included.

644

Innocent
People Caught
In The Grip Of
TERROR!

These thrilling novels—where deranged minds create sinister schemes, placing victims in mortal danger and striking horror in their hearts—will keep you in white-knuckled suspense!

BROTHERLY LOVE
by William D. Blankenship 44765/$3.50

HORROR STORY by Oliver McNab
83215/$2.95

SOMEONE'S WATCHING
by Andrew Neiderman 42831/$3.50

THE MALL by Steve Kahn 42504/$3.50

OFFICE PARTY by Michael A. Gilbert
45524/$2.95

HUSH, LITTLE BABY by Judi Miller
43182/$2.95

If your bookseller does not have the titles you want, you may order them by sending the retail price (plus 75¢ postage and handling—New York State and New York City residents please add appropriate sales tax) to: POCKET BOOKS, Dept. TER, 1230 Avenue of the Americas, New York, N.Y. 10020. Send check or money order—no cash or C.O.D.s and be sure to include your name and address. Allow six weeks for delivery. For purchases over $10.00, you may use VISA: card number, expiration date and customer signature must be included.

351